THE WORLD'S BEST
FAIRY TALES

A READER'S DIGEST ANTHOLOGY

THE WORLD'S BEST FAIRY TALES

Edited by
BELLE BECKER SIDEMAN

Illustrations by
FRITZ KREDEL

The Reader's Digest Association, Inc.
Pleasantville, New York   Montreal

The acknowledgments that appear on page 383 are
hereby made a part of this copyright page.

Library of Congress Catalog Card Number 79-89496
ISBN 0-89577-076-8 (Volume One)
ISBN 0-89577-078-4 (Set)

Printed in the United States of America

Third Printing (Two-Volume Edition), September 1983

CONTENTS

THE PIED PIPER OF HAMELIN

A VERY LONG time ago, the town of Hamelin in Germany was invaded by bands of rats, the likes of which had never been seen before nor ever will be again. They were great black creatures which ran boldly in broad daylight through the streets and swarmed all over the houses, so that people at last could not put hand or foot down anywhere without touching one.

When dressing in the morning they found rats in their breeches and petticoats, in their pockets and in their boots; and when they wanted a morsel to eat, the voracious horde had swept away everything from cellar to garret. The nighttime was even worse. As soon as the lights were out, these untiring nibblers set to work. And everywhere—in the ceilings, in the floors, in the cupboards, at the doors—there was a chase and a rummage, and so furious a noise of gimlets, pincers and saws that a deaf man could not rest for even one hour. Neither cats nor dogs, nor poison nor traps, nor prayers, nor candles burned to all the saints—nothing did any good. The more rats they killed the more came.

But one Friday there arrived in the town a man with a queer face, who played the bagpipes and sang this refrain:

> Who lives shall see:
> This is he,
> The ratcatcher.

He was a tall, gawky fellow, dry and bronzed, with a crooked nose, a long rattail mustache, two great yellow piercing and mocking eyes under a large felt hat set off by a scarlet cock's feather. He was dressed in a green jacket with a leather belt and orange breeches, and on his feet were sandals fastened by thongs passed around his legs in the gypsy fashion. That is how he may be seen to this day, painted on a window of the cathedral of Hamelin.

He stopped in the great marketplace before the town hall, turned his back to the church and went on with his music, singing:

> Who lives shall see:
> This is he,
> The ratcatcher.

The town council had just assembled to consider once more this plague of Egypt, from which no one could save the town. The stranger sent word to the councilors that if they would make it worth his while, he would rid them of all their rats before night fell.

"Then he is a sorcerer!" cried the citizens with one voice. "We must beware of him."

The chief town councilor, who was considered clever, reassured them. He said, "Sorcerer or no, if this bagpiper speaks the truth, it was he who sent us this horrible vermin he wants to rid us of today for money. Well, we must learn to catch the devil in his own snares. You leave it to me."

"Leave it to the town councilor," said the citizens one to another.

And the stranger was brought before them. "Before night," said he, "I shall have dispatched all the rats in Hamelin if you will but pay me a schilling a head."

"A schilling a head!" cried the citizens. "But that will come to millions of taler!"

The town councilor simply shrugged his shoulders and said to the stranger, "A bargain! The rats will be paid for at one schilling a head as you ask."

The bagpiper announced he would begin that very evening when the moon rose. He added that the inhabitants should at that hour leave the streets free and content themselves with looking out of their windows at the pleasant spectacle that was passing.

When the people of Hamelin heard of the bargain, they too exclaimed, "A schilling a head! But this will cost us a deal of money!"

"Leave it to the town councilor," said the town council with a malicious air. And the good people of

Hamelin repeated, "Leave it to the town councilor."

Toward evening the bagpiper reappeared in the marketplace. As at first, he turned his back to the church, and the moment the moon rose on the horizon, the bagpipes resounded: *Trarira, trari!*

It was first a slow, caressing sound, then more and more lively and urgent, and so sonorous and piercing that it penetrated the farthest alleys and retreats of the town. Soon—from the bottom of cellars, the top of garrets, from under all the furniture, from all the nooks and corners of the houses—out came the rats, searching for the door, flinging themselves into the street, and—trip, trip, trip—they began to run in file toward the front of the town hall, so squeezed together that they covered the pavement like the waves of a flooded torrent.

When the square was quite full, the bagpiper faced about and, still playing briskly, turned toward the river that runs at the foot of the walls of Hamelin.

Arriving there, he turned around; the rats were following. "Hop! Hop!" he cried, pointing with his finger to the middle of the stream where the water whirled and was drawn down as if through a funnel. And, hop, hop, without hesitating, the rats took the leap, swam straight to the funnel, plunged in head foremost and disappeared.

The plunging continued thus without ceasing till midnight. At last, dragging himself with difficulty, came a big rat, white with age, who stopped on the bank. It was the king of the band.

"Are they all there, Friend Blanchet?" asked the bagpiper.

"They are all there," replied the white rat.

"And how many were they?"

"Nine hundred and ninety thousand, nine hundred and ninety-nine."

"Well reckoned?"

"Well reckoned."

"Then go and join them, old sire, and *au revoir*."

And the old white rat sprang in his turn into the river, swam to the whirlpool and disappeared.

When the bagpiper had thus concluded his business, he went to bed at his inn. And for the first time in three months the people of Hamelin slept quietly through the night.

The next morning at nine o'clock, the bagpiper appeared at the town hall, where the town council awaited him. "All your rats took a jump into the river yesterday," said he to the councilors, "and I guarantee that not one of them comes back. They were nine hundred and ninety thousand, nine hundred and ninety-nine, at a schilling a head. Reckon!"

"Let us reckon the heads first. One schilling a head is one head the schilling. Where are the heads?"

The piper did not expect this treacherous stroke. He paled with anger, and his eyes flashed fire. "The heads!" cried he. "If you care about them, go and find them in the river."

"So," replied the chief councilor, "you refuse to honor the terms of your agreement? We ourselves could refuse you all payment. But you have been of use to us, and we will not let you go without a recompense." With this, he offered him fifty taler.

"Keep your recompense for yourself," replied the piper proudly. "If you do not pay me, I will be paid by your heirs." Thereupon he pulled his hat down over his eyes, went hastily out of the hall and left the town without speaking to a soul.

When the people of Hamelin heard how the affair had ended, they rubbed their hands and, with no more scruple than their town councilors, laughed about the bagpiper who, they said, had been caught in his own trap. But what made them laugh above all was his threat of getting himself paid by their heirs. Ha! They wished they could only have such creditors for the rest of their lives.

Next day, which was a Sunday, they went gaily to church, thinking that afterward they would at last be able to eat some good thing that the rats had not tasted before them. They never suspected the terrible surprise that awaited them on their return home: no children anywhere! They had all disappeared!

"Our children! Where are our poor children?" was the cry that was soon heard in all the streets.

Then through the east gate of the town came three little boys who cried and wept, and this is the story they told:

While the parents were at church, a wonderful music had sounded in the streets. Soon all the little boys and all the little girls who had been left at home, attracted by the magic sounds, had gone out to the great marketplace. There they found the piper playing his bagpipes. Then the stranger started to walk quickly, and they had followed—running, singing and dancing to the sound of the music, as far as the foot of the mountain which one sees on entering Hamelin. At their approach the mountain had opened a little, and the bagpiper had gone in with them, after which it had closed again.

Only the three little ones who told of the adventure had remained outside, as if by a miracle. One was lame and could not run fast enough; the second, who had left the house in haste, one foot shod, the other bare, had hurt himself against a big stone and could scarcely walk; the third had arrived on time, but while hurrying to go in had struck so violently against the wall of the mountain that he fell backward at the moment it closed upon his comrades.

Hearing this story, the parents redoubled their lamentations. They ran with pikes and mattocks to the mountain and searched till evening to find the opening through which their children had disappeared, without success. At last, the night falling, they returned desolate to Hamelin.

But the most unhappy was the town councilor who had bargained with the piper, for he had lost three boys and two girls, and to crown all, the people of Hamelin overwhelmed him with reproaches, forgetting that the day before they had agreed with him.

What had become of these unfortunate children?

The parents always hoped they were not dead and that the piper, who certainly must have come out of the mountain, would have taken them with him to his own country. That is why for several years they sent in search of them to different countries, but no one ever found a trace of the poor little ones.

It was not till much later that anything was to be heard.

About a hundred and fifty years after the event, when there were no longer any of the fathers, mothers, brothers or sisters of that day left, there arrived one evening in Hamelin some merchants of Bremen returning from the East, who asked to speak with the citizens. They told how, in crossing Hungary, they had sojourned in a mountainous country called Transylvania where the inhabitants spoke only German, while all around them nothing was spoken but Hungarian. These people also declared that they came from Germany, but they did not know how they chanced to be in this strange country.

"Now," said the merchants of Bremen, "these Germans cannot be other than the descendants of the lost children of Hamelin."

The people of Hamelin did not doubt it; and since that day they have regarded it as certain that the Transylvanians of Hungary are their countryfolk, whose ancestors, as children, were taken from Hamelin by the bagpiper. There are more difficult things to believe than that.   CHARLES MARELLES, ANDREW LANG COLLECTION

SNOW WHITE AND ROSE RED

A POOR WIDOW once lived in a little cottage, in front of which grew two rose trees, one bearing white roses and the other red. She had two little girls who were just like the two trees. One was called Snow White and the other Rose Red, and they were the sweetest and best children in the world.

Rose Red loved to run about the fields and meadows and to pick flowers and catch butterflies, but Snow White sat at home with her mother and helped her in the household or read aloud to her when there was no work to do. The two children loved each other so dearly they always walked about hand in hand whenever they went out together, and when Snow White said, "We will never desert each other," Rose Red answered, "No, not so long as we live." And the mother added, "Whatever one gets she shall share with her sister."

They often roamed about in the woods gathering berries, and no beast ever hurt them; on the contrary, they came up to them in the most confiding manner. The little hare would eat a cabbage leaf from their hands, the deer grazed beside them, the stag would bound past them merrily, and the birds remained on the nearby branches and sang to them. No evil ever befell them. If they forgot about the time and night overtook them, they lay down on the moss and slept till morning, and their mother knew they were quite safe and never felt anxious about them.

Once, when they had slept the night in the wood and had been wakened by the morning sun, they perceived a beautiful child in a shining white robe sitting close to their resting place. The figure looked at them kindly, but said nothing and vanished into the wood. And, when they looked around, they saw they had slept quite close to a precipice, over which they would certainly have fallen had they gone on a few steps farther in the darkness.

When they told their mother of their adventure, she said what they had seen must have been the angel that guards good children.

Snow White and Rose Red kept their mother's cottage so clean and neat it was a pleasure to step into it. In summer Rose Red looked after the house and, every morning before her mother awoke, she placed two flowers beside the bed, a rose from each tree. In winter Snow White lit the fire and put a shining brass kettle on to boil.

In the long winter evenings when snowflakes fell, their mother would say, "Snow White, go close the shutters." They gathered around the fire, while their mother put on her spectacles and read aloud from a big book. The two girls listened and spun quietly. Beside them on the ground lay a little lamb, and behind them perched a little white dove with its head tucked under its wing.

One evening, as they sat thus cozily together, someone knocked at the door. The mother said, "Rose Red, open the door quickly. It must be some poor traveler seeking shelter from the snow and cold."

Rose Red hastened to unbar the door and thought she saw a poor man standing in the darkness outside. But it was a Bear who poked his thick black head through the door. Rose Red screamed aloud and sprang back in terror, the lamb began to bleat, the dove flapped its wings, and Snow White ran and hid behind her mother's bed. But the Bear said, "Don't be afraid. I won't hurt you. I am half frozen and only wish to warm myself a little."

"You poor Bear," said the mother, "lie down by the fire, but take care not to burn your fur."

Then she called, "Snow White and Rose Red, come out. The Bear will do you no harm; he is a good, honest creature."

So they both came out of their hiding places, and gradually the lamb and dove drew near too, and they all forgot their fear. The Bear asked the children to beat the snow out of his fur, and they fetched a brush and scrubbed him till he was dry. Then the beast stretched himself in front of the fire and growled happily and comfortably. The girls soon grew quite playful with him and treated their guest like a big dog. They rolled him about here and there and teased him gaily, and if he growled they only laughed.

The Bear submitted to everything with the greatest good nature, only when they went too far, he cried:

> Oh, spare my life!
> Snow White and Rose Red,
> Don't beat your lover dead.

When it was time to retire for the night, and the others went to bed, the mother said to the Bear, "You can lie there on the hearth; it will be a shelter for you from the cold and wet outside."

As soon as day dawned the children let him out, and he trotted off through the snow into the wood. From this time on the Bear came every evening at the same hour and lay down by the hearth and let Snow White and Rose Red play what pranks they liked with him. They grew so accustomed to his visits that the door was never locked at night till their friend had made his appearance.

When spring came, and all the world outside was green, the Bear said one morning to Snow White, "Now I must leave you and I will not return again the whole summer."

"Where are you going, dear Bear?" asked Snow White.

"I must go to the forest and protect my treasure from the wicked dwarfs. In winter, when the earth is frozen hard, they remain underground, for they cannot work their way through. But now, when the snow has thawed and the sun has warmed the ground, they come out to spy the land and steal what they can. Anything that falls into their hands and disappears into their caves with them is not easily brought to light again."

Snow White was quite sad over their friend's departure. When she unbarred the door for him, the Bear caught a piece of his fur in the door knocker as he stepped out, and Snow White thought she caught sight of glittering gold beneath it, but she could not be certain. The Bear ran hastily away and soon disappeared behind the trees.

A short time later, their mother sent the children into the wood to collect brushwood. They came upon a big tree fallen on the ground, and on the trunk among the long grass they noticed something jumping up and down, but what it was they could not distinguish.

When they came closer they perceived a dwarf with a wizened face and a beard a yard long. The end of the beard was caught in a cleft of the tree, and the little man sprang about like a dog on a chain and did not seem to know what to do. He glared at the girls with his fiery red eyes and screamed out, "What are you standing there for? Come and help me!"

"What were you doing, little man?" Rose Red asked him.

"You stupid, inquisitive goose!" replied the dwarf. "I wanted to split the tree in order to get chips of wood for our kitchen fire. I drove in the wedge, and all was going well, but the wood was so slippery it suddenly sprang out. There was no time to remove my beautiful white beard, so here I am caught fast. I can't get away, and you silly, smooth-faced, milk-and-water girls just stand and laugh at me! Ugh, what wretches you are!"

The girls did everything in their power, but they could not get the little man's beard out; it was wedged in far too firmly.

"I will run and fetch somebody," said Rose Red.

"Blockheads!" snapped the dwarf. "What is the good of calling anyone else? You two are already too many for me. Does nothing better occur to you than that idea?"

"Do not be so impatient," said Snow White. "I will help you." And taking her scissors out of her pocket she snipped the end off his beard. As soon as the dwarf was free, he seized a bag full of gold which was hidden among the roots of the tree, and muttered aloud, "Curse these rude wretches, cutting off a piece of my splendid beard!" With these words he swung the bag over his back and disappeared without another look at the children.

A few days later Snow White and Rose Red went out to catch some fish for supper. As they approached the stream they saw something which looked like an enormous grasshopper springing toward the water as if it were going to jump in. They ran forward and recognized their old friend the dwarf.

"Where are you going?" asked Rose Red. "You are surely not going to jump into the water?"

"I am not such a fool!" screamed the dwarf. "That wretched fish is trying to drag me in!"

The little man had been sitting on the bank fishing, when the wind had unfortunately entangled his beard in the line. Immediately afterward, a big fish bit, but the feeble little creature had no strength to pull it out and the fish was dragging the dwarf toward him. He clung with all his might to every rush and blade of grass, but it did not help him much. He had to follow every movement of the fish and was in great danger of being dragged into the water.

The girls had come just at the right moment. They held him firm and did all they could to disentangle his beard from the line; but in vain, for beard and line were in a hopeless muddle. Nothing remained but to produce the scissors and cut the beard, and a small part of it was sacrificed.

When the dwarf saw what they were doing, the ungrateful little man yelled, "Do you call that manners, to disfigure a fellow's face? It wasn't enough that you shortened my beard before, but now you cut off the best bit of it. I won't dare show myself like this before my own people. I wish you'd never come at all." Then he picked up a sack of pearls that lay among the rushes, and, without saying another word, he dragged it away and disappeared behind a stone.

Soon after this the mother sent the two girls to the town to buy needles, thread, laces and ribbons. The road led over a field where huge boulders of rock lay scattered. As they walked along they saw a big bird hovering in the air, circling slowly above them, but always descending lower, till at last it settled on a rock not far from them. Immediately afterward they heard a sharp, piercing cry.

They ran forward and saw with horror that the eagle had pounced on their old friend the dwarf and was about to carry him off. The tenderhearted girls seized hold of the little man and struggled so long with the bird that at last he let go his prey. When the dwarf had recovered from the first shock he screamed in his screeching voice, "Couldn't you have treated me more carefully? You have torn my fine little coat all to shreds, awkward hussies that you are!" Then he took up a bag of precious stones and vanished under the rocks into his cave.

The girls were accustomed to his ingratitude, and continued on to the town. On their way home, they passed the field again and were surprised to see the dwarf pouring out his precious jewels on an open space, for he had thought no one would pass by at so late an hour. The evening sun shone on the glittering stones, and they sparkled so beautifully that the girls stood still and gazed at them.

"What are you two standing there gaping for?" shrieked the dwarf, and his ashen-gray face became scarlet with rage.

He was about to run off with these angry words when a sudden growl was heard, and a black Bear trotted out of the wood. The dwarf jumped up in great fright, but he had no time to reach his hiding place, for the Bear was already upon him. Then he cried in terror, "Dear Mister Bear, spare me! I'll give you all my treasure. Look at those beautiful precious stones lying there. Spare my life! What pleasure would you get from a poor, feeble little fellow like me? You wouldn't feel me between your teeth. There, lay hold of these two wicked girls; they will be a tender morsel for you, as fat as young quails. Eat them instead."

The Bear, paying no attention to his words, gave the evil little creature one blow with his paw, and he never moved again. The girls had run away, but the Bear called after them, "Snow White and Rose Red, do not be afraid. Wait, and I will come with you." Then they recognized his voice and stood still. When he was quite close to them his bear skin suddenly fell off, and a handsome young man stood beside them, all dressed in gleaming gold.

"I am a king's son," he said, "and was bewitched by that wicked dwarf. Not only had he stolen my treasure, but I was doomed to roam about the woods as a wild bear till his death should set me free. Now he has the punishment he deserves."

Snow White married the Prince, and Rose Red married his brother, and they divided the great treasure the dwarf had collected between them. The old mother lived peacefully with her children for many years. She carried the two rose trees with her. They stood in front of her window, and every year they bore the loveliest red and white roses.

JAKOB AND WILHELM GRIMM, TRANSLATED BY MAY SELLAR

IT'S PERFECTLY TRUE!

"IT'S A DREADFUL busi-
ness," said a hen, and she said it in a part of the town
where the incident had not taken place.

"It's a dreadful business to happen in a hen house.
I wouldn't dare to sleep alone tonight. Thank goodness
there are so many of us up here on the perch!"

And then she told the story she had heard in such a
way that the feathers of the other hens stood on end
as she spoke, and even the Rooster's comb drooped.
It's perfectly true!

But let's begin at the beginning.

It happened in a hen house at the other end of the
town. The sun went down, and the hens flew up. One
of them was a white-feathered, short-legged little thing
who laid her eggs regularly—a most respectable hen
in every way. She settled on the perch, preening herself with her beak. As she did this, one tiny feather
fluttered down.

"There's that feather gone!" said the Hen. "Well,
well, the more I preen myself, the prettier I shall become, no doubt!"

She said it only in fun, you know. She was the life and soul of that crowd, but otherwise, as we've said, most respectable. Then she fell asleep.

All was dark. There sat the hens, packed closely together.

But the white Hen's neighbor wasn't asleep; she had heard and not heard, as one must do in this world for the sake of peace and quiet.

But she couldn't resist telling her neighbor on the other side: "Did you hear? Well, my dear, I won't mention names, but there's one hen I know who is going to pluck out all her feathers just because she thinks it makes her look smart. Humph! If I were a rooster I should simply treat her with the greatest contempt."

Up above the hens lived Mother Owl, Father Owl and all the little Owls. They were a sharp-eared family, and they heard every word; they rolled their eyes, and old Mother Owl flapped her wings. "Don't take any notice—you heard what she said, of course, and I heard it with my own ears. Upon my word, I don't know what the world is coming to! One of the hens, so utterly lost to all sense of henly decency, is sitting there plucking out her feathers with the Rooster looking on the whole time!"

"Little pitchers have big ears," said Father Owl, motioning toward their children. "Be careful what you are saying!"

"Oh, but I shall have to tell the owl across the road," said Mother Owl. "She is somebody well worth associating with, you know." And off she flew to spread the news.

"Tu-whit, tu-whoo, tu-whit, tu-whoo," they hooted together outside the pigeon house over the way. "Have you heard the news? Have you heard the news? There is a hen who has pulled out all her feathers just to please the Rooster. She is freezing to death, if she isn't dead already—tu-whit, tu-whoo, tu-whit, tu-whoo. . . ."

"Where? Where?" asked the pigeons.

"In the yard opposite; I saw it, so to speak, with my own eyes! It's not at all a nice story to tell, but it's perfectly true!"

"Trrrue, too trrrue—trrrue, too trrrue," cooed the pigeons, and they immediately flew down to tell the story in the chicken run below. "There's a hen—in fact, some say there are two hens—who have plucked out all their feathers to be different from the rest and to attract the attention of the Rooster. It was certainly a dreadful thing to do, what with the risk of chills and fever; and they caught cold and died, both of them!"

"Cock-a-doodle-doo! Wake up! Wake up!" crowed the Rooster, flying up onto the fence. He was still half asleep, but he crowed all the same. "Three hens have died of a broken heart, all for the sake of the Rooster;

they've plucked out all their feathers, and now they are dead! It's a dreadful business, it really is, but it's no good trying to keep it quiet. Tell anyone you please!"

"We'll tell, we'll tell!" squeaked the bats; and the Rooster crowed and the hens clucked, "Tell, tell, tell, tell," and so the story flew from one hen house to another, until at last it came back to the place where it had really started: "Five hens . . ." (that's how it was told) "five hens have plucked out all their feathers to show which one has lost the most weight for love of the Rooster; then they pecked at one another till they bled and all five dropped down dead—a shame and a disgrace to their relations, and a serious loss to their owner!"

The Hen who had dropped the little loose feather naturally didn't recognize her own story and, as she was a respectable hen, she exclaimed, "I despise such hens! But there are others just as bad! Things like that ought not to be hushed up; I must do what I can to make certain that the story gets into the papers, then it will soon be known throughout the country and it will surely serve the wretches right and their relations too!"

It was put into the papers, all clearly written in plain print. And it's perfectly true—one little feather can easily become five hens.

HANS CHRISTIAN ANDERSEN, TRANSLATED BY PAUL LEYSSAC

TOM THUMB

In the days of the great King Arthur there lived a mighty magician called Merlin, the most learned and skillful enchanter the world has ever seen.

This famous magician, who could take any form he pleased, was once traveling about as a poor beggar and, being very tired, he stopped at the cottage of a peasant to rest himself, and asked for food.

The farmer bade him welcome, and his wife, who was a goodhearted woman, soon brought him some milk in a wooden bowl and some coarse brown bread on a platter.

Merlin was much pleased with the kindness of the peasant and his wife, but he could not help noticing that though everything was neat and comfortable in the cottage, they both seemed to be very unhappy. He therefore asked them why they were so melancholy, and learned that they were miserable because they had no children.

The poor woman said, with tears in her eyes, "I should be the happiest creature in the world if I had a son; even if he was no bigger than my husband's thumb, I would be satisfied."

Merlin was so amused with the idea of a boy no bigger than a man's thumb that he determined to grant the poor woman's wish.

Accordingly, in a little while the peasant's wife had a son who, wonderful to relate, was not a bit bigger than his father's thumb.

The Queen of the Fairies, wishing to see the little fellow, came in the window while his mother was sitting up in bed admiring him. The Queen kissed the child and, giving him the name of Tom Thumb, sent for some of the fairies, who dressed her little godson according to her orders:

> An oak-leaf hat he had for his crown;
> His shirt of web by spiders spun;
> With jacket wove of thistle's down;
> His trousers were of feathers done.
> His stockings, of apple-rind, they tie
> With eyelash from his mother's eye:
> His shoes were made of mouse's skin,
> Tanned with the downy hair within.

Tom never grew any larger than his father's thumb, which was only of ordinary size; but as he got older he became very cunning and full of tricks. When he was old enough to play with the boys and had lost all his own marbles, he would creep into the bags of his playfellows and fill his pockets with theirs. Then, getting out without their noticing him, Tom would again join in the game.

One day, however, as he was coming out of a bag of marbles, where he had been stealing as usual, the boy to whom it belonged chanced to see him. "Ah, ah, my little Tommy," said the boy, "so I have caught you stealing my marbles at last, and you shall be rewarded for your thievish tricks." On saying this, he drew the string tight around Tom's neck and gave the bag such a hearty shake that poor little Tom's legs, thighs and body were sadly bruised. He roared out with pain and begged the fellow to let him out, promising never to steal again.

A short time afterward Tom's mother was making a batter-pudding, and, being very anxious to see how it was made, he climbed up to the edge of the bowl. But his foot slipped, and he plumped head over heels into the bowl without his mother noticing him. She stirred him into the pudding and set him into the pot to boil.

The batter filled Tom's mouth and prevented him from crying out. But the hot water began to scald him, and he kicked and struggled so much in the pot that his mother thought the pudding was bewitched and, pulling it out of the pot, she threw it outside the door. A poor tinker who was passing by picked up the pudding and, putting it into his knapsack, walked off.

As Tom had now got his mouth cleared of the batter, he began to cry aloud, which so frightened the tinker that he flung down the pudding and ran away. The pudding broke to pieces in the fall, and Tom crept out, covered all over with the batter, and walked home. His mother, who was very sorry to see her darling in such a woeful state, put him into a teacup and soon washed off the batter, after which she kissed him and put him into bed.

Soon after the adventure of the pudding, Tom's mother went to milk her cow in the meadow, and she took Tom along with her. The wind was very high, and, fearing he would be blown away, she tied him to a thistle with a piece of fine thread. The cow soon observed Tom's little oak-leaf hat and, liking the appearance of it, took poor Tom, his hat and the thistle at one mouthful.

While the cow was chewing the thistle, Tom was afraid of her great teeth which threatened to crush him in pieces, and he roared out as loud as he could, "Mother, Mother!"

"Where are you, Tommy, my dear Tommy?" said his mother.

"Here, Mother, in the red cow's mouth."

His mother began to cry and wring her hands. But the cow, surprised at the odd noise in her throat, opened her mouth and let Tom drop out.

Fortunately his mother caught him in her apron as

he was falling, or he might have been dreadfully hurt. She then put Tom inside her blouse and quickly ran home with him.

Tom's father made him a whip of a barley straw to drive the cattle with, and having one day gone into the fields, Tom slipped and rolled into a furrow. A raven which was flying past picked him up, flew with him over the sea and there dropped him.

A large fish swallowed Tom the moment he fell into the sea. Soon after, this fish was caught and bought for the table of King Arthur. When they opened the fish in order to cook it, everyone was very astonished at finding such a little boy. Tom was quite delighted at being free again. They carried him to the King, who made Tom his dwarf, and he soon became a great favorite at court. By his tricks and gambols he not only amused the King and Queen, but the Knights of the Round Table as well. It is said that when the King rode out on horseback he often took Tom along, and if a shower came, Tom would creep into His Majesty's vest pocket and sleep till the rain was over.

King Arthur one day asked Tom about his parents, wishing to know if they were as small as he was and whether they were well off. Tom told the King that his father and mother were as tall as anybody in the court, but that they were in poor circumstances. On hearing this, the King carried Tom to his treasury, where he kept his money, and told him to take as much money

as he could carry home to his parents, which made the poor fellow caper with joy. Tom went to procure a purse, which was made out of a water bubble, and King Arthur gave him a large silver piece to put into it.

Our little hero had some difficulty in lifting the burden upon his back, but at last he succeeded in getting it placed to his liking, and set forward on his journey. Without meeting with any accident, and after resting himself more than a hundred times by the wayside, in two days and two nights he reached his father's house in safety. Tom had traveled forty-eight hours with a huge silver piece on his back and was almost tired to death when his mother ran out to meet him and carried him into the house. But he soon returned to King Arthur's court.

As Tom's clothes had suffered much in the batterpudding and the inside of the fish, His Majesty ordered him a new suit of clothes, and announced he would be mounted as a knight on a mouse.

Of butterfly's wings his shirt was made,
His boots of chicken's hide;
And by a nimble fairy blade,
Well learnèd in the tailoring trade,
His clothing was supplied.
A needle dangled by his side;
A dapper mouse he used to ride;
Thus strutted Tom in stately pride!

It was certainly very diverting to see Tom in this dress and mounted on the mouse as he rode out hunting with the King and nobility, who were ready to expire with laughter at the sight of Tom and his fine prancing charger.

The King was so charmed with his manner that he ordered a little chair to be made, in order that Tom might sit upon the Round Table, and a palace of gold, a foot high, with a door an inch wide, to live in. He also gave Tom a coach drawn by six small mice.

The Queen was so enraged at the honors that were being conferred on Sir Thomas that she resolved to ruin him, and told the King that the little knight had been saucy to her.

The King sent for Tom in great haste, but being fully aware of the danger of royal anger, Tom crept into an empty snail shell where he lay for a long time until he was almost starved with hunger. At last he ventured to peep out and, seeing a fine large butterfly on the ground near his hiding place, he got close to it and, jumping astride it, was carried up into the air. The butterfly flew with him from flower to flower and from tree to tree and from field to field and at last returned to the court, where the King and nobility all strove to catch hold of him, but poor Tom finally fell from his seat into a watering pot, in which he was almost drowned.

When the Queen saw him, she was angry and said

he should be beheaded, and so Tom was put into a mousetrap to wait for his execution.

However, a cat, observing something alive in the trap, patted it about till the wires broke, and set Thomas at liberty.

The King received Tom into favor once again. But Tom did not live to enjoy it, for a large spider one day attacked him, and although he drew his sword and fought well, the spider's poison at last overcame him.

He fell dead on the ground where he stood,
And the spider sucked every drop of his blood.

King Arthur and his whole court were so sorry at the loss of their little favorite that they went into mourning and raised a fine white marble monument over his grave with the following epitaph:

Here lies Tom Thumb, King Arthur's knight,
Who died by a spider's cruel bite.
He was well known in Arthur's court,
Where he afforded gallant sport;
He rode a tilt and tournament,
And on a mouse a-hunting went.
Alive he filled the court with mirth;
His death to sorrow soon gave birth.
Wipe, wipe your eyes, and shake your head
And cry, Alas! Tom Thumb is dead!

OLD ENGLISH TALE, RETOLD BY JOSEPH JACOBS

THE NIGHTINGALE

IN CHINA, the Emperor is Chinese, as you can well understand, and all his courtiers are also Chinese. It happened many years ago, but the story is worth telling again, before it is forgotten.

The Emperor's palace was the most splendid in the world, all made of priceless porcelain, but so brittle and delicate one had to take great care in touching it. In the garden were the most beautiful flowers, and the loveliest of them were hung with silver bells which tinkled as you passed—you could not help admiring them. Everything was admirably arranged for a pleasing effect, and the garden was quite large; even the gardener himself did not know where it ended. Beyond it was a stately forest with great trees and deep lakes. The forest sloped down to the sea, which was a clear blue. Large ships could sail in under the branches of the trees, where lived a Nightingale.

This Nightingale sang so beautifully that even the poor fisherman, who had much to do, stopped to listen when he came at night to haul in his nets. "How beautiful it is!" he said. But he had to attend to his work and forgot about the bird.

Travelers came to the Emperor's capital from many countries and were astonished at the palace and the garden. But as they heard the Nightingale, they all said, "This is the finest of all!"

The travelers told about it when they returned home, and learned scholars wrote many books about the town, the palace and the garden. But they did not forget the Nightingale. She was praised above everything else in the empire, and the poets composed splendid verses about the Nightingale in the forest by the deep blue sea.

These books were sent everywhere in the world, and some of them reached the Emperor. He sat in his golden chair and read and read. He nodded his head now and then, for he liked the brilliant accounts of the town, the palace and the garden. "But the Nightingale is the most wonderful," the books said.

"What!" said the Emperor. "I don't know anything about the Nightingale. Is there such a bird in my empire, and in my own garden? I have never heard of her. Fancy reading about her for the first time in a book written by someone who never lived here!"

He called his first lord, who was so grand that if anyone of lower rank ventured to speak to him, he would say only "Pfft!"—and that means nothing at all.

"There is said to be a most remarkable bird called

a Nightingale," said the Emperor. "They say she is the most glorious wonder of my kingdom. Why has no one ever said anything to me about her?"

"I have never before heard the Nightingale mentioned," said the first lord. "I know that she has never been presented at court! But I will seek her out!"

But where was she to be found? The first lord ran upstairs and downstairs, through the halls and corridors; but no one he met had ever heard of the Nightingale. So the first lord ran again to the Emperor and told him that it must all be imagination on the part of those who had written the books.

"Your Imperial Majesty cannot really believe whatever is written. There are some inventions called the black art."

"But one book in which I read this," said the Emperor, "was sent me by the powerful Emperor of Japan, so it cannot be untrue. The Nightingale must be here this evening! She has my gracious permission to appear before me, and if she does not, the whole court shall be trampled underfoot after supper!"

"Tsing pe!" said the first lord; and he ran upstairs and downstairs, through the halls and corridors, and half the court ran with him, for they did not want to be trampled underfoot.

Everyone was asking about the wonderful Nightingale, of which all the world knew except those at the court of the Chinese Emperor.

At last they met a poor little maid in the kitchen who said, "Oh, I know the Nightingale well. How she sings! Every evening I carry the leftover scraps from the court table to my poor sick mother. When I am going home at night, tired and weary, and I stop to rest for a while in the woods, then I hear the Nightingale singing. It brings tears to my eyes, and I feel as if my mother were kissing me."

"Little kitchen maid," said the first lord, "I will give you a place as the court cook, and you shall have leave to see the Emperor at dinner every night, if you will lead us to the Nightingale. She is invited to appear at court this evening."

So they all went into the forest where the Nightingale usually sang, and half the court went too. On the way they heard a cow mooing.

"Oh," said one of the courtiers, "we have found her! What wonderful power for such a small creature! I am sure I have heard her before."

"No, that is a cow mooing," said the little kitchen maid. "We are still a long way off."

Then the frogs began to croak in the marsh.

"Splendid," said the court chaplain. "That must be the Nightingale. It sounds like distant church bells."

"No, no, those are frogs," said the little kitchen maid. "But I think we shall soon hear her now!"

Then the Nightingale began to sing.

"There she is!" cried the girl. "Listen! She is sitting

there." And she pointed to a small gray bird up in the branches.

"Is it possible?" said the first lord. "I should never have thought it. How ordinary she looks! She must have lost her color, seeing so many distinguished men around her."

"Dear little Nightingale," called the kitchen maid, "our gracious Emperor would like to have you sing for him."

"With the greatest of pleasure," said the Nightingale, and she sang so gloriously that it was a joy to hear her.

"It sounds like crystal bells," said the first lord. "Look how her tiny throat throbs! It is strange we have never heard her before. She will be a great success at court."

"Shall I sing once more for the Emperor?" asked the Nightingale, thinking that he was one of the men standing below.

"My esteemed little Nightingale," said the first lord, "I have the honor to invite you to court this evening, where his gracious Imperial Highness will be enchanted with your charming song!"

"My song sounds best among the trees," said the Nightingale; but she went with them gladly when she heard that the Emperor wished it.

At the palace everything was prepared for the glorious occasion. The porcelain walls and floors glittered in the light of many thousands of golden lamps; gorgeous flowers with tinkling bells were placed in the corridors. There was such hurrying and doors opening and closing that all the bells jingled so one could scarcely hear oneself speak.

In the center of the great hall, where the Emperor sat on his throne, a golden perch had been placed for the Nightingale. The whole court was there, and the little kitchen maid was allowed to stand behind the door, now that she was court cook. Everyone was dressed in his best, and everyone was looking toward the little gray bird to whom the Emperor nodded most kindly.

The Nightingale sang so gloriously that tears came into the Emperor's eyes and rolled down his cheeks. Then the Nightingale sang even more beautifully, and her music melted every heart.

The Emperor was filled with such delight that he said she should wear his gold slipper around her neck. But the Nightingale thanked him and said she had reward enough already: "I have seen tears in the Emperor's eyes; that is the richest reward. An Emperor's tears have great power." Then she sang again with her entrancingly sweet voice.

"That is the most charming coquetry I have ever heard," said the ladies, and all of them held water in their mouths that they might make a jug-jugging sound whenever anyone spoke to them. Then they thought themselves nightingales. The lackeys and chambermaids announced they also were pleased, which means a great deal, for they are most difficult of all to satisfy. In short, the Nightingale was a real success.

She had to stay at court now. She had her own cage, with permission to walk out twice in the day and once at night. She was given twelve servants, each of whom held a silken ribbon which was fastened around one of her tiny legs, so there was not much fun in an outing like this.

The whole town was talking about the wonderful bird, and, when two people met, one would say "Nightin—" and the other "—gale," and then they would sigh and understand each other. Yes, and eleven grocers' children were named after the Nightingale, but not one of them could sing a note.

One day the Emperor received a large parcel, on which was written, "The Nightingale."

"Here is another new book about our famous bird, I am sure," said the Emperor.

It was not a book, however, but a little mechanical toy, which lay in a box—an artificial nightingale, very like the real one, but studded with diamonds, rubies and sapphires. When it was wound up, it could sing one of the songs the real bird sang, and its tail moved up and down, glittering with silver and gold. Around its neck was a little collar on which was written, "The

Nightingale of the Emperor of Japan is nothing compared to that of the Emperor of China."

"Wonderful!" everyone said, and the man who had brought the artificial bird received the title of "Bringer of the Imperial First Nightingale."

"Now they must sing together. What a duet we shall have!"

And so they sang together, but their voices did not blend, for the real Nightingale sang in her way, and the other bird sang waltzes.

"It is not its fault!" said the music master. "It always keeps very good time and is quite correct in every way."

Then the artificial bird had to sing alone. It gave just as much pleasure as the real one, and some said it was much prettier to look at, for it sparkled like bracelets and necklaces. Three-and-thirty times it sang the same piece without being tired.

The courtiers wanted to hear it once again, but the Emperor thought that the living Nightingale should sing for them now—but where was she? No one had noticed that she had flown out of the open window, back to her green woods.

"What shall we do?" said the Emperor.

And all the court scolded and said that the Nightingale was very ungrateful.

"But we still have the better bird!" they said joyfully. Then the artificial one had to sing again, and that was the thirty-fourth time they had heard the same piece, but they did not yet know it by heart; it was much too difficult.

The music master praised the bird and assured them it was better than a real nightingale, not only because of its beautiful diamond-studded plumage, but because of its mechanical interior as well.

"For see, my lords and ladies and Your Imperial Majesty, with the real Nightingale one can never tell which song will come out, but with the artificial bird everything is set beforehand. You can explain its mechanism and show people how man's skill arranged the waltzes and how one note follows the other in perfect order!"

"That is just what I think!" said everyone, and the music master requested permission to show the bird to the people the next Sunday. "They shall hear it sing," commanded the Emperor. And they heard it and were as pleased as if they had had too much tea, after the Chinese fashion. They all said, "Oh!" and held up their forefingers and nodded time. But the poor fisherman who had heard the real Nightingale suddenly remembered its voice and said, "This one sings well enough, but there is something wanting. I don't know what."

The real Nightingale was banished from the kingdom, while the artificial bird was put on a silken cushion by the Emperor's bed. All the presents which it received of gold and precious stones lay around it. It was given the title of "Imperial Night Singer, First from the Left." The Emperor considered that side the more distinguished, for even an Emperor's heart is on the left.

And the music master wrote twenty-five volumes about the artificial bird, all learned, lengthy and full of the hardest Chinese words—yet the people in the court said they had read and understood them, for they remembered that once they had been very stupid about a book and had been trampled underfoot in consequence.

So a whole year passed. The Emperor, the court and the other Chinese knew every note of the artificial bird's song by heart, and they liked it the better for that. They could even sing with it, and they did so. The young street boys sang "Tra-la-la-la-la," and the Emperor sang with the bird too, sometimes. It was indeed delightful.

But one evening, when the artificial bird was singing its best, and the Emperor lay in bed listening to it, something inside the bird snapped! Whir-r-r! All the wheels ran down and then the music ceased. The Emperor sprang up and had his physician summoned, but what could he do?

Then the watchmaker came, and, after a great deal of talking and examining, he repaired the bird as well as he could. But he said the bird must be used as little as possible, as the works were nearly worn out and could not be replaced.

Here was a calamity! Only once a year was the artificial bird allowed to sing, and even that was almost too much for it; but then the music master made a little speech full of difficult words, saying that it was just as good as before, and so, of course, it was just as good as before.

Five years passed, and then a great sorrow befell the nation. The Chinese were fond of their Emperor, and now he lay ill and, it was said, was not likely to live. Already a new Emperor had been chosen, and the people stood in the street and asked the first lord how the old Emperor was.

"Pfft!" said he, and shook his head.

Cold and pale lay the Emperor in his regal bed; all the courtiers believed him dead, and one after the other left him to pay their respects to the new Emperor. Everywhere in the halls and corridors cloth was laid down so no footstep could be heard, and everything was still—very, very still—and nothing came to break the silence.

The Emperor longed for something to relieve the monotony of this deathlike stillness. If only someone would speak to him. If only someone would sing to him. Music would carry his thoughts away and break the spell lying on him. The moon shone in at the open window, but that, too, was silent, quite silent.

"Music! Music!" cried the Emperor. "Precious little golden bird, sing! Sing! I gave you gold and jewels; I hung my gold slipper around your neck with my own hand. Sing! Sing!"

But the bird was silent, for there was no one to wind it up. And everything was silent, terribly still!

All at once there came in through the window the most glorious burst of song. It was the little living Nightingale, who had been sitting on a bough outside. She had heard of the need of her Emperor and had come to sing to him of comfort and hope. As she sang, the blood flowed quicker and quicker in the Emperor's weak body, and life began to return.

"Thank you, thank you," said the Emperor, "you divine little bird. I know you. I banished you from my kingdom, and yet you have given me life again. How can I reward you?"

"You have done that already," said the Nightingale. "I brought tears to your eyes the first time I sang; I shall never forget that. They are jewels that rejoice a singer's heart. But now sleep and grow strong again. I will sing you a lullaby."

And the Emperor fell into a deep, calm sleep as the Nightingale sang.

The sun was shining through the window when he awoke, strong and well. None of his servants had come back yet, for they thought he was dead. But the Nightingale still sang to him.

"You must stay with me always," said the Emperor. "You shall sing only when you like, and I will break the artificial bird into a thousand pieces."

"Don't do that," said the Nightingale. "It did what it could. Keep it as you have done. I cannot build my nest in the palace and live here, but let me come whenever I like. In the evening I will sit on the branch outside the window and sing something to make you feel happy. I will sing of joy and of sorrow; I will sing of the evil and the good which lie hidden from you. The little singing bird flies everywhere—to the poor fisherman's hut or the farmer's cottage, to all those who are far away from you and your court. I love your heart more than your crown, though that has about it a brightness as of something holy.

"Now I will sing to you again, but you must promise me one thing."

"Anything that you ask," said the Emperor, standing up in his beautiful imperial robes, which he had put on himself, and fastening on his sword richly embossed with gold.

"One thing only I beg of you! Do not tell anyone you have a little bird who tells you everything; it will be much better not to have it known."

Then the Nightingale flew away.

When the servants came in to attend their dead Emperor, the Emperor said, "Good morning!"

HANS CHRISTIAN ANDERSEN, ANDREW LANG COLLECTION

CHICKEN LITTLE

ONCE UPON a time there was a tiny little chicken whom everyone called Chicken Little. One day, while she was out in the garden (where she had no right to be), a rose leaf fell on her tail. Away she ran in great fright, for she thought the sky was falling.

As she ran along she met Henny Penny.

"Oh, Henny Penny," cried Chicken Little, "the sky is falling!"

"How do you know that?" asked Henny Penny.

"Oh, I saw it with my eyes; I heard it with my ears; and part of it fell on my tail," said Chicken Little.

"Let us run and tell the King," said Henny Penny.

So they ran along together until they met Ducky Lucky.

"Oh, Ducky Lucky," cried Chicken Little, "the sky is falling!"

"How do you know that?" asked Ducky Lucky.

"Oh, I saw it with my eyes; I heard it with my ears; and part of it fell on my tail," said Chicken Little, "and we are going to tell the King."

"May I go, too?" asked Ducky Lucky.

"Oh, yes," said Chicken Little, and they all ran along together. Presently they met Goosey Loosey.

"Oh, Goosey Loosey," cried Chicken Little, "the sky is falling!"

"How do you know that?" asked Goosey Loosey.

"Oh, I saw it with my eyes; I heard it with my ears; and part of it fell on my tail," said Chicken Little, "and we are going to tell the King."

"May I go, too?" asked Goosey Loosey.

"Oh, yes," said Chicken Little, and they all ran along together. Presently they met Turkey Lurkey.

"Oh, Turkey Lurkey," cried Chicken Little, "the sky is falling!"

"How do you know that?" asked Turkey Lurkey.

"Oh, I saw it with my eyes; I heard it with my ears; and part of it fell on my tail," said Chicken Little, "and we are going to tell the King."

"May I go, too?" asked Turkey Lurkey.

"Oh, yes," said Chicken Little, and they all ran along together. Presently they met Foxy Loxy.

"Oh, Foxy Loxy," cried Chicken Little, "the sky is falling."

"How do you know that?" asked Foxy Loxy.

"Oh, I saw it with my eyes; I heard it with my ears; and part of it fell on my tail," said Chicken Little, "and we are going to tell the King."

"Come with me," said Foxy Loxy, "and I will show

you where the King lives." So Chicken Little, Henny Penny, Ducky Lucky, Goosey Loosey and Turkey Lurkey all followed Foxy Loxy; but, oh! he led them into his den, and they never, never came out again!

ENGLISH FOLK TALE, RETOLD BY CLARA M. LEWIS

THE FROG PRINCE

IN THE OLDEN days, when wishing was still of some use, there lived a King. He had several beautiful daughters, but the youngest was so fair that even the sun, who sees so many wonders, could not help marveling every time he looked into her face.

Near the King's palace lay a large, dark forest, and there, under an old linden tree, was a well. When the day was very warm, the little Princess would go off into this forest and sit at the rim of the cool well. There she would play with her golden ball, tossing it up and catching it deftly in her little hands. This was her favorite game and she never tired of it.

Now it happened one day that, as the Princess

tossed her golden ball into the air, it did not fall into her uplifted hands as usual. Instead, it fell to the ground, rolled to the rim of the well and then into the water. Plunk, splash! The golden ball was gone.

The well was deep and the Princess knew it. She felt sure she would never see her beautiful ball again, so she cried and cried and could not stop. "What is the matter, little Princess?" said a voice behind her. "You are crying so that even a hard stone would have pity on you."

The little girl looked around and there she saw a Frog. He was in the well and stretching his fat, ugly head out of the water. "Oh, it's you—you old water-splasher!" said the girl. "I'm crying over my golden ball. It has fallen into the well."

"Oh, as to that," said the Frog, "I can bring your ball back to you. But what will you give me if I do?"

"Whatever you wish, dear old Frog," said the Princess. "I'll give you my dresses, my beads and all my jewelry—even the golden crown on my head."

The Frog answered, "Your dresses, your beads and all your jewelry, even the golden crown on your head —I don't want them. But if you can find it in your heart to like me and take me for your playfellow, if you will let me sit beside you at the table, eat from your little golden plate and drink from your little golden cup, and if you are willing to let me sleep in your own little bed besides: if you promise me all this, little Princess, then I will gladly go down to the bottom of the well and bring back your golden ball."

"Oh, yes," said the Princess, "I'll promise anything you say if you'll only bring back my golden ball to me." But to herself she thought: What is the silly Frog chattering about? He can only live in the water and croak with the other frogs; he could never be a playmate to a human being.

As soon as the Frog had heard her promise, he disappeared into the well. Down, down, down, he sank; but he soon came up again, holding the golden ball in his mouth. He dropped it on the grass at the feet of the Princess, who was wild with joy when she saw her favorite plaything once more. She picked up the ball and skipped away, thinking no more about the little creature who had returned it to her. "Wait!" cried the Frog. "Take me with you, I can't run that fast."

But what good did it do him to cry out his "Quark! Quark!" after her as loud as he could? She didn't listen to him but hurried home, where she soon forgot the poor Frog, who now had to go back into his well again.

The next evening, the Princess was eating her dinner at the royal table when—plitch, plotch, plitch, plotch—something came climbing up the stairs. When it reached the door, it knocked and cried:

> Youngest daughter of the King,
> Open the door for me!

The Princess rose from the table and ran to see who was calling her. When she opened the door, there sat the Frog, wet and green and cold! Quickly she slammed the door and sat down at the table again, her heart beating loud and fast. The King could see well enough that she was frightened and worried, and he said, "My child, what are you afraid of? Is there a giant out there who wants to carry you away?"

"Oh, no," said the Princess. "It's not a giant, but a horrid old Frog!"

"And what does he want of you?" asked the King.

"Oh, dear Father, as I was playing under the linden tree by the well, my golden ball fell into the water. And because I cried so hard, the Frog brought it back to me; and because he insisted so much, I promised him that he could be my playmate. But I never, never thought that he would ever leave his well. Now he is out there and wants to come in and eat from my plate and drink from my cup and sleep in my little bed. But I couldn't bear that, Papa, he's so wet and ugly and his eyes bulge out!"

While she was talking, the Frog knocked at the door once more and said:

> Youngest daughter of the King,
>   Open the door for me.
> Mind your words at the old well spring;
>   Open the door for me!

At that the King said, "If we make promises, Daughter, we must keep them. So you had better go and open the door."

The Princess still did not want to do it but she had to obey. When she opened the door, the Frog hopped in and followed her until she reached her chair. Then he sat on the floor and said, "Lift me up beside you."

She hesitated—the Frog was so cold and clammy— but her father looked at her sternly and said, "You must keep your promise."

After the Frog was on her chair, he wanted to be put on the table. When he was there, he said, "Now shove your plate a little closer so we can eat together like real playmates."

The Princess shuddered, but she had to do it. The Frog enjoyed the meal and ate heartily, but the poor girl could not swallow a single bite. At last the Frog said, "Now I've eaten enough and I feel tired. Carry me to your room so I can go to sleep."

The Princess began to cry. It had been hard enough to touch the cold, fat Frog, and worse still to have him eat out of her plate, but to have him beside her in her little bed was more than she could bear.

"I want to go to bed," repeated the Frog. "Take me there and tuck me in."

The Princess shuddered again and looked at her father, but he only said, "He helped you in your trouble. Is it fair to scorn him now?"

There was nothing for her to do but pick up the creature—she did it with both hands—and carry him up into her room, where she dropped him in a corner on the floor, hoping he would be satisfied. But after she had gone to bed, she heard something she didn't like. Ploppety, plop! Ploppety, plop! It was the Frog, hopping across the floor, and when he reached her bed he said, "I'm tired and the floor is too hard. I have as much right as you to sleep in a good soft bed. Lift me up or I will tell your father."

At this the Princess was bitterly angry, but she picked the Frog up and put him at the foot of her bed. There he stayed all night; but when the dark was graying into daylight, the Frog jumped down from the bed, out of the door and away, she knew not where.

The next night it was the same. The Frog came back, knocked at the door and said:

> Youngest daughter of the King,
>   Open the door for me.
> Mind your words at the old well spring;
>   Open the door for me!

The only thing the Princess could do was let him in. Again he ate out of her golden plate, sipped out of her golden cup, and again he slept at the foot of her bed. In the morning he went away as before.

The third night he came again. But this time he was not content to sleep at her feet. "I want to sleep under your pillow," he said. "I'd like it better there."

The girl thought she would never be able to sleep with a horrid, damp, goggle-eyed Frog under her pillow. She began to weep softly to herself and couldn't stop until at last she cried herself to sleep.

When the night was over and the morning sunlight burst in at the window, the Frog crept out from under her pillow and hopped off the bed. But as soon as his feet touched the floor something happened to him. In that moment he was no longer a cold, fat, goggle-eyed Frog—he had turned into a young Prince with handsome, friendly eyes!

"You see," he said, "I wasn't what I seemed to be! A wicked old woman bewitched me. No one but you could break the spell, little Princess, and I waited and waited at the well for you to help me."

The Princess was speechless with surprise, but her eyes sparkled.

"And will you let me be your playmate now?" said the Prince, laughing. "Mind your words at the old well spring!"

At this the Princess laughed too, and they both ran out to play with the golden ball.

For years they were the best of friends and the happiest of playmates, and it is not hard to guess, I'm sure, that when they were grown up they were married and lived happily ever after.

JAKOB AND WILHELM GRIMM, TRANSLATED BY WANDA GÁG

CINDERELLA

ONCE THERE was a gentleman who married, for his second wife, the proudest and most haughty woman that was ever seen. She had, by a former husband, two daughters who possessed their mother's temper and who were, indeed, exactly like her in all things. The man had a young daughter of his own, who had an unusually sweet disposition which she took from her mother, who had been the nicest person in the world.

No sooner were the ceremonies of their wedding over than the stepmother began to show her true colors. She could not bear the good qualities of her pretty stepdaughter, and all the less because they made her own daughters appear the more odious. She employed her in the meanest work of the house: scouring the dishes and tables and scrubbing madam's room and those of her daughters. The girl slept in a miserable garret upon a wretched straw bed, while her sisters occupied fine rooms with beds of the very newest fashion, and where they had looking glasses so large they could view themselves from head to foot.

The poor girl bore all of this patiently and dared not tell her father, who would have scolded her, for his wife ruled him entirely. When she had done her work, she used to go into the chimney corner and sit down among the cinders and ashes, which is the reason why they called her Cinderwench. But the younger of the sisters, who was not so rude and mean as the elder, called her Cinderella. However, Cinderella, notwithstanding her shabby attire, was a hundred times more beautiful than her sisters, though they were always dressed very richly.

It happened that the King's son gave a ball and invited all persons of fashion to it. The two sisters were among those invited, for they cut a very grand figure. They were delighted with this invitation and became wonderfully busy choosing such gowns, petticoats and headdresses as might become them. This meant new trouble for Cinderella, for it was she who ironed her sisters' linen and pleated their ruffles, while they talked of nothing but how they should be dressed for the ball.

"For my part," said the elder, "I will wear my red velvet suit with French trimming."

"And I," said the younger, "shall have my usual silk skirt. But then, to make amends for that, I will put on my gold-flowered cloak and my diamond necklace, which is far from being the most ordinary one in the world."

They sent for the best milliner to make up their

headdresses and adjust their double-frilled caps, and they ordered their rouge and beauty patches from Mademoiselle de la Poche.

Cinderella was also consulted in all these matters, for she had excellent ideas, and she offered her services to dress their hair, which they were very willing she should do. As she was doing this, they said to her, "Cinderella, would you not like to go to the ball?"

"Alas," she said, "it is not for such as I."

"You are right," they replied. "It would make people laugh to see a cinderwench at a palace ball."

The two sisters went almost two days without eating, so much were they transported with joy. They broke more than a dozen laces in trying to be laced up tightly so that they might have fine slender shapes, and were continually at their looking glasses. At last the happy day came. They went to court, and Cinderella followed them with her eyes as long as she could and, when she had lost sight of them, she began to cry.

Her godmother found her all in tears, and asked her what was the matter. "I wish I could——I wish I could——" But Cinderella was not able to speak the rest, being interrupted by her tears and sobbing.

This godmother of hers, who was a fairy, said, "You wish to go to the ball—is that not so?"

"Yes," cried Cinderella, with a great sigh.

"Well," said her godmother, "be a good girl, and I will arrange that you shall go!" Then she said to Cinderella, "Run into the garden and bring me a pumpkin."

Cinderella went immediately to gather the finest one and brought it to her godmother, not being able to imagine how this pumpkin could help her go to the ball. Her godmother scooped out all of the inside, leaving nothing but the rind. Then she struck it with her wand, and the pumpkin was instantly turned into a fine coach. She then found six live mice in the mousetrap. She told Cinderella to lift up the little door, and—after she gave each mouse, as it went out, a little tap with her wand—every mouse was turned into a fine horse. Altogether they made a very handsome set of six beautiful horses with blond manes.

Being at a loss for a coachman, Cinderella said, "I will go and see if there is a rat in the rattrap—we may make a coachman of him."

"Yes," replied her godmother. "Go and look."

Cinderella brought the trap to her, and in it there were three huge rats. The fairy chose the one which had the largest beard, and, touching him with her wand, she turned him into a fat, jolly coachman with the smartest mustachios that eyes ever beheld. Then she said to Cinderella, "Go again into the garden, and you will find six lizards; bring them to me."

Cinderella had no sooner done so than her godmother turned them into six footmen, who skipped up immediately behind the coach, their green liveries trimmed with silver.

The fairy then said to Cinderella: "Well, you see here an equipage fit to take you to the ball."

"Oh, yes," cried Cinderella, "but must I go as I am, in these old rags?"

Her godmother barely touched her with her wand, and at that same instant her rags were turned into clothes of silver, all trimmed with gold and jewels. This done, she gave her a pair of glass slippers, the prettiest in the whole world. Thus decked out, Cinderella climbed into her coach. Then her godmother commanded her above all things not to stay after midnight, telling her that—if she stayed one moment later —the coach would be a pumpkin again, her horses mice, her coachman a rat, her footmen lizards and her clothes would become just as they were before.

Cinderella promised her godmother she would not fail to leave the ball before midnight. And then away she drove, scarcely able to contain herself for joy. The King's son, who was told that a great Princess, whom nobody knew, had come, ran out to receive her. He gave her his hand as she alighted from the coach and led her into the hall, among all the company. There was immediately a profound silence; the other guests stopped dancing, and the violins ceased to play, so attentive was everyone to the singular beauties of the unknown newcomer. Nothing was then heard but: "Ha! How lovely she is! Ha! How lovely she is!"

The King himself, old as he was, could not help

watching her, and he told the Queen softly that it was a long time since he had seen so beautiful a creature. All the ladies were busy observing her clothes and headdress, so they might have some made next day after the same pattern, provided they could find such fine materials and able hands to make them.

The King's son conducted her to the seat of honor, and afterward took her out to dance with him, and she danced so gracefully that all admired her more and more. A fine supper was served, but the young Prince ate nothing, so intently was he gazing on Cinderella.

She sat down by her sisters, showing them a thousand civilities, giving them part of the oranges and lemons with which the Prince had presented her, and this surprised them very much, for they did not recognize her. While Cinderella was thus amusing her two sisters, she heard the clock strike eleven and three quarters; she immediately made a curtsy to the company and hastened away as fast as she could.

Reaching home, she ran to seek out her godmother and, after having thanked her, said she could not but heartily wish she might go to the ball the next day, because the King's son had asked her. As she was eagerly telling her godmother all that had happened that evening, her two sisters knocked at the door, which Cinderella ran and opened.

"How long you have stayed!" she cried, rubbing her eyes and stretching herself as if she had just been waked out of her sleep. (She had not, of course, had any inclination to sleep since they had left home.)

"If you had been at the ball," said one of her sisters, "you would not have been tired with it. There came unexpectedly the finest Princess, the most beautiful ever seen with mortal eyes; she showed us a thousand civilities and gave us oranges and lemons."

Cinderella seemed very indifferent, but she asked them the name of that Princess. They told her they did not know it and that the King's son would give all the world to know who she was. At this Cinderella smiled and replied, "She must, then, be very beautiful indeed. How happy you have been! Could I not see her? Ah, dear Miss Charlotte, do lend me your yellow dress which you wear every day."

"Ah, to be sure," cried Miss Charlotte, "lend my clothes to a dirty cinderwench! I should be a fool."

Cinderella, indeed, had expected such an answer and was very glad of the refusal, for she would have been sadly put to it if her sister had done what she asked for jestingly.

The next day the two sisters were at the ball, and so was Cinderella, but dressed more magnificently than before. The King's son was always by her side and never ceased his compliments and kind speeches to her. All this was so far from being tiresome that she quite forgot what her godmother had commanded her. At last, she counted the clock striking twelve when she had thought it to be no more than eleven. She then rose up and fled, as nimble as a deer.

The Prince followed but could not overtake her. But she lost one of her glass slippers, which the Prince picked up most carefully. Cinderella reached home quite out of breath and in her old clothes, having nothing left of her finery but one of the little slippers, mate to the one she had dropped.

The guards at the palace gate were asked if they had seen a Princess go out. But no, they had seen nobody except a young girl, very poorly dressed, who had more the air of a country wench than a gentlewoman.

When the two sisters returned from the ball, Cinderella asked them if they had been well entertained, and if the fine lady had been there. They told her yes, but that she had hurried away immediately when it struck twelve and with such haste that she dropped one of her little glass slippers, which the Prince had picked up. He had done nothing but look at her during the ball, and he was very much in love with the beautiful girl who owned the glass slipper.

What they said was true, for a few days afterward the King's son caused it to be proclaimed, by sound of trumpet, that he would marry her whose foot this slipper would just fit. His gentlemen-in-waiting began to try it upon the princesses, then the duchesses and all the court, but in vain. It was brought to the two sisters, who each did what she possibly could to thrust her foot into the slipper. But they could not manage it. Cinderella, who knew her slipper, said to them, smiling, "Let me see if it will not fit me."

Her sisters burst out laughing and began to tease her. The gentleman who was sent to try the slipper looked earnestly at Cinderella and, finding her very lovely, said it was only fair that she should try and that he had orders to let everyone do so.

He bade Cinderella sit down and, putting the slipper to her foot, he found it went on easily and fitted her as if it had been made of wax. The astonishment of her two sisters was great, but it was greater still when Cinderella pulled out of her pocket the other slipper. At this, there appeared her godmother, who touched Cinderella's clothes with her wand, making them more magnificent than any she had ever worn before.

Her two sisters threw themselves at her feet to beg pardon for all the ill-treatment they had made her undergo. Cinderella embraced them and cried that she forgave them with her whole heart and desired them always to love her.

She was conducted to the young Prince. He thought her more charming than ever and, a few days afterward, married her. Cinderella, who was no less good than she was beautiful, gave her two sisters lodging in the palace and, that very same day, matched them with two great lords of the court.

CHARLES PERRAULT, ANDREW LANG COLLECTION

THE PRINCESS AND THE PEA

HERE WAS once upon a time a Prince who wanted to marry a princess, but she had to be a true princess. So he traveled through the whole world to find one, but there was always something against each one he met. There were plenty of princesses, but he could not find out if they were true princesses. In every case there was some little defect which showed the right person had not yet been found. So he came home again in very low spirits, for he had wanted very much to have a true princess for his bride.

One night there was a dreadful storm; it thundered, the lightning flashed and the rain streamed down in torrents. It was fearful! In the midst of the storm there was a knocking heard at the palace gate, and the old King went to open it.

There stood a Princess outside the gate; but, oh, in what a sad plight she was from the rain and the storm! The water was running down from her hair and her dress into the tips of her shoes and out at the heels again. And yet this girl said that she was really a true princess!

Well, we shall soon find out! thought the old Queen, when the King had brought her in. But she said nothing and went into one of the bedchambers, took off the bedclothes and laid a pea on the bottom of the bed.

Then she put twenty mattresses on top of the pea and twenty eiderdown quilts on top of the mattresses. And this was the bed in which the Princess was to spend the night.

The next morning the Queen asked the girl how she had slept.

"Oh, very badly!" said the Princess. "I scarcely closed my eyes all night! I am sure I don't know what was in the bed. I lay on something so hard that my whole body is black and blue. It is dreadful!"

Now they perceived that she was indeed a true princess, as she had claimed, because she had felt the pea through the twenty mattresses and the twenty eiderdown quilts.

No one, surely, but a true princess could be as sensitive as that.

So the Prince married her, for he knew that at last he had found a true princess. And the pea was put into the Royal Museum, where it is still to be seen if no one has stolen it.

Now, this is a true story.

HANS CHRISTIAN ANDERSEN, COLLECTION OF
KATE DOUGLAS WIGGIN AND NORA ARCHIBALD SMITH

ALI BABA AND
THE FORTY THIEVES

IN A TOWN in Persia there dwelled two brothers, one named Cassim, the other Ali Baba. Cassim was married to a rich wife and lived in wealth and plenty, while Ali Baba had to maintain his wife and children by cutting wood in a neighboring forest and selling it in the town.

One day, when Ali Baba was in the forest, he saw a troop of men on horseback coming toward him in a cloud of dust. He was afraid they were robbers and climbed up among some rocks for safety.

When they came up to him and dismounted, he counted forty of them. They unbridled their horses and tied them to trees.

The finest man among them, whom Ali Baba took to be their captain, went a little way into the bushes and said, "Open, Sesame!" so plainly that Ali Baba heard him. A door opened in the rocks and, having made the troops go in, the captain followed them, and the door shut again of itself.

They stayed some time inside, and Ali Baba, fearing

they might come out and catch him, was forced to sit patiently hidden in the rocks. At last the door opened again, and the forty thieves came out. As the captain had gone in last he came out first and made them all pass by him. He then closed the door, saying, "Shut, Sesame!" Every man bridled his horse and mounted, the captain put himself at their head, and they departed as they had come.

Then Ali Baba climbed down and went to the door concealed in the bushes and said, "Open, Sesame!" and it flew open. Ali Baba, who expected a dull, dismal place, was greatly surprised to find it large and well lighted and hollowed by the hand of man in the form of a vault, which received the light from an opening in the ceiling. He saw rich bales of merchandise—silk stuffs and brocades all piled together, gold and silver in heaps, and money in leather purses. He went in, and the door shut behind him. He did not look at the silver but brought out as many bags of gold as he thought his donkeys, which were browsing outside, could carry, loaded them with the bags and covered the bags with firewood.

Using the words "Shut, Sesame!" he closed the door after him and went home.

Then he drove his donkeys into his own yard, shut the gates, carried the bags to his wife and emptied them out before her. He bade her keep his adventure a secret and told her that he would bury the gold.

"Let me first measure it," said his wife. "I will borrow a measure from someone while you dig the hole."

So she ran to the wife of Cassim and borrowed a measure. Knowing Ali Baba's poverty, the sister-in-law was curious to find out what sort of grain his wife wished to weigh and artfully put some suet at the bottom of the measure. Ali Baba's wife went home and set the measure on the heap of gold and filled it and emptied it often, to her great content. She then took the measure back to her sister-in-law, without noticing that a piece of gold was sticking to it.

Cassim's wife saw it as soon as her back was turned. She grew very curious and said to her husband when he came home that evening, "Cassim, your brother is richer than you. He does not count his money; he measures it."

He begged her to explain this riddle, which she did by showing him the piece of money and telling him where she had found it. Then Cassim grew so envious that he could not sleep and went to his brother in the morning before sunrise.

"Ali Baba," he said, showing him the gold piece, "how is it that you pretend to be poor and yet you measure gold?"

By this Ali Baba realized that, through his wife's folly, Cassim and his wife knew his secret, so he confessed all and offered Cassim a share.

"That I expect," said Cassim, "but I must know

where to find the treasure, otherwise I will try to discover it for myself and you will lose it all."

Ali Baba, more out of kindness than fear, told him of the cave and the very words to use. Cassim left Ali Baba immediately, meaning to reach the cave before his brother and get the treasure for himself. He rose early next morning and set out with three mules loaded with great chests. He soon found the place and the door in the rock.

He said, "Open, Sesame!" and the door opened and shut behind him.

He could have feasted his eyes all day on the treasure, but he now hastened to gather together as much of it as possible; but when he was ready to go he could not remember what to say, for he was thinking only of his great riches. Instead of "Open, Sesame!" he said, "Open, Barley!" and the door remained fast. He named several other sorts of grain—for sesame is a kind of grain—all but the right one, and the door still stuck fast. He was so frightened at the danger he was in that he had as much forgotten the word as if he had never heard it.

About noon the robbers returned to their cave and saw Cassim's mules roving about with great chests on their backs. This gave them the alarm. They drew their sabers and went to the door, which opened on the captain's saying, "Open, Sesame!"

Cassim, who had heard the trampling of their

horses' feet, resolved to sell his life dearly, so when the door opened he leaped out and threw the captain down. In vain, however, for the robbers soon killed him with their sabers. On entering the cave they saw all the bags laid ready and could not imagine how he had entered in without knowing their secret. They cut Cassim's body into four quarters and nailed them up inside the cave in order to frighten anyone who should venture in. Then they went away in search of more treasure.

As night drew on, Cassim's wife grew very uneasy, and she ran to her brother-in-law to tell him where her husband had gone. Ali Baba did his best to comfort her and set out for the forest in search of Cassim. The first thing he saw on entering the cave was his dead brother. Full of horror, he put the body on one of the mules and bags of gold on the other two and, covering all with firewood, returned home. He drove the two mules laden with gold into his own yard and led the other to Cassim's house. The door was opened by the slave Morgiana, whom Ali Baba knew to be both brave and cunning.

Unloading the mule, he said to her, "This is the body of your master, who has been murdered, but whom we must bury as though he had died in his bed. I will speak with you again, but now tell your mistress that I have come."

The wife of Cassim, on learning the fate of her husband, broke out into cries and tears, but Ali Baba offered to take care of her for life if she would promise to keep his counsel and leave everything to Morgiana. She agreed to this and dried her eyes.

Morgiana, meanwhile, sought out an apothecary and asked him for some lozenges. "My poor master," she said, "can neither eat nor speak and no one knows what his illness is." She carried home the lozenges and returned next day, weeping, and asked for an essence only given to those almost dead. Thus, in the evening, no one was surprised to hear the shrieks and cries of Cassim's wife and Morgiana, telling everyone that Cassim had just died.

The next day Morgiana went to an old cobbler named Baba Mustapha, who opened his stall early near the gates of the town. She put a piece of gold in his hand and, having bound his eyes with a handkerchief, bade him follow her with his needle and thread. She took him to the room where the body lay, pulled off the bandage and bade him sew the quarters together, after which she covered his eyes again and led him back to his stall.

Then they buried Cassim, and Morgiana, his slave, followed him to the grave, weeping and tearing her hair, while Cassim's wife stayed at home uttering lamentable cries. Next day Ali Baba and his family went to live in Cassim's house, and Cassim's shop was given to Ali Baba's eldest son.

The forty thieves, meanwhile, on their return to the cave were much astonished to find Cassim's body gone as well as some of their money bags.

"We are certainly discovered," said the captain, "and shall be undone if we cannot find out who it is that knows our secret. Two men must have known it; we have killed one—we must now find the other. To this end one of you who is bold and artful must go into the city, dressed as a traveler, and discover whom we have killed and whether men talk of the strange manner of his death. If the messenger fails, he must lose his life, lest we be betrayed."

One of the thieves started up and offered to do this; and, after the rest had highly commended him for his bravery, he disguised himself and happened to enter the town at daybreak, just by Baba Mustapha's stall. The thief bade Baba Mustapha good day, saying to him, "Honest man, how can you possibly see to stitch at your age?"

"Old as I am," replied the cobbler, "I have very good eyes, and you will believe me when I tell you that I have sewn a dead body together in a place where I had less light than I have now."

The robber was overjoyed at his good fortune and, giving the cobbler a piece of gold, desired to be shown the house where he had stitched up the dead body. At first Mustapha refused, saying that he had been blind-folded. But when the robber gave him another piece of gold he began to think he might remember the turnings if blindfolded as before. This means succeeded. The robber partly led him and was partly guided by him right to the front of Cassim's house, the door of which the robber marked with a piece of chalk.

Then, well pleased, he bade farewell to Baba Mustapha and returned to the forest. By and by Morgiana, going out, saw the mark the robber had made, quickly guessed that some mischief was brewing and, fetching a piece of white chalk, marked two or three doors on each side, without saying anything to her master or mistresses.

The thief, meanwhile, told his comrades of his discovery. The captain thanked him and bade him show them the house he had marked. But when they came to it they saw that five or six of the houses were chalked in the same manner. The guide was so confounded that he knew not what answer to make, and when they returned to the cave he was at once beheaded for having failed in his mission.

Another robber was dispatched and, having won over Baba Mustapha, marked the house in red chalk. But Morgiana was again too clever for them, and the second messenger was put to death also.

The captain now resolved to go himself but, wiser than the others, he did not mark the house but looked at it so closely he could not fail to remember it. He returned and ordered his men to go into the neighboring villages and buy nineteen mules and thirty-eight leather jars, all empty, except one which was full of oil. The captain put one of his men, fully armed, into each, rubbing the outside of the jars with oil from the full vessel. Then the nineteen mules were loaded with the jar of oil and thirty-seven robbers in jars, and they reached the town at dusk.

The captain stopped his mules in front of the house and said to Ali Baba, who was sitting outside in the cool evening air, "I have brought some oil from a distance to sell at tomorrow's market, but it is now so late that I know not where to pass the night, unless you will do me the favor to take me in."

Though Ali Baba had seen the captain of the robbers in the forest, he did not recognize him in the disguise of an oil merchant. He bade him welcome, opened his gates for the mules to enter and went to Morgiana to bid her prepare a bed and supper for his guest. He brought the stranger into his hall and, after they had supped, went again to speak to Morgiana in the kitchen, while the captain went into the yard under the pretense of seeing after his mules but really to tell his men what to do.

Beginning at the first jar and ending at the last, he said to each man, "As soon as I throw some stones from the window of the chamber where I lie, cut the jars open with your knives and come out, and I will be with you in a trice."

He returned to the house and Morgiana led him to his chamber. She then told her fellow slave, Abdallah, to make some broth for her master, who had gone to bed. Meanwhile, her lamp had gone out and there was no more oil in the house.

"Do not be uneasy," said Abdallah. "Go into the yard and take some out of one of those jars."

Morgiana thanked him for his advice, took the oil pot and went into the yard. When she came to the first jar the robber inside said softly, "Is it time?"

Any other slave but Morgiana, on finding a man in the jar instead of the oil she wanted, would have screamed and called for help. But she, knowing the danger her master was in, bethought herself of a plan and answered quietly, "Not yet, but presently."

She went to all the jars, giving the same answer, till she came to the jar of oil. Morgiana now saw that her master, thinking he was entertaining an oil merchant, had let thirty-eight robbers into his house. She filled her oil pot, went back to the kitchen and, having lit her lamp, went again to the oil jar and filled a large kettle full of oil. As soon as it boiled, she went and poured enough oil into every jar to stifle and kill the robber inside. When this brave deed was done she went back to the kitchen, put out the fire and the lamp and waited to see what would happen.

In a quarter of an hour the captain of the robbers awoke, got up and opened the window. As all seemed quiet, he threw down some little pebbles which hit the jars. He listened and, when none of his men stirred, he grew uneasy and went down into the yard. On going to the first jar and saying, "Are you asleep?" he smelled the hot boiled oil and knew at once that his plot to murder Ali Baba and his household had been discovered. He found all the thieves were dead and, missing the oil out of the last jar, became aware of the manner of their death. He then forced the lock of a door leading into a garden and, climbing over several walls, made his escape.

Morgiana saw all this and, rejoicing at her success, went to bed and fell asleep.

At daybreak Ali Baba arose and, seeing the oil jars there still, asked why the merchant had not left with his mules. Morgiana bade him look in the first jar and see if there was any oil. Seeing a man, he started back in terror. "Have no fear," said Morgiana, "the man cannot harm you; he is dead."

Ali Baba, when he had recovered from his astonishment, asked what had become of the merchant.

"Merchant!" said she. "He is no more a merchant than I am!" And she told him the whole story, assuring him that it was a plot of the forty robbers of the forest, of whom she thought three were still alive, and that the white and red chalk marks had something to do with it. Ali Baba at once gave Morgiana her freedom, saying that he owed her his life. They then buried the bodies in Ali Baba's garden, while the mules were sold in the market by his slaves.

The captain returned to his lonely cave, which seemed frightful to him without his lost companions, and firmly resolved to avenge them by killing Ali Baba. He dressed himself carefully and went back into the town, where he lodged at an inn. In the course of a great number of journeys to the forest, he carried away many rich stuffs and much fine linen and set up a shop opposite that of Ali Baba's son. He called himself Cogia Hassan and, as he was both civil and well dressed, he soon made friends with Ali Baba's son and through him with Ali Baba, whom he was continually asking to sup with him.

Ali Baba, wishing to return his kindness, invited him into his house and received him smiling, thanking him for his kindness to his son. When the merchant was about to take his leave, Ali Baba stopped him, saying, "Where are you going, sir, in such haste? Will you not stay and sup with me?"

The merchant refused, saying that he had a reason and, on Ali Baba's asking him what that was, he replied, "It is, sir, that I can eat no foods that have any salt in them."

"If that is all," said Ali Baba, "let me tell you there shall be no salt in either the meat or the bread that we eat tonight."

He went to give this order to Morgiana, who was

much surprised, as custom made sacred the friendship of those who partook of salt together.

"Who is this man you speak of," she said, "who eats no salt with his meat?"

"He is an honest man, Morgiana," returned Ali Baba, "therefore do as I bid you."

But she could not withstand a desire to see this strange man, so she helped Abdallah carry up the dishes and saw in a moment that Cogia Hassan was the robber captain and carried a dagger under his garment. "I am not surprised," she said to herself, "that this wicked man who intends to kill my master will eat no salt with him, but I will hinder his plans."

She sent up the supper with Abdallah, while she made ready for one of the boldest acts that could be thought of. When the dessert had been served, Cogia Hassan was left alone with Ali Baba and his son, whom he thought to make drunk and then murder.

Morgiana, meanwhile, put on a headdress like a dancing girl's and clasped a jeweled belt around her waist, from which hung a dagger with a silver hilt. She said to Abdallah, "Take your tambourine, and let us go and divert our masters and their guest."

Abdallah took his instrument and played before Morgiana until they came to the door, where Abdallah stopped playing and Morgiana made a low curtsy.

"Come in, Morgiana," said Ali Baba. "Let Cogia Hassan see how you can dance."

Cogia Hassan was by no means pleased, for he feared that his chance of killing Ali Baba was gone for the present, but he pretended great eagerness to see Morgiana, and Abdallah began to play and Morgiana to dance. After she had performed several dances she drew her dagger and made passes with it, sometimes pointing it at her own breast, sometimes at her masters', as if it were part of the dance. Suddenly, out of breath, she snatched the tambourine from Abdallah with her left hand and held it out to her master, clutching the dagger in her right. Ali Baba and his son put a piece of gold into it, and Cogia Hassan, seeing that she was coming to him, pulled out his purse to make her a present, but while he was putting his hand into it Morgiana plunged the dagger into his heart.

"Unhappy girl!" cried Ali Baba and his son. "What have you done to ruin us?"

"It was to preserve you, master, not to ruin you," answered Morgiana. "See here"—opening the false merchant's garment and showing the dagger—"see what an enemy you have entertained! Remember, he would eat no salt with you; what more would you have? Look at him! He is both the false oil merchant and the captain of the forty thieves."

Ali Baba was so grateful to Morgiana for thus saving his life that he offered her in marriage to his son, who readily consented; and the wedding was celebrated with great splendor a few days after.

At the end of a year, Ali Baba, having heard nothing of the two remaining robbers, judged they were dead and set out to the cave. The door opened on his saying, "Open, Sesame!" Going in, he saw that nobody had been there since the captain had left it. He brought away as much gold as he could carry and returned to town. He told his son the secret of the cave, which his son handed down in turn, so the children and grandchildren of Ali Baba were rich to the end of their lives.

ARABIAN NIGHTS, TRANSLATED BY ANTOINE GALLAND

THE GOLDEN GOOSE

THERE WAS once a man who had three sons. The youngest of them was called Simpleton, and he was sneered and jeered at and snubbed on every possible opportunity. One day it happened that the eldest son wished to go into the forest to cut wood, and before he started out his mother gave him a fine rich cake and a bottle of wine so that he might be sure not to suffer from hunger or thirst.

When he reached the forest he met a little gray old man who wished him "Good morning" and said, "Do give me a piece of that cake you are carrying and a drink from your bottle of wine—I am so hungry and thirsty."

But this clever son replied, "If I give you my cake and wine I shall have none for myself; you just go your own way." And he left the little gray man standing there and went farther on into the forest. There he began to cut down a tree, but before long he made a false stroke with his axe, and cut his own arm so badly that he was obliged to go home and have it bound up by his mother.

Then the second son went to the forest, and his mother gave him a good cake and a bottle of wine as she had to his elder brother. He too met the little gray old man, who begged him for a morsel of cake and a drink of wine.

But the second son spoke most sensibly also, and said, "Whatever I give to you I deprive myself of. Just go your own way, will you?"

Not long afterward his punishment overtook him, for no sooner had he struck a couple of blows with his axe than he cut his leg so badly that he had to be carried back home.

Then the youngest son said, "Father, let me go out and cut wood."

But his father answered, "Both your brothers have

injured themselves. You had better not; you know nothing about it."

The boy begged him so hard to be allowed to go that at last his father said, "Very well, then—go! Perhaps when you have hurt yourself, you may learn to know better." His mother gave him only a very plain cake, made with water and baked in the cinders, and a bottle of sour beer.

When he came to the forest, he too met the little gray old man, who greeted him and said, "Give me a piece of your cake and a drink from your bottle. I am so hungry and thirsty."

The boy replied, "I have just a cinder cake and some sour beer, but if you care to have that, let us sit down and eat."

So they sat down, and when the boy brought out his cake he found it had turned into a fine rich loaf, and the sour beer into excellent wine. Then they ate and drank all they wanted.

When they had finished eating, the little gray man said, "Now I will bring you luck, because you have a kind heart and are willing to share what you have with others. There stands an old tree. Cut it down, and among its roots you'll find something."

With that the little man took his leave.

Then the boy began at once to hew down the tree, and when it fell he found among its roots a goose whose feathers were all of pure gold. He lifted it out, carried it off and took it with him to an inn where he meant to spend the night.

Now the landlord of the inn had three daughters, and when they saw the goose they were filled with curiosity about this wonderful bird, and each longed to have one of its golden feathers.

The eldest said to herself, "No doubt I shall soon find a good opportunity to pluck out one of its feathers," and the first time Simpleton happened to leave the room she caught hold of the goose by its wing. But, lo and behold! her fingers seemed to stick fast to the goose, and she could not take her hand away. Soon afterward the second daughter came in and thought to pluck a golden feather for herself too; but hardly had she touched her sister than she stuck fast as well. At last the third sister came with the same intention, but the other two cried out, "Keep off! For Heaven's sake, keep off!"

The youngest sister could not imagine why she was to keep off, and thought: If they are both there, why should not I be there too? So she sprang toward them; but no sooner had she touched one of them than she stuck fast to her. And they all three had to spend the night with the goose.

Next morning the boy tucked the goose under his arm and went off, without in the least troubling himself about the three girls who were hanging on to it. They just had to run after him right or left as best they could. In the middle of a field they met the parson, and when he saw this procession he cried, "For shame, you bold girls! What do you mean by running after a young fellow through the fields like that?"

And with that he caught the youngest girl by the arm to draw her away. But directly he touched her he stuck on and had to run along with the rest.

Not long afterward the town clerk came that way and was much surprised to see the parson following the footsteps of the three girls. "Why, where is Your Reverence going so fast?" cried he. And he ran after him, grabbed his coat and hung on to it himself.

As the five of them trotted along in this fashion one after the other, two peasants were coming from their work with their hoes. On seeing them, the parson called out and begged them to come and rescue him and the clerk. But no sooner did the first one touch the clerk than they were stuck too, and so there were seven of them running after Simpleton and his goose.

After a time they came to a town where a King reigned whose daughter was so serious and solemn that no one could ever manage to make her laugh. So the King had decreed that whoever should succeed in making her laugh could marry her.

When Simpleton heard this he marched before the Princess with his goose and its appendages, and as soon as she saw these seven people continually running after each other, she burst out laughing and could not stop

herself. Then he claimed her as his bride, but the King, who did not much fancy him as a son-in-law, made all sorts of objections and told him he must first find a man who could drink up a whole cellarful of wine.

Simpleton bethought him of the little gray old man, who could, he felt sure, help him. So he went off to the forest, and on the very spot where he had cut down the tree he saw a man with a most dismal expression on his face.

He asked the man what he was taking so much to heart, and the man answered, "I don't know how I am ever to quench this terrible thirst I am suffering from. Cold water doesn't suit me at all. To be sure, I've emptied a whole barrel of wine, but what is one drop on a hot stone?"

"I think I can help you," said the boy. "Come with me, and you shall drink to your heart's content."

So he took him to the King's cellar, and the man sat down before the huge casks and drank and drank till he had drunk up the whole contents of the cellar before the day closed.

Then Simpleton asked once more for his bride, but the King felt vexed at the idea of a stupid fellow whom people called Simpleton carrying off his daughter, and he began to make fresh conditions. He required Simpleton to find a man who could eat a mountain of bread. The boy did not wait to consider long but went straight off to the forest, and there on the same spot sat a man who was drawing in a strap as tightly as he could around his body, and making a most woeful face the while.

Said he, "I've eaten up a whole ovenful of loaves, but what's the good of that to anyone who is as hungry as I am? I declare my stomach feels quite empty, and I must draw my belt tight if I'm not to die of starvation."

Simpleton was delighted, and said, "Get up and come with me, and you shall have plenty to eat," and he brought him to the King's court.

Now the King had given orders to have all the flour in his kingdom brought together and to have a huge mountain baked of it. But the man from the wood just took up his stand before the mountain and began to eat, and in one day it had all vanished.

For the third time Simpleton asked for his bride, but again the King tried to make some evasion, and demanded a ship which could sail on land or water. "When you come sailing in such a ship," said he, "you shall have my daughter without further delay."

Again the boy started off to the forest, and there he found the little gray old man with whom he had shared his cake and who said, "I have eaten and I have drunk for you, and now I will give you the ship. I have done all these things for you because you were kind and merciful to me."

Then he gave him a ship which could sail on land or

water, and when the King saw it he felt he could no longer refuse him his daughter. So they celebrated the wedding with great rejoicings, and after the King's death Simpleton succeeded to the kingdom, and lived happily with his wife for many years.

JAKOB AND WILHELM GRIMM, TRANSLATED BY MAY SELLAR

WHY THE SEA IS SALT

ONCE UPON a time long, long ago, there were two brothers, the one rich and the other poor. When Christmas Eve came, the poor one had not a bite in the house, either of meat or bread. So he went to his brother and begged him, in Heaven's name, to give him something for Christmas Day. It was by no means the first time his brother had been forced to give some food to him, and he was no more pleased at being asked now than he generally was.

"If you will do what I ask you, you shall have a whole ham," said he. The poor one immediately thanked him and promised.

"Well, here is the ham, and now you must go

straight to Dead Man's Hall," said the rich brother, throwing the ham to him.

"Well, I will do what I have promised," said the poor man, and he took the ham and set off. He went on and on for the livelong day, and at nightfall he came to a place where there was a bright light. I have no doubt this is the place, thought the man with the ham.

An old man with a long white beard was chopping yule logs.

"Good evening," said the man with the ham.

"Good evening to you. Where are you going at this late hour?" asked the old man.

"I am going to Dead Man's Hall, if only I am on the right track," answered the poor man.

"Oh, yes, you are right enough, for it is here," the old man said. "When you go inside they will all want to buy your ham, for they don't get much meat to eat there. But you must not sell it unless you can get for it the hand mill which stands behind the door. When you come out again I will teach you how to stop the hand mill, which is useful for almost everything."

So the man with the ham thanked the other for his good advice and rapped at the door. When he went in, everything happened just as the old man had said. All the people, great and small, came around him like ants on an anthill, and each tried to outbid the other for the ham.

"By rights, my old woman and I should have it for

our Christmas dinner, but since you have set your hearts upon it, I must just give it up to you," said the man. "But, if I sell it, I will have the hand mill standing there behind the door."

At first they would not hear of this, and haggled and bargained with the man, but he stuck to what he had said, and the people were forced to give the hand mill to him. When the man returned to the yard, he asked the old woodcutter how to stop the hand mill. And when he had learned that, he thanked him and set off with all the speed he could, but did not arrive home until after the clock had struck twelve on Christmas Eve.

"But where in the world have you been?" asked the old woman, his wife. "Here I have sat waiting for you hour after hour, and have not even two sticks to lay across each other underneath the Christmas porridge pot."

"Oh, I could not come before. I had something of importance to see about, and a long way to go, too. But now you shall just see!" said the man. Then he set the mill on the table and bade it first grind light, then a tablecloth, then meat and beer and everything else that was good for a Christmas Eve supper.

And the mill ground all that he ordered.

"Bless me!" said the old woman, as one thing after another appeared. She wanted to know where her husband had gotten the mill, but he would not tell her.

"Never mind where I got it. You can see it is a good one, and the water that turns it will never freeze," said the man. So he ground meat and drink and all kinds of good things, to last through Christmastide, and on the third day he invited friends to come to a feast.

Now when the rich brother saw what there was at the banquet and in the house, he was both vexed and angry, for he grudged everything his brother had. On Christmas Eve he was so poor he came to me and begged for a trifle, and here he gives a feast as if he were both a count and a king! thought he. "But, for Heaven's sake, tell me where you got your riches," said he to his brother.

"From behind the door," said he who owned the mill, for he did not choose to satisfy his brother on that point. But later in the evening, when he had taken a drop too much, he could not refrain from telling how he had come by the hand mill. "There you see what has brought me all my wealth!" And he brought out the mill from the cupboard and made it grind first one thing and then another.

When the brother saw that, he insisted on having the mill and after a great deal of persuasion got it. But he had to give three hundred dollars for it, and the poor brother was to keep it till haymaking time, for he thought: If I keep it that long, I can make it grind meat and drink that will last many a long year.

During that time the mill did not grow rusty, and, when hay harvest came, the rich brother took it, but the other had taken good care not to teach him how to stop it. It was evening when the rich man reached home, and in the morning he bade the old woman who tended his rooms and kitchen go out and spread the hay after the mowers, for he would attend to the house himself that day.

So, when dinner time drew near, he set the mill on the kitchen table and said, "Grind herrings and milk pudding, and do it both quickly and well."

So the mill began to grind herrings and milk pudding, and first all the dishes and tubs were filled, and then it covered the kitchen floor. The man twisted and turned the mill and did all he could to make it stop, but howsoever he turned it and screwed it, the mill went on grinding, and in a short time the pudding rose so high that the man was almost drowned. So he threw open the parlor door, but it was not long before the mill had ground the parlor full too, and it was with difficulty and danger that the man got through the mess of pudding and grabbed hold of the door latch. When the door was open, he did not stay long in the room, but ran out, and the herrings and pudding came after him and streamed out over both farm and field.

Now the old woman, who was out spreading the hay, began to think dinner was long in coming, and

said to the women and the mowers, "Though the master does not call us home, we may as well go. It may be he finds he is not good at making dinner, and I should go to help him." So they began to straggle homeward, but a little way up the hill they met the herrings and pudding, all pouring forth and winding about one over the other, and the man himself in front of the flood.

"Would to Heaven that each of you had a hundred stomachs! Take care that you are not drowned in the pudding!" he cried as he ran by them as if Mischief were at his heels, down to where his brother dwelled. Then he begged him to take the mill back again, and to do so in that instant, for, said he, "If it grind one hour more the whole district will be destroyed by herrings and pudding!" But the brother would not take it until the other paid him another three hundred dollars, and that he was obliged to do.

Now the poor brother had both the money and the mill again. So it was not long before he had a farmhouse much finer than his brother's, but the mill ground him so much money that he covered his house with blocks of gold, and, as it lay close by the seashore, it shone and glittered far out to sea. Everyone who sailed by put in to visit the rich man in the gold farmhouse, and everyone wanted to see the wonderful mill, for the report of it spread far and wide, and there was no one who had not heard tell of it.

After a long, long time there came a skipper who wished to see the mill. He asked if it could make salt. "Yes, it can make salt," said he who owned it, and when the skipper heard that, he wished with all his might and main to have the mill, no matter what it cost. He thought that if he had it he would not have to sail far away over the perilous sea for his cargo of salt. At first the owner would not hear of parting with the mill, but the skipper begged and prayed, and at last the man sold it to him, for many, many thousands of dollars. When the skipper had the mill he did not stay long, for he was afraid the man would change his mind, and he had no time to ask how he was to stop it grinding, but went on board his ship as fast as he could.

When he had gone a little way out to sea he took the mill on deck. "Grind salt, and grind both quickly and well," said the skipper.

So the mill began to grind salt, till it spouted out like water, and when the skipper had the ship filled he wanted to stop the mill, but whichsoever way he turned it, and howsoever he tried, it went on grinding, and the heap of salt grew higher and higher, until at last the ship sank.

There lies the mill at the bottom of the sea, and still, day by day, it grinds on: and that is why the sea is salt.
PETER C. ASBJÖRNSEN AND JÖRGEN E. MOE,
ANDREW LANG COLLECTION

THE UGLY DUCKLING

IT WAS SO lovely in the country—it was summer! The wheat was yellow, the oats were green, the hay was stacked in the meadows and the stork went tiptoeing about on his red legs, jabbering Egyptian, a language his mother had taught him. Around the fields and meadows were great forests, and in the midst of those forests lay deep lakes. Yes, it was indeed lovely in the country! An old manor house stood there, bathed in sunshine, surrounded by a deep moat, and from the walls down to the water's edge the bank was covered with great wild rhubarb leaves which were growing so high that little children would have been able to stand upright under the biggest of them. The place was as much of a wilderness as the densest forest.

There sat a Duck on her nest, busy hatching her ducklings, but she was almost tired of it, because sitting is such a tedious business, and she had very few callers. The other ducks thought it more fun to swim about in the moat than to come and have a gossip with her under a wild rhubarb leaf.

At last one eggshell after another began to crack open. "Cheep, cheep!" All the yolks had come to life and were sticking out their heads.

"Quack, quack," said the Duck, and her little ducklings came scurrying as fast as they could, looking about under the green leaves, and their mother let them look as much as they liked, because green is good for the eyes.

"How big the world is!" said the ducklings, for they felt far more comfortable now than when they were lying in their eggs.

"Do you imagine this is the whole of the world?" asked their mother. "It goes far beyond the other side of the garden, right into the rector's field, but I've never been there yet. I hope you're all here," she went on, and hoisted herself up. "No, I haven't got every one of you even now; the biggest egg is still there. I wonder how much longer it will take! I'm getting rather bored with the whole thing." And she squatted down again on the nest.

"Well, how are you getting on?" asked an Old Duck who came to call on her.

"That last egg is taking an awfully long time," said the Mother Duck. "It won't break; but let me show you the others, they're the sweetest ducklings I've ever seen. They are all exactly like their father; the scamp— he never comes to see me!"

"Let me look at the egg that won't break," said the

Old Duck. "You may be sure it's a turkey's egg. I was fooled like that once, and the trouble and bother I had with those youngsters, because they were actually afraid of the water! I simply couldn't get them to go in! I quacked at them and I snapped at them, but it was no use. Let me see the egg—of course, it's a turkey's egg. Leave it alone, and teach the other children to swim."

"Oh, well, if I've taken so much trouble I may just as well sit a little longer," said Mother Duck.

"Please yourself," said the Old Duck, and she waddled off.

At last the big egg cracked. "Cheep, cheep!" said the youngster, scrambling out. He was so big and ugly! Mother Duck looked at him.

"What a frightfully big Duckling that one is," she said. "None of the others looked like that! I wonder if he could possibly be a turkey chick. Well, we'll soon find out; he'll have to go into the water, even if I have to kick him in myself!"

The next day the weather was simply glorious, and Mother Duck appeared with her family down by the moat. Splash! There she was in the water! "Quack, quack," she said, and one duckling after another plunged in. The water closed over their heads, but they were up again in a second and floated beautifully. All of them were out in the water now, and even the ugly gray creature was swimming along with them.

"That's no turkey!" she said. "Look how nicely he uses his legs, and how straight he holds himself! He isn't really so bad when you take a good look at him. Quack, quack—come along with me, I'll bring you out into the world and introduce you to the duck yard, but keep close to me or you may get stepped on, and look out for the cat!"

So they made their entrance into the duck yard. What a pandemonium there was! Two families were quarreling over an eel's head; but in the end the cat got it after all.

"There you are, that's the way of the world!" said Mother Duck, licking her lips, for she did so want the eel's head herself. "Now use your legs," she said. "Move about briskly and bow to the Old Duck over there; she is the most aristocratic person here and of Spanish blood; that's why she is so stout. And be sure to observe that red rag around her leg. It's a great distinction and the highest honor that can be bestowed upon a duck. It means that her owner wishes to keep her and that she is to be specially noticed by man and beast. Now hurry! Don't turn your toes in; a well-brought-up duckling turns his toes out just as his father and mother do—like that."

And they did as they were told; but the other ducks looked at them and said out loud, "There now, have we got to have that crowd, too? As if there weren't enough of us already. Ugh, what a dreadful-looking

creature that Duckling is! We won't put up with him."
And immediately a duck rushed at him and bit him in
the neck.

"Leave him alone," said the mother. "He's not
bothering any of you."

"I know," said the duck who had bitten him, "but
he's too big and funny looking. What he wants is a
good smacking."

"Those are pretty children you've got, Mother,"
said the Old Duck with the rag around her leg. "They
are all nice looking except that one—he didn't turn out
so well."

"Your Grace," said Mother Duck, "he's not handsome, but he's as good as gold, and he swims as well
as any of the others, I daresay even a little better. He
was in the egg too long, that's why he isn't properly
shaped." And she pecked his neck and brushed up the
little creature. "As it happens, he's a drake," she
added, "so it doesn't matter quite so much."

But the poor Duckling who was the last to be
hatched, and who looked so ugly, was bitten and buf-
feted about and made fun of by all the ducks as well as
the hens.

"He's too big!" they all said. And the turkey-cock,
who was born with spurs and consequently thought he
was an emperor, blew himself up like a ship in full sail
and made for him, gobbling and gabbling till his wat-
tles were quite purple. The poor Duckling did not

know where to turn: he was so miserable because of his ugliness and because he was the butt of the whole barnyard.

And so it went on all the first day, and after that matters grew worse and worse. His own brothers and sisters were downright nasty to him and always said, "I hope the cat gets you, you skinny bag of bones!" And even his mother said, "I wish you were miles away!" And the ducks bit him and the hens pecked him, and the girl who fed them tried to kick him with her foot.

So one day, half running and half flying, he scrambled over the fence.

The little birds in the bushes rose up in alarm. That's because I'm so ugly, thought the Duckling, and closed his eyes, but he kept on running and finally came out into the great marsh where the wild ducks lived. There he lay the whole night long, very tired and very sad.

In the morning the wild ducks flew up and looked at their new companion. "What sort of a fellow are you?" they asked, and the Duckling turned in all directions, bowing to everybody around him as nicely as he could.

"You're appallingly ugly!" said the wild ducks, "but why should we care so long as you don't marry into our family?"

Poor thing! As if he had any thought of marrying!

All he wanted to do was to lie among the reeds and to drink a little marsh water.

So he lay there for two whole days, and then came two wild geese, or rather ganders, for they were young males. They had not been out of the egg very long, and that was why they were so cocky.

"Listen, young fellow," they said. "You're so ugly that we actually like you. Will you join us and be a bird of passage? There are some lovely wild geese, all nice young girls, in a marsh nearby. You're so ugly that you might appeal to them."

Two shots rang out—bang! bang! Both ganders fell dead among the reeds, and the water was reddened with their blood. Bang! bang! was heard again, and large flocks of wild geese flew up from the reeds. Then —bang! bang! bang! again and again. A great hunt was going on. The men were lying under cover around the marsh, and some of them were even up in the trees. Blue smoke drifted in among the dark trees and was carried far out over the water. Through the mud came the gundogs—splash! splash!—sniffing through the reeds and rushes. The poor Duckling was scared out of his wits and tried to hide his head under his wing, when suddenly a ferocious-looking dog came close to him, his tongue hanging far out of his mouth and his wild eyes gleaming horribly. He opened his jaws wide, showed his sharp teeth and—splash! splash!—off he went without touching the Duckling.

"Thank Heaven!" he sighed. "I'm so ugly that even the dog won't bother to bite me!" And so he lay perfectly still, while the shots rattled through the reeds as gun after gun was fired.

It was toward evening when it was quiet again; even then the poor Duckling dared not stir. He waited several hours before he looked about him, and then hurried away from the marsh as fast as he could. He ran over field and meadow, hardly able to fight against the strong wind.

Late that night he reached a wretched little hut, so wretched, in fact, that it did not know which way to fall, and that is why it remained standing upright. The wind whistled so fiercely around the Duckling that the poor thing simply had to sit down on his tail to keep from being knocked over.

The storm grew worse and worse. Then he noticed that the door had come off one of its hinges and hung so crookedly that he could slip inside through the opening, and that is what he did.

An old woman lived here with her Tomcat and her Hen. The Cat, whom she called "Sonny," knew how to arch his back and purr; in fact, he could even give out sparks, but for that she had to rub his fur the wrong way. The Hen had little short legs and was called "Stumpy." She produced many, many eggs, and the old woman loved her as her own child.

Next morning they at once noticed the strange

Duckling; the Cat began to purr and the Hen to cluck. "What's the matter?" asked the old woman, looking all about her; but her eyes were not very good and so she mistook the Duckling for a fat duck that had lost her way.

"What a windfall!" she said. "Now I shall have duck's eggs—if it doesn't happen to be a drake. We must make sure of that." So the Duckling was taken into the house on trial for three weeks, but not a single egg came along.

Now the Cat was master of the house, and the Hen was mistress, and they always said, "We, and the world," for they imagined themselves to be not only half the world, but by far the better half.

The Duckling thought that other people might be allowed to have an opinion too, but the Hen could not see that at all.

"Can you lay eggs?" she asked.

"No."

"Well, then, you'd better keep your mouth shut!"

And the Cat said, "Can you arch your back, purr and give out sparks?"

"No."

"Well, then, you can't have any opinion worth offering when sensible people are speaking."

The Duckling sat in a corner, feeling very gloomy and depressed; then he suddenly thought of the fresh air and the bright sunshine, and such a longing came over him to swim in the water that he could not help telling the Hen about it.

"What's the matter with you?" asked the Hen. "You haven't got anything to do, that's why you get these silly ideas. Either lay eggs or purr and you'll soon be all right."

"You don't understand me," said the Duckling.

"Well, if we don't understand you, then who would? You surely don't imagine you're wiser than the Cat or the old woman—not to mention myself, of course. Don't give yourself such airs, child. Believe me, I only wish you well. I tell you unpleasant things, but that's the way to know one's real friends. Come on, hurry up, see that you lay eggs, and do learn how to purr or to give out sparks!"

"I think I had better go out into the wide world," said the Duckling.

"Please yourself," said the Hen.

So the Duckling went away. He walked on the land and swam in the water and dived down into it, but he was still snubbed by every creature because of his ugliness.

Autumn set in. The leaves turned yellow and brown; the wind caught them and whirled them about; and up in the air it looked very cold. The clouds hung low, heavy with snowflakes, and on the fence perched the raven, trembling with the cold, and croaking, "Caw! Caw!" The mere thought of it was enough to make anybody shiver. The poor Duckling was certainly to be pitied!

One evening, when the sun was setting in all its splendor, a large flock of big handsome birds came out of the bushes. The Duckling had never before seen anything quite so beautiful as they were—dazzlingly white, with long supple necks—they were swans! They uttered a most uncanny cry, and spread their splendid great wings to fly away to warmer countries and open lakes. They rose so high, so very high in the air that a strange feeling came over the ugly little Duckling as he watched them. He turned around and around in the water like a wheel, craned his neck to follow their flight and uttered a cry so loud and strange that it frightened him.

He could not forget those noble birds, those happy birds, and when they were lost to sight he dived down to the bottom of the water; then when he came up again he was quite beside himself. He did not know what the birds were called, nor where they were flying to, and yet he loved them more than he had ever loved anything. He did not envy them in the least; it would never have occurred to him to want such beauty for himself. He would have been quite content if only the ducks would have put up with him—the poor ugly creature!

And the winter grew so cold, so bitterly cold. The Duckling was forced to swim about to keep the water

See page 118

from freezing altogether, but every night the opening became smaller and smaller; at last it froze so hard that the ice made cracking noises, and the Duckling had to keep on paddling to prevent the opening from closing up. In the end he was exhausted and lay quite still, caught in the ice.

Early next morning a farmer came by, and when he saw him he went onto the ice, broke it with his wooden shoe and carried him home to his wife. There the Duckling revived.

The children wanted to play with him, but he thought they meant to do him harm, so he fluttered, terrified, into the milk pail, splashing the milk all over the room. The farmer's wife screamed and threw up her hands in fright. Then he flew into the butter tub, and from that into the flour barrel and out again. What a sight he was! The woman shrieked and struck at him with her tongs. Laughing and shouting, the children fell on each other trying to catch him. Fortunately, the door was open, so the Duckling dashed out of the house and into the bushes and lay there in a daze in the newly fallen snow.

It would be too sad, however, to tell of the trouble and misery he had to suffer during that cruel winter. But when the sun began to shine warmly he found himself once more in the marsh among the reeds. The larks were singing—it was spring, beautiful spring!

Then suddenly he spread his wings; the sound of

their whirring made him realize how much stronger they had grown, and they carried him powerfully along. Before he knew it, he found himself in a great garden where the apple trees stood in bloom and the lilac filled the air with its fragrance.

It was so lovely here, so full of the freshness of spring. And floating down the stream in front of him came three beautiful white swans, ruffling their feathers proudly. The Duckling recognized the glorious creatures, and felt a strange sadness come over him.

"I will fly near those royal birds, and they will peck me to death for daring to bring my ugly self near them. But that doesn't matter in the least! Better to be killed by them than to be bitten by the ducks, pecked by the hens, kicked by the girl in charge of the hen run and suffer untold agony in winter."

Then he flew into the water and swam toward the beautiful swans. They saw him and dashed at him with outspread, rustling feathers. "Kill me," said the poor creature, and he bowed his head down upon the surface of the stream, expecting the worst. But what was this he saw mirrored in the clear water? He saw beneath him his own image, but it was no longer the image of an awkward, dirty, gray bird, ugly and repulsive—he himself was a swan!

It does not matter if one was born in a duck yard, if only one has lain in a swan's egg.

The great swans swam around him and stroked him

with their beaks. He felt quite glad to have been through so much trouble and adversity, for now he could fully appreciate not only his own good fortune, but also the beauty that greeted him.

Some little children came into the garden to throw bread and corn into the water, and the youngest exclaimed, "There's a new one!" And the other children chimed in, "Yes, there's a new one!" They clapped their hands, danced about and ran to fetch their father and mother.

Bread and cake were thrown into the water, and everyone said, "The new one is the most beautiful! He's so young and handsome!" And the old swans bowed to him.

That made him feel quite embarrassed, and he put his head under his wing, not knowing what it was all about. An overwhelming happiness filled him, and yet he was not a bit proud, for a good heart never becomes proud. He remembered how once he had been despised and persecuted; and now he heard everyone saying that he was the most beautiful of beautiful birds.

And the lilac bushes dipped their branches into the water before him, and the sun shone warm and mild. He rustled his feathers and held his graceful neck high, and from the depths of his heart he joyfully exclaimed, "I never dreamt that so much happiness was possible when I was the Ugly Duckling."

HANS CHRISTIAN ANDERSEN, TRANSLATED BY PAUL LEYSSAC

JACK AND THE BEANSTALK

ONCE UPON a time there was a poor widow who lived in a little cottage with her only son Jack, who was a simple but kindhearted boy. There had been a terribly hard winter, and the poor woman saw there would be no means of keeping Jack and herself from starvation but by selling her cow. So one morning she said to her son, "I am too weak to go myself, Jack. You must take the cow to market for me and sell her."

"Cheer up, Mother, I'll go and get work somewhere," said Jack.

"We've tried that before and nobody would take you," said his mother.

So Jack took the cow and left for the market. On the way, he met a butcher who had some beautiful beans in his hand.

Jack stopped to look at the beans, and the butcher told the boy that they were very valuable, and persuaded the silly lad to sell him the cow in exchange for these beans.

When he brought them home to his mother instead

of the money she had expected, she was vexed and shed many tears, scolding Jack for his folly. He was very sorry, and when mother and son went to bed sadly that night their last hope seemed gone.

At daybreak Jack rose and went out into the garden. At least, he thought, I can sow the wonderful beans. Mother says that they are just common scarlet runners and nothing else, but I may as well try and see. So he took a piece of stick, made some holes in the ground and put in the beans.

That day they had very little dinner and again went sadly to bed, knowing that the next day there would be none. Jack, unable to sleep from grief and vexation, got up at dawn and went out into the garden.

What was his amazement to find that the beans had grown in the night, and had climbed up and up till they covered the high cliff that sheltered the cottage and disappeared above it! The stalks had twined themselves together till they formed a sturdy ladder.

It would be easy to climb it, thought Jack. And, having thought of it, he at once resolved to do so. So climb he did, and went up and up on the ladderlike beanstalk till everything he had left behind him—the cottage, the village and even the tall church tower—looked quite small, and still he could not see the top of the beanstalk.

Jack felt tired and thought for a moment that he would go down again; but he was a very persevering

boy and he knew that the way to succeed in anything
is not to give up. So after resting for a few minutes he
went on.

After climbing higher and higher, till he grew afraid
to look down for fear he would become dizzy, Jack at
last reached the top of the beanstalk and found himself in a beautiful country with fine meadows dotted
with grazing sheep. A crystal stream ran through the
pastures, and not far from the place where he had
gotten off the beanstalk stood a fine, strong castle.

While Jack was standing looking at the castle, a very
strange-looking woman came out of the wood and advanced toward him. She wore a pointed cap of quilted
red satin turned up with ermine, her hair streamed
loose over her shoulders and she walked with a staff.
Jack took off his cap and made her a bow.

"If you please, ma'am," said he politely, "is this
your house?"

"No," said the old woman. "Listen, and I will tell
you the story of that castle.

"Once upon a time there was a noble knight who
lived in this castle, which is on the borders of Fairyland. He had a fair and beloved wife and several lovely
children. And as his neighbors, the little people, were
very friendly toward him, they bestowed on him many
excellent and precious gifts.

"Rumor whispered of these treasures, and a mon-
strous giant, who lived at no great distance and who

was a very wicked being, resolved that he would take possession of them.

"So he bribed a false servant to let him inside the castle, when the knight was asleep, and he killed him as he lay. Then he went to the part of the castle which was the nursery and also killed all the poor little ones he found there.

"Happily for her, the knight's lady was not there. She had gone with her infant son, who was only two or three months old, to visit her old nurse who lived in the valley, and she had been detained there all night by a storm.

"The next morning, as soon as it was light, one of the servants who had managed to escape from the castle came to tell the poor lady of the sad fate of her husband and her pretty babes. She could scarcely believe him at first, and, in her sorrow, was eager at once to go back and share the fate of her dear ones. But the old nurse, with many tears, besought her to remember that she still had a child and that it was her duty to live for his sake.

"The lady yielded to this reasoning and consented to remain in concealment at her nurse's house, for the servant told her that the giant had vowed, if he could find her, he would kill both her and her baby. Years went by. The old nurse died, leaving her cottage and its few articles of furniture to her poor mistress, who lived in it, working as a peasant for her daily bread.

Her spinning wheel and the milk of a cow which she had purchased with the little money she had with her sufficed for the scanty subsistence of herself and her growing son. There was a nice little garden attached to the cottage, in which they cultivated peas, beans and cabbages, and the old lady was not ashamed to go out and work in the fields to supply her son's wants.

"Jack, that poor lady is your mother. This castle was once your father's and must again be yours."

Jack uttered a cry of surprise. "My mother! Oh, ma'am, what ought I to do?"

"Your duty requires you to win it back for your mother," the woman said. "But the task is a very difficult one and full of peril, Jack. Have you courage to undertake it?"

"I fear nothing when I am doing right," said Jack, bravely.

"Then," said the lady in the red cap, "you are one of those who slay giants. You must get into the castle, and if possible gain possession of the hen that lays golden eggs and the harp that talks. Remember, all the giant possesses is really yours."

As she ceased speaking, the lady of the red hat suddenly disappeared, and of course Jack then knew she was a fairy.

Jack determined at once to attempt the adventure. He advanced and blew the horn which hung at the castle portal. The door was opened in a moment by a frightful giantess with one great eye in the middle of her forehead.

As soon as Jack saw her he turned to run away, but the giantess caught him and began to push and pull him toward the castle.

"Ho, ho!" she laughed terribly. "You didn't expect to see me here, that is clear! No, I shan't let you go. I am overworked, and I don't see why I should not have a page the same as other ladies. And you shall clean the knives and black the boots and make the fires, and help me generally when the giant is out. When he is at home I must hide you, for he has eaten up my other pages, and you would be a dainty morsel, my little lad."

While she spoke she dragged Jack right into the castle. The poor boy was very frightened, but he struggled to be brave and make the best of things. "I am quite ready to help you and do what I can to serve you, madam," he said, "only I beg you be good enough to hide me from your husband, for I should not like to be eaten at all."

"That's a good boy," said the giantess, nodding her head. "Come here, child. Go into my wardrobe; he never ventures to open that. You will be safe there."

She opened a huge wardrobe which stood in the great hall and shut him into it. The keyhole was so large that it admitted plenty of air, and through it Jack could see everything that took place in the room. By and by he heard a heavy tramp on the stairs, like the lumbering along of a great cannon, and then a voice booming:

> Fee-fi-fo-fum,
> I smell the blood of an Englishman.
> Be he alive or be he dead,
> I'll grind his bones to make my bread.

"Wife," cried the giant, "there is an Englishman in the castle. Let me have him for breakfast."

"You have grown old and stupid," cried the giantess in her loud tones. "It is only a nice fresh elephant steak which you smell. Sit down and have breakfast."

And she placed a huge dish before him of savory steaming meat, which greatly pleased him and made him forget his idea of an Englishman being in the castle. When he had breakfasted he went for a walk, and then the giantess made Jack come out to help her, which he busily did all day. She fed him well and, when evening came, put him back in the wardrobe.

The giant came in to supper. Jack watched him through the keyhole and was amazed to see him pick a wolf's bone and put half a fowl at a time into his enormous mouth. When the supper was ended he bade his wife bring him his hen that laid the golden eggs.

"It lays as well as it did when it belonged to that paltry knight," he said. "Indeed I think the eggs are heavier than ever."

The giantess went away, and soon returned with a

little brown hen, which she placed on the table before her husband.

"And now, my dear," she said, "I am going for a walk, if you don't want me any longer."

"Go," said the giant, "I shall be glad to have a nap in a little while."

Then he took up the brown hen and said to her: "Lay!" And she instantly laid a golden egg.

"Lay!" said the giant again. And she laid another.

"Lay!" he repeated the third time. And again a golden egg lay on the table.

Now Jack was sure this hen was the one of which the fairy had spoken. By and by the giant put the hen down on the floor, and soon went fast asleep, snoring so loudly that it sounded like thunder.

When Jack perceived that the giant was fast asleep, he pushed open the door of the wardrobe and crept out. Very softly he stole across the room and, picking up the hen, hurried away. He knew the way to the kitchen, the door of which he found ajar. He opened it, then shut and locked it after him, and flew back to the beanstalk, which he descended just as fast as his feet would move.

When his mother saw him she wept for joy, for she had feared the fairies had carried him off or that the giant, whom she had always secretly feared, had found him. But Jack put the brown hen down before her, and told her he had been in the giant's castle, and all his adventures. She was very glad to see the hen, which would surely make them rich.

Jack made another journey up the beanstalk to the giant's castle one day while his mother had gone to the market; but first he dyed his hair and disguised himself. The old giantess did not recognize him and dragged him in as she had done before to help do the work; but she heard her husband coming and hid him in the wardrobe, not thinking that he was the same boy who had stolen the hen. She bade him stay quite still there, afraid the giant would eat him.

Then the giant came in, saying:

> Fee-fi-fo-fum,
> I smell the blood of an Englishman.
> Be he alive or be he dead,
> I'll grind his bones to make my bread.

"Nonsense!" said the wife. "It is only a roasted ox that I thought would be a tidbit for your supper. Sit down and I will bring it at once."

The giant sat down, and soon his wife brought up a roasted ox on a large dish, and they began their supper. Jack was amazed to see them pick its bones as if it had been a small bird. As soon as they had finished their meal, the giantess rose and said, "Now, my dear, with your leave I am going up to my room to finish the story I am reading. If you want me, call for me."

"First," answered the giant, "bring me my money

bags, that I may count my gold pieces before I sleep."

The giantess obeyed. She soon brought two large bags over her shoulders, which she put down by her husband. "There," she said, "that is all that is left of the knight's money. When you have spent it you must go and take another baron's castle."

"That he shan't do, if I can help it," Jack vowed to himself.

The giant, when his wife was gone, took out heaps and heaps of gold pieces, counted them and put them in stacks, till he was bored. Then he swept them back into their bags and, leaning back in his chair, fell fast asleep, snoring so loudly that no other sound was audible.

Jack stole softly from the wardrobe and, taking up the bags of money, which were really his own because the giant had stolen them from his father, he ran off. After descending the beanstalk with great difficulty, he laid the bags of gold on his mother's table. She had just returned from town and was crying because Jack was not at home.

"There, Mother, I have brought you the gold that my father lost."

"Oh, Jack, you are a very good boy, but I wish you would not risk your precious life in the giant's castle! Tell me how you came to go there again."

And Jack told her all about it. His mother was very glad to have the money, but she did not like him to run any risk for her. But after a time Jack made up his mind to go again to the giant's castle.

So he climbed the beanstalk once more and blew the horn at the giant's gate. The giantess soon opened the door. She was very stupid and did not recognize him. She stopped a moment before she took him in, because she feared another robbery. But Jack's fresh face looked so innocent she bade him come in, and again she hid him away in the wardrobe.

By and by the giant came home, and as soon as he had crossed the threshold, he roared out:

> Fee-fi-fo-fum,
> I smell the blood of an Englishman.
> Be he alive or be he dead,
> I'll grind his bones to make my bread.

"You stupid old giant," said his wife, "you only smell the nice sheep I grilled for your dinner."

The giant sat down, and his wife brought up a whole sheep for his dinner. When he had eaten it all, he said, "Now bring me my harp, and I will have a little music while you take your walk."

The giantess obeyed and returned with a beautiful harp. The framework was all sparkling with diamonds and rubies, and the strings were all of gold.

"This is one of the nicest things I took from the knight," said the giant. "I am very fond of music, and my harp is a faithful servant."

So he drew the harp toward him, and said, "Play!"
And the harp played a very soft, sad air.

"Play something merrier!" said the giant.

And the harp played a gay tune.

"Now play me a lullaby," roared the giant. And the harp played a sweet lullaby, and at the sound its master fell asleep.

Then Jack stole softly out of the wardrobe and went into the huge kitchen to see if the giantess had gone out. He found no one there, so he went to the door and opened it softly. Then he entered the giant's room, seized the harp and ran away with it. But as he jumped over the threshold the harp called out loudly, "Master! Master!"

The giant woke up. With a tremendous roar he sprang from his seat and in two strides reached the door. Jack was very nimble and he fled like lightning with the harp, talking to it as he went, for he saw it was a fairy, and told it he was the son of its old master, the knight. Still the giant came on so fast that he was quite close to poor Jack and he stretched out his great hand to catch him. But, luckily, just at that moment he stepped upon a loose stone, stumbled and fell flat on the ground, where he lay at his full length.

Jack had just time to get on the beanstalk and hasten down it; but as he reached their own garden he beheld the giant descending after him. "Mother! Mother!" cried Jack. "Make haste and give me the axe."

His mother ran to him with the axe in her hand, and Jack with one tremendous blow cut through all the beanstalks except one. "Now, Mother, stand out of the way!" said he.

Jack's mother shrank back, and it was well she did, for just as the giant took hold of the last branch of the beanstalk, Jack cut the stem through and darted away. Down came the giant with a terrible crash, and that was the end of him. Before Jack and his mother had recovered from their alarm, a beautiful lady stood before them.

"Jack," said she, "you have acted like a brave knight's son and deserve to have your inheritance restored to you. Dig a grave and bury the giant, and then go and kill the giantess."

"But," said Jack, "I could not kill anyone unless I were fighting with him, and I could not draw my sword upon a woman. Moreover, the giantess was always very kind to me."

The fairy smiled on Jack. "I am much pleased with your generous feeling," she said. "Nevertheless, return to the castle, and act as you will find needful."

Jack asked the fairy to show him the way to the castle, as the beanstalk was now down. She told him she would drive him there in her chariot, which was drawn by two peacocks. Jack thanked her and sat down in the chariot with her.

The fairy drove him a long distance till they reached

a village which lay at the bottom of the hill. Here they found a number of wretched-looking men assembled. The fairy stopped her carriage and addressed them. "My friends," said she, "the cruel giant who oppressed you and ate up all your flocks and herds is dead, thanks to this young gentleman. He is the son of your kind old master, the knight."

The men gave a loud cheer at these words and pressed forward to say that they would serve Jack as faithfully as they had served his father. The fairy bade them follow her to the castle, and they marched there in a body. When they arrived, Jack blew the horn and demanded admittance.

The old giantess saw them coming from the turret loophole. She was very frightened, for she guessed that something had happened to her husband. As she came downstairs very quickly she caught her foot in her dress and fell from the top to the bottom.

When the people outside found that the door was not open, they took crowbars and forced the portal. Nobody was to be seen, but on going into the castle they found the body of the dead giantess at the foot of the stairs.

Thus Jack took possession of the castle. The fairy brought his mother to him, with the hen and the harp. He had the giantess buried and endeavored to help those whom the giant had robbed. Before her departure for Fairyland, the fairy explained to Jack that she had sent the butcher to meet him with the beans, to test what sort of lad he was.

"If you had looked at the gigantic beanstalk and just wondered stupidly about it," she said, "I should have left you where misfortune had placed you, only restoring her cow to your mother. But you showed an inquiring mind and great courage and enterprise, therefore you deserve to rise; and when you mounted the beanstalk you climbed the ladder of fortune."

She then took her leave of Jack and his mother.

OLD ENGLISH TALE, ANDREW LANG COLLECTION

TWO FROGS

ONCE UPON a time, in the country of Japan, there lived two Frogs, one of whom made his home in a ditch near the town of Osaka, on the seacoast, while the other dwelled in a clear little stream which ran through the city of Kyoto. At such a great distance apart, they had never even heard of each other; but, oddly enough, the idea came into both their heads at the same time that they should like to see a little of the world, and the Frog who lived in Kyoto wanted to visit Osaka, and the Frog who lived near Osaka wished to go to Kyoto, where the great Mikado had his palace.

So one fine morning in the spring they both set out along the road that led from Kyoto to Osaka, one Frog coming from Osaka and the other from Kyoto. The journey was more tiring than they expected, for they did not know much about traveling nor that halfway between the two towns there rose a mountain which had to be climbed. It took them a long while and a great many hops to reach the top, but there they were at last, and what was the surprise of each to see another frog before him!

They looked at each other for a moment without speaking and then fell into conversation, explaining the cause of their meeting so far from their homes. It was delightful to find that they both felt the same wish —to learn a little more of their native country—and, as there was no sort of hurry, they stretched themselves out in a cool, damp place and agreed that they would have a good rest before they parted to go their separate ways.

"What a pity we are not bigger," said the Osaka Frog, "for then we could see both towns from here and tell if it is worth our while going on."

"Oh, that is easily managed," returned the Kyoto Frog. "We have only to stand up on our hind legs and

hold on to each other, and then we can each look at the town we are traveling to."

This idea pleased the Osaka Frog so much that he at once jumped up and put his front feet on the shoulders of his friend, who had risen also. There they both stood, stretching themselves as high as they could, and holding to each other tightly so that they might not fall down.

The Kyoto Frog turned his nose toward Osaka, and the Osaka Frog turned his nose toward Kyoto. But the foolish things forgot that when they stood up their great eyes lay in the back of their heads, and that, though their noses might point to the places to which they wanted to go, their eyes beheld the places from which they had come.

"Dear me," cried the Osaka Frog, "Kyoto is exactly like Osaka! It is certainly not worth such a long journey. I shall go home!"

"If I'd had any idea that Osaka was only a copy of Kyoto I should never have traveled all this way!" exclaimed the Frog from Kyoto. And as he spoke he took his hands from his friend's shoulders and they both fell down on the grass.

Then the two Frogs took a polite farewell of each other and set off for home again, and to the end of their lives they believed that Osaka and Kyoto, which are as different to look at as two towns can be, were alike as two peas. FROM TALES OF JAPAN, ANDREW LANG COLLECTION

THE SNOW QUEEN

THERE WAS once a dreadfully wicked hobgoblin. One day he was in high good spirits because he had made a mirror which reflected everything that was good and beautiful in such a way that it dwindled almost to nothing, but anything that was bad and ugly stood out very clearly and appeared much worse. The most beautiful landscapes looked like boiled spinach. The nicest people looked repulsive or seemed to stand on their heads or had no middles, and their faces were so distorted that they could not be recognized. And if anyone had a single freckle you might be sure it would look as if it had spread over his whole nose and mouth. That's the funniest thing about it, thought the hobgoblin.

One day the hobgoblin was flying high among the clouds, maliciously flashing his mirror on all the countries below. Suddenly it slipped from his hands and crashed to the earth, shattered into millions and billions of pieces. And now came the greatest mischief of all, for most of the pieces were hardly as large as a grain of sand, and they flew about all over the world.

If anyone got a speck of the mirror in his eye there it stayed. From then on he would see everything crooked, or else could see only the ugly side of things. For every tiny splinter of the glass possessed the same power as the whole mirror.

Some people got a splinter in their hearts, and that was dreadful, for then the heart would turn into a lump of ice. A few of the fragments were large enough to be used as windowpanes, but how terrible it would be to look at one's friends and neighbors through such a window!

The hobgoblin was so pleased he laughed till his sides ached, as the tiny bits of glass continued to whirl about in the air.

And now we will hear what happened.

A Little Boy and a Little Girl

In a large town, where there were so many people and houses that there was not enough room for everybody to have a garden, lived two poor children. They were not brother and sister, but they loved each other just as much as if they were. Their parents lived opposite one another in two attics, and each family had planted a rose tree and sweet peas in a window box. In summer the two children were allowed to sit out underneath the rose trees and play lovely games together all afternoon.

In the winter they could not do this, so they heated pennies on the stove and put them against the frozen windowpanes. These made perfect peepholes through which they could gaze at each other across the frozen gutters.

His name was Kay, and hers was Gerda.

One day it was snowing very hard.

"Those are the white bees swarming," said the old grandmother.

"Have they got a queen bee too?" asked the little boy, for he knew that the real bees have one.

"To be sure," said the grandmother. "She flies wherever they swarm the thickest. She is the Snow Queen and is the biggest of them all. She never remains still upon the earth, but always returns to the black clouds. Often at midnight she flies through the streets of the town and peeps in at all the windows, and then the snowflakes freeze in pretty patterns and look like flowers."

"Yes, we have seen that," said both children; they knew that it was true.

"Can the Snow Queen come in here?" asked the little girl.

"Just let her!" cried the boy. "I would put her on the stove and melt her!"

But the grandmother stroked his hair, and told some more stories.

That evening, when little Kay was going to bed, he

jumped on the chair by the window and peeped through the little hole. A few snowflakes were falling, and one of them, the largest, lay on the edge of one of the window boxes. The snowflake grew larger and larger till it took the form of a maiden, dressed in finest white gauze.

She was so beautiful and delicate, but all ice—hard, glittering ice.

She nodded at the window, and beckoned to Kay with her hand. The little boy was frightened at the sight of her and sprang down from the chair. Suddenly it seemed as if a great white bird had flown past the window.

The next day the weather cleared. Not long after, a thaw set in—and spring appeared. With the warm spring sunshine, the countryside turned a soft green, the swallows worked busily on their nests and Kay and Gerda played together once more in their little garden high on the rooftop. They knew that summer had come at last when their little rose trees burst into glorious bloom.

One day the children were looking at a picture book. The clock in the great church tower had just struck five, when Kay suddenly exclaimed, "Oh! Something has stung my heart, and now I've got something in my eye!" Gerda threw her arms around his neck. He blinked his eyes again and again; but no, she could see nothing in them.

"I think it is gone now," said he. But it had not gone. It was one of the tiny splinters from the magic mirror we have heard about, the mirror that turned whatever was fine and good reflected in it into something small and ugly. And a splinter had found its way to poor Kay's heart, which began to change into a lump of ice. His heart did not hurt him at all, but the splinter was still there.

"Why are you crying?" he asked Gerda. "It makes you look so ugly! There's nothing the matter with me. Just look! That rose is all worm-eaten, and this one is stunted! What ugly roses they are!"

And he began to pull them to pieces.

"Kay, what *are* you doing?" cried the little girl, and she threw up her hands.

When he saw how frightened she was he pulled off another rose and ran inside to his window, away from dear little Gerda.

When she came later on with a picture book, he said that it was only fit for babies, and when his grandmother told them stories, he always interrupted with, "But——" and then he would get behind her and put on her spectacles and mimic everything she did. Very soon he could imitate whatever was odd or ugly about the people who lived on their street.

When winter came, he began to love the cold. Each day he would take a magnifying glass and hold it over his blue coat while the snowflakes fell on it. "Look in the glass, Gerda! They are much more perfect than real flowers. If only they did not melt!"

One morning Kay went out with his warm gloves on and his little sled hung over his shoulder. He shouted to Gerda, "I don't want to play with you. I am going to the marketplace to be with the other boys," and away he went.

In the marketplace the boldest boys often used to fasten their sleds to the rears of the carts of the farmers, and then they got a good ride. That day, when Kay and the other boys were in the middle of their games, there drove into the square a large white sleigh, and in it sat a figure dressed in a white fur cloak and a white fur cap.

The sleigh drove around the square twice. Suddenly it came to a short stop, and Kay fastened his little sled behind it and was pulled away. The sleigh began to go more and more quickly. The driver turned around from time to time and nodded to Kay in a friendly way, as if they had known each other before. Every time Kay tried to unfasten his sled the driver nodded again, and Kay sat still, and so they drove swiftly out of the town.

The snow began to fall so thickly that the little boy could not see his hand before him as they sped along. He tried to unfasten the cord to get free of the big sleigh, but it was no use; his little sled could not be loosened and on they went like the wind. He cried out, but nobody heard him. He was dreadfully frightened.

The snowflakes grew larger and larger till they looked like great white birds. All at once the large sleigh stopped, and the figure who was driving stood up. It was a lady, tall and slim and glittering. Her fur cloak and cap were made entirely of snow. It was the Snow Queen.

"We have made good time," she said. "But you are almost frozen. Creep in under my cloak."

And she held him close to her in the sleigh and drew the cloak over him. He felt as though he were sinking into a snowdrift.

"Are you still cold?" she asked, and kissed him on the forehead. The kiss was as cold as ice and reached down to his heart, which was already frozen into half a lump of ice.

"My sled! Don't forget my sled!" He thought of that first, and they fastened it to one of the white birds, who flew behind with the sled on its back.

The Snow Queen kissed Kay again, and he forgot all about little Gerda, his grandmother and everybody else at home.

"Now I must not kiss you anymore," she said, "or I will kiss you to death."

Then away they flew over forests and lakes, over sea and land. Around them whistled the cold wind, the wolves howled and the snow hissed; over them flew the black shrieking crows. But high up the moon shone

large and bright, and thus Kay passed the long, long winter night. During the day he slept at the Snow Queen's feet.

The Old Woman and Her Magic Garden

But what happened to little Gerda when Kay did not come back? What had become of him? Nobody knew. The other boys told how they had seen him fasten his sled to a large one which had driven out of the town gate. Gerda cried a great deal. The winter was long and dark to her.

Then the spring came and with it the warm sunshine. "I will go and look for Kay," said Gerda.

So she went down to the river and climbed into a little boat that lay on the bank. Presently the stream began to carry it away. The boat glided along, passing trees and fields; then Gerda saw a large cherry orchard, in which stood a house with strange red, blue and yellow windows and a straw roof. Before the door stood two wooden soldiers at attention.

Gerda thought they were alive and called to them, but naturally they did not answer. The current swept the boat straight toward the bank. Gerda called still louder, and a very old woman came out of the house. She leaned upon a crutch and wore a large sun hat painted with the most beautiful flowers.

"You poor child!" said the old woman.

And then she stepped into the water, brought the boat in close with her crutch and lifted little Gerda out.

"And now come and tell me who you are and how you came here," she said, and taking Gerda's hand she led her into the house and shut the door.

The windows were very high and painted red, blue and yellow, so that the light came through in strange colors. On the table was a bowl of the most delicious cherries, and the old woman let Gerda eat as many as she liked, while she combed her hair with a gold comb. The beautiful sunny hair rippled and shone around the friendly face. "I have always longed to have a dear little girl like you," said the old woman. "You shall see how happy we will be together."

And as she combed Gerda's hair, Gerda thought less and less about Kay, for the old woman was a witch, but not a wicked witch. She only enchanted now and then to amuse herself. She did want to keep little Gerda very much, and so she went into the garden and waved her crooked stick over all the rosebushes, and they disappeared into the black earth, leaving no trace of where they had been. The witch was afraid that if Gerda saw the roses they would remind her of her own roses and of Kay, and she would run away.

Then she led Gerda out into the garden. How glorious it was, and what lovely scents filled the air!

Gerda jumped for joy and played in the garden till the sun set behind the tall cherry trees. Then she went to sleep in a beautiful bed with red silk pillows filled with violets, and she slept soundly and dreamed as a queen does on her wedding day.

The next day she played again among the flowers in the warm sunshine, and so many days passed by. Gerda knew every flower, but although there were so many, it seemed to her as if one was missing, but she could not remember which.

One day she happened to look at the old woman's sun hat, the one with painted flowers on it, and there she saw a rose. The good witch had forgotten about that one when she made the other roses disappear into the black earth. It is so difficult to think of everything! "Why, there are no roses here!" cried Gerda, and then she sat down and cried, but her tears fell on the spot where a rosebush had sunk, and when her warm tears watered the earth, the bush came up in full bloom just as it had been before. Gerda kissed the roses and thought of the lovely ones at home, and with them came the thought of Kay. "Oh, what have I been doing!" said the little girl. "I wanted to look for Kay."

She ran to the end of the garden. The gate was shut, but she pushed against the rusty lock so that it swung open, then ran barefoot out of the garden. No one came after her. At last she could not run any longer, and she sat down on a large stone. When she looked around she saw that the summer was over; it was late autumn. The seasons had never changed in the old woman's

beautiful garden, where there were sunshine and flowers all the year round.

"My goodness, how much time I've wasted," said
Gerda. "It's almost winter! I cannot rest any longer!"
And she sprang up to run on.

Oh, how tired and sore her little feet were, and all
around her it became colder and colder.

The Prince and the Princess

After a while, Gerda had to rest again. While she
was sitting, she looked up and there on the snow in
front of her was a large Crow.

It had been looking at her for some time, and it
nodded its head and said, "Caw! Caw! Good day."
Then it asked the little girl where she was going all
alone like that in the world. Gerda told the Crow her
story, and asked if he had seen Kay.

The Crow nodded very thoughtfully and said, "It
might be! It *might* be!"

"What! Do you think you have?" cried the little
girl, and she smothered him with her kisses.

"Gently, gently," said the Crow. "It might be little
Kay, but now he has forgotten you for the Princess!"

"Does he live with a Princess?" asked Gerda.

Then the Crow told her everything he knew.

"In the kingdom in which we are now sitting lives
a Princess who is dreadfully clever. She has read all the

newspapers in the world and then forgotten them again. She is as clever as that. The other day she was sitting on the throne, and that is not such fun as people think. Then she began to say, 'Why should I not marry?' But she wanted a husband who knew how to answer when spoken to, not one who would stand up stiffly looking superior—that would be too boring.

"When she told all the ladies of the court, they were delighted. You can believe every word I say," continued the Crow. "I have a tame sweetheart in the palace, and she tells me everything." (Of course his sweetheart was a crow.)

"Every newspaper came out next morning with a border of hearts and the Princess' initials, and inside you could read that every handsome young man might come into the palace and speak to the Princess, and whoever spoke best should become her husband.

"Indeed," said the Crow, "you can certainly believe me. It is as true as that I am sitting here.

"Young men arrived in streams, but nothing came of it on the first or the second day. The suitors were talkative enough in the streets, but once they went inside the palace gates and saw the guards in silver-braided uniforms and the footmen in gold-braided uniforms lining the stairs and the great hall all lit up, then their wits left them entirely. When they stood in front of the throne where the Princess sat, they could think of nothing to say except to repeat the last word she had spoken, and she did not care to hear that again. It seemed as if they were walking in their sleep until they went out into the street again and were able to speak once more.

"There was a line of young men stretching from the town gate up to the castle. They were hungry and thirsty, but in the palace they did not even get a glass of water. Some of the cleverest had thought to bring slices of bread and butter with them, but they did not share with their neighbor, for they thought: If he looks hungry, the Princess will not have him!"

"But what about Kay?" asked Gerda. "When did he come? Was he in the crowd?"

"Wait a bit; we are coming to him! On the third day, a little figure without horse or carriage walked jauntily up to the palace. His eyes shone as yours do; he had lovely curly hair, but very shabby clothes."

"That was Kay!" cried Gerda with delight. "Oh, I have found him!" And she clapped her hands.

"He had a little bundle on his back," said the Crow.

"It must have been his sled."

"Possibly," said the Crow, "I did not see for certain. But I know, from my sweetheart, that when he came to the palace gate and saw the royal guards in silver and the footmen in gold on the stairs, he was not the least bit put out. He nodded to them, saying, 'It must be rather dull standing on the stairs. I would rather go inside.'

"The halls were ablaze with lights; counselors and ambassadors were walking about carrying gold trays. It was enough to make one nervous! The boy's boots creaked noisily, but he was not frightened."

"That must be Kay!" said Gerda. "I know he had new boots on; I've heard them creaking in his grandmother's room!"

"They did creak, certainly!" said the Crow. "And, not one bit afraid, up he went to the Princess, who was sitting on a large pearl as round as a spinning wheel. All the ladies-in-waiting were standing around with their attendants, and the lords-in-waiting with their attendants."

"It must have been dreadful," said little Gerda. "And Kay did win the Princess?"

"I heard from my tame sweetheart that he was cheerful and quick-witted. He had not come to woo, he said, but to listen to the Princess' wisdom. And the end of it was that they fell in love with each other."

"That must have been Kay! He was always so clever; he could do sums with fractions. Oh, won't you lead me to the palace?" begged Gerda.

"That's easily asked!" said the Crow, "but how are we to manage that? I must talk it over with my tame sweetheart. She may be able to advise us, but I may as well tell you that a little girl like you could never get permission to enter the palace."

"Oh, I will get in!" said Gerda. "When Kay hears

that I am there he will come out at once and fetch me!"

"Wait for me by the fence," said the Crow, and he nodded his head and flew away.

It was late in the evening when he came back.

"Caw, caw!" he cried, "I am to give you her love, and here is a little roll for you. She took it out of the kitchen; there's plenty there, and you must be hungry. The guards in silver braid and the footmen in gold will not allow you to come into the palace. But don't cry! You shall get in all right. My sweetheart knows a little back staircase which leads to the bedchamber, and she knows where to find the key."

Later that evening they went into the palace garden, and when the lights were put out one by one, the Crow led Gerda to a back door.

Oh, how Gerda's heart beat with anxiety and longing! It seemed as if she were going to do something wrong, but she only wanted to know if it was little Kay. Yes, it must be he! She remembered so well his clever eyes, his curly hair. She could see him smiling as he did when they were at home under the rose trees! He would be so pleased to see her and to hear how they all were at home.

Now they were on the stairs; a little lamp was burning, and on the landing stood the tame Crow. She put her head on one side and looked at Gerda, who bowed as her grandmother had taught her.

"My fiancé has told me many nice things about you,

my dear young lady," the Crow said. "Will you take the lamp while I go in front? We go this way so as to meet no one."

They walked through many beautiful rooms until they came to the bedchamber. In the middle of it were two beds shaped like lilies, one all white, in which the Princess lay, and the other red, in which Gerda hoped to find Kay. She pushed aside the curtain, and saw a slim brown neck. Oh, it *was* Kay! She called his name out loud, holding the lamp toward him.

He woke up and turned his head, and she saw that it was *not* Kay!

It was only his neck that was like Kay's, but he was young and handsome. The Princess sat up in her lily-bed and asked who was there. Then Gerda cried, and told her story and all that the Crows had done.

"You poor child!" said the Prince and Princess, and they praised the Crows and said that they were not angry with them, but that they must not do it again. Now they should have a reward.

"Would you like to fly away free?" the Princess asked the birds, "or will you take a permanent place as Court Crows with what you can get in the kitchen?"

They both bowed and asked for a permanent appointment, for they thought of their old age.

They put Gerda to bed, and she folded her hands, thinking, as she fell asleep, "How good people and animals are to me!"

The next day she was dressed from head to foot in silk and satin. The Prince and Princess wanted her to stay on in the palace, but she begged for a little carriage, a horse and a pair of shoes so that she might go out again into the world to look for Kay.

They gave her a muff as well as some shoes. She was warmly dressed, and when she was ready, there in front of the door stood a coach of pure gold, with a coachman, footmen and outriders, all wearing fine gold crowns.

The Prince and Princess helped her into the carriage and wished her good luck.

"Good-bye, good-bye!" called the Prince and Princess; and little Gerda cried, and the Crow cried.

The wild Crow, who was now married, drove with her for the first three miles; his wife could not come because she had a bad headache.

When the wild Crow had said good-bye, he flew up to a tree and flapped his big black wings for as long as the carriage was in sight.

The Little Robber Girl

They drove on and came to a dark forest, which the coach lit up like a torch as it passed through. When a band of robbers saw the carriage, they rushed out, exclaiming, "Gold! It's gold!"

And they seized the horses, killed the coachman,

footmen and outriders, and dragged Gerda out of the carriage.

"What a plump and tender morsel! I will eat her for my supper," said the old robber queen, and she drew her long knife, which glittered horribly.

"You shall not kill her!" cried the queen's little daughter. "She shall play with me. She shall give me her muff and her beautiful dress, and she shall sleep with me in my bed."

The little robber girl was as big as Gerda, but she was stronger and broader, with dark hair and black eyes that looked a little sad. She threw her arms around Gerda and said, "I will not let them kill you, so long as you do not make me angry. Are you a princess?"

"No," answered Gerda, "I'm not," and she began to tell all that had happened to her, and how dearly she loved little Kay.

The robber girl listened attentively and, when the tale was finished, she took Gerda to a corner of the robbers' camp where she slept.

Perched on rafters all around were more than a hundred Pigeons, who seemed to be asleep, but who fluttered a little when the two girls appeared. A Reindeer came up and nuzzled the robber girl while she teased it by tickling it with her long sharp knife.

Gerda lay awake for some time, for she did not know whether she was going to live or die in the robbers' camp.

"Coo, coo!" said the Pigeons. "We have seen little Kay. A white bird carried his sled while he was sitting in the Snow Queen's sleigh. They drove over the forest as we were sitting in our nests. She breathed on our young, and all died except two. Coo, coo!"

"What are you saying up there?" cried Gerda. "Where was the Snow Queen going? Do you know anything at all?"

"She was probably traveling to Lapland, where there is always ice and snow. Ask the Reindeer."

"There is marvelous ice and snow there!" said the Reindeer. "One can run about in the great sparkling valleys. There the Snow Queen has her summer palace, but her best palace is up by the North Pole, on one of the islands called Spitsbergen."

In the morning Gerda told the little robber girl all that the Pigeons had said. She nodded. "Do you know where Lapland is?" she asked the Reindeer.

"Who should know better than I?" said the beast, and his eyes sparkled. "I was born and bred there on the snowfields."

"Listen!" said the robber girl to Gerda, "you see that all the robbers have gone. Only my mother is left, and she takes a nap in the afternoon—then I shall do something for you!"

When her mother had fallen asleep, the robber girl went up to the Reindeer and said, "I am going to set you free so that you can run to Lapland. But you must go quickly and carry this little girl to the Snow Queen's palace, where her playmate is. You must have heard all that she told me, for she spoke loud enough!"

The Reindeer leaped high for joy. The robber girl lifted up little Gerda and tied her firmly onto the Reindeer. She even gave her a little pillow for a saddle.

"You must wear your fur boots," she said, "for it will be cold; but I shall keep your muff, it's such a pretty one! And I'm going to give you my mother's big fur gloves so that you won't freeze. They will come right up to your elbows."

And Gerda wept for joy.

"Don't make such faces!" said the robber girl. "You should look very happy now. And here are two loaves of bread and a sausage, so you won't be hungry!"

When these were tied to the Reindeer's back, the robber girl opened the door, called in all the big dogs, cut through the Reindeer's halter with her sharp knife and said to him, "Off with you now! But take good care of the little girl."

And Gerda stretched out her hands with the large fur gloves toward the little robber girl and said, "Good-bye!"

Then the Reindeer flew over the ground, through the great forest, as fast as he could. The wolves howled, the ravens screamed, the sky seemed on fire. "Those are my dear old Northern Lights," said the Reindeer. "Look how they glow."

And he ran faster and faster still, day and night. The loaves and the sausage were eaten, and then they came to Lapland.

The Lapp Woman and the Finn Woman

They stopped at a wretched little house. The roof almost touched the ground, and the door was so low that you had to creep in and out. There was no one in the house except an old Lapp woman who was cooking fish over an oil lamp. The Reindeer told Gerda's whole history, but first he told his own, for that seemed to him much more important, and Gerda was so cold that she could not speak.

"Ah, you poor creatures!" said the Lapp woman. "You have still farther to go! You must go over a hundred miles into Finland, for there the Snow Queen lives, and every single night she burns blue flares. I will scribble a few words on a dried codfish, for I have no paper, and you must give it to the Finn woman, for she can give you better advice than I can."

And when Gerda was warmed up and had had something to eat and drink, the Lapp woman wrote a few lines on a dried cod and told Gerda to take care of it. Then she tied her securely onto the Reindeer's back, and away they went again.

The whole night was ablaze with Northern Lights, and then they came to Finland and knocked at the Finn woman's chimney, for it was so cold she had no door at all.

Inside it was so hot that the Finn woman wore almost nothing. She drew off Gerda's fur gloves and boots and loosened her clothes. Finally she read what was written on the codfish. She read it over three times, till she knew it by heart, and then put the fish in her saucepan to cook, for she never wasted anything.

Soon the Reindeer told his story and, after his, little Gerda's, and the Finn woman blinked her eyes but said nothing.

"You are very clever, I know," said the Reindeer. "Won't you give the little girl a drink so that she may have the strength of twelve men and overpower the Snow Queen?"

"The strength of twelve men!" said the Finn woman. "That would not help much. It's true that little Kay is with the Snow Queen, and he likes everything there very much and thinks it the best place in all the world. That is because he has a splinter of glass in his heart and a tiny chip of it in his eye. If these do not come out, he will never be free, and the Snow Queen will keep him in her power."

"But can't you give little Gerda something so that she can have power over the Snow Queen?"

"I can give her no greater power than she already has. Don't you see how great it is? Don't you see how men and beasts help her when she wanders into the wide world with her bare feet? She is powerful already, because she is a dear little innocent child. If she herself cannot conquer the Snow Queen and remove the glass splinters that are in little Kay, *we* cannot help her! The Snow Queen's garden begins two miles from here. You can carry the girl so far; put her down by the large bush with red berries that stands in the snow. And you must come back here as fast as you can." Then the Finn woman lifted Gerda onto the Reindeer, and away he sped.

"Oh, I have left my gloves and boots behind!" cried Gerda. She missed them in the piercing cold, but the Reindeer did not dare to stop. On he ran till he came to the bush with red berries. There he sat Gerda down and kissed her, and big tears ran down his cheeks. Then he ran back, leaving the poor girl without shoes or gloves in the middle of the bitter cold of Finland.

She went on as fast as she could. A regiment of gigantic snowflakes came against her, but they melted even before they touched her, and she continued with fresh courage.

The Snow Queen's Palace

And now we must see what Kay was doing. He was not thinking of Gerda and never dreamed that she was standing right outside the Snow Queen's palace.

The walls of the palace were built of driven snow,

and the doors and windows of piercing winds. There were more than a hundred halls in it—the largest several miles long—all made of frozen snow. The bright Northern Lights lit them up, and very large and empty and cold and glittering they were! In the middle of the great hall was a frozen lake which had cracked in a thousand pieces. Here the Snow Queen used to sit when she was at home.

Little Kay was almost black and blue with cold, but he never felt it, for the Snow Queen had kissed away his feelings and his heart was a lump of ice. He was sitting in the hall, pulling about some sharp, flat pieces of ice and trying to put them together into a pattern. He thought they were beautiful, but that was because of the splinter of glass in his eye. He was able to fit them into a great many shapes, but he really wanted to make them spell the word "Love." The Snow Queen had said, "If you can spell out that word you will be your own master. I shall give you the whole world and a new sled." But Kay could not do it.

"Today I must fly to warmer countries," said the Snow Queen. "I must go and stir up my black kettles!" (This was what she called Mount Etna and Mount Vesuvius.) And off she flew, leaving Kay alone in the great hall trying to do his puzzle. He sat so still that you would have thought he was frozen.

Then little Gerda stepped into the palace hall. The raging winds quieted down as if they had fallen asleep when she appeared. She caught sight of Kay and ran to put her arms around his neck, crying, "Kay! Dear little Kay! I have found you at last!"

But Kay sat quite still and cold. Gerda wept hot tears, which fell on his breast and thawed his heart so that the glass splinter was dissolved. He looked at her and burst into tears. He cried so much that the splinter swam out of his eye. Then he recognized her and cried out, "Gerda! Dear little Gerda! Where have you been so long? And where have I been?"

And he looked around him. "How cold it is here! How huge and empty!" He threw his arms around Gerda, and she laughed and wept for joy. It was such a happy time that the pieces of ice even danced around them for joy. When they grew tired, Kay and Gerda lay down, and as they slept they melted the ice, forming the word that the Snow Queen had said Kay must spell in order to become his own master.

Gerda kissed his cheeks and they grew rosy. She kissed his eyes and they sparkled like hers. She kissed his hands and feet and he became warm and glowing. The Snow Queen might come home now, but they had his release—the word "Love" stood written in the sparkling ice.

They took each other's hands and wandered out of the great palace. They talked about the grandmother and the roses in the window boxes, and wherever they went the winds calmed down and the sun came out.

When they reached the bush with red berries there stood the Reindeer waiting for them.

He carried Kay and Gerda first to the Finn woman, who warmed them in her hot room and gave them advice for their journey home.

Then they went to the Lapp woman, who gave them new clothes and let them borrow her sleigh until they reached the border of their own country. The Reindeer ran alongside the sleigh till they came to fields fresh with the first spring green. There he said good-bye.

When they reached the forest, which was bursting into bud, there came riding out of it a young girl on a splendid horse. She was wearing a red cap and carrying pistols in her belt. It was the little robber girl, who was tired of staying at home and wanted to go out into the world. She and Gerda recognized each other at once.

"You are a fine one!" she said to Kay. "I wonder if you deserve to be run after all over the world!"

But Gerda patted her cheeks and asked after the Prince and Princess.

"They are traveling about," said the robber girl.

"And the Crow?" asked Gerda.

"Oh, the Crow is dead," answered the robber girl. "His tame sweetheart is a widow now and hops about with a bit of black crepe on her leg. She makes a great fuss, but it's all nonsense. Now tell me what happened to you, and how you found him."

And Kay and Gerda told her all.

"What a story!" said the robber girl. She shook hands with them and promised that if she ever passed through their town she would come and see them. Then she rode on.

Gerda and Kay went home hand in hand. There they found the grandmother and everything just as it had been, but when they went through the doorway they found they were grown up.

There were the roses in the window boxes. It was summer—warm, glorious summer.

HANS CHRISTIAN ANDERSEN, ANDREW LANG COLLECTION

SIX SILLIES

ONCE UPON a time there was a girl who had reached the age of thirty-seven without ever having had a suitor, for she was so foolish that no one wanted to marry her.

One day, however, a young man arrived to pay court to her, and her mother, beaming with joy, sent the girl down to the cellar to draw a jug of beer.

As her daughter did not come back, the mother

went down to see what had become of her and found her sitting on the stairs, her head in her hands, while by her side the beer was running all over the floor, for she had forgotten to close the tap.

"What are you doing?" asked the mother.

"I was thinking what I shall call my first child, after I am married to that young man. All the names in the calendar are taken already."

The mother sat down on the staircase beside her daughter and said, "I will think about it with you, my dear."

The father, who had stayed upstairs with the young man, was surprised that neither his daughter nor his wife came back, and he in turn decided to go down to look for them.

He found them both sitting on the stairs, while beside them the beer was running all over the ground from the tap, which was wide open.

"What are you doing there? The beer is running all over the cellar."

"We were thinking what we should call the children that our daughter will have when she marries that young man. All the names in the calendar are taken already."

"Well," said the father, "I will think about it with the two of you."

As neither daughter nor mother nor father came upstairs again, the suitor grew impatient waiting for them and went down into the cellar to see what they could all be doing.

He found the three sitting on the stairs, while beside them beer was running all over the ground from the tap, which was still wide open.

"What in the world are you all doing that you don't come upstairs and that you allow the beer to run all over the cellar?"

"Yes, I know the beer is flowing, my boy," said the father, "but if you marry our daughter, what shall you call your children? All the names in the calendar are already taken."

When the young man heard this answer he replied, "Well, good-bye, I am going away. When I have found three people sillier than you, I will come back and marry your daughter."

So he started his journey and, after walking a long way, he reached an orchard. There he saw a man knocking down walnuts from a tree and trying to throw them into a cart with a fork.

"What are you doing there?" the young man asked.

"I want to load the cart with walnuts, but cannot manage to do it."

The young man advised him to get a basket and put all the walnuts in it, and then turn the basket over into the cart.

"Well," he said to himself, "I have already found someone more foolish than those three."

So he went on his way, and by and by he came to a wood. There he saw a man who wanted to give his pig some acorns to eat and was trying with all his might to make the pig climb up the oak tree.

"What are you doing, my good man?" asked he.

"I want to make my pig eat some acorns, but I can't get him to go up the tree."

"If you were to climb up and shake down the acorns, the pig would pick them up."

"Oh, I never thought of that."

"Here is the second foolish one," said the young man to himself.

Some way farther along the road, he came upon a man who had never worn any trousers and who was trying to put on a pair. He had fastened them between two trees and was jumping with all his might high up in the air and trying to hit the two legs of the trousers as he came down.

"It would be much better if you held them in your hands," said the young man, "and then put your legs in, one after the other."

"Dear me, to be sure! You are sharper than I am, for that never occurred to me."

And, having found three people more foolish than the girl or her father or her mother, the young man went back to marry the young lady. And, in the course of time, they had a great many children.

HENRI CARNOY, ANDREW LANG COLLECTION

THE HEDGEHOG AND
THE RABBIT

This is a lying story, my children, but it's true just the same, for my grandfather, who told it to me, used to say: "It must be true, my child, or else how could one tell it, after all?"

But this is the way the story goes:

It happened on the Buxtehuder Heath on a Sunday morning at harvesttime, just as the buckwheat was coming into flower. The sun was climbing up into the heavens, a breeze blew gently over the stubble, larks trilled in the sky, bees buzzed in the buckwheat and everybody was going to church in their Sunday best— in short, all creatures, great and small, were contented; and the Hedgehog was, too.

This Hedgehog, he was standing in his doorway with his arms crossed on his chest, pointing his nose to the wind and singing a little tune—that is, as good or bad a tune as a hedgehog might be expected to sing on a lovely Sunday morning.

While he was humming contentedly to himself in this charming fashion, a thought came into his head.

While my wife is busy washing and brushing the little ones, he thought, I might as well go for a Sunday stroll and take a look at my turnip patch. The turnip patch was in the field next to his house and belonged to a farmer, but, because the Hedgehog and his family had fallen into the habit of eating there, they had come to think of it as their own.

Well, no sooner said than done. The Hedgehog closed the door after him and sauntered down the road. But just as he reached the blackthorn bush which grew beside the turnip patch, he met a Rabbit who was out on the same business—that is to say, he had come to see how his garden, the cabbage patch, was getting along on this fine day.

Bowing and smiling, the Hedgehog wished the Rabbit a pleasant good morning, but the Rabbit—who was a grand gentleman in his own community, and most haughty about it, too—this Rabbit did not return the Hedgehog's neighborly greeting. Instead, he said with a mocking air, "Hm! And how do you happen to be running around in this field so early on a Sunday morning?"

"It's such a fine Sunday," said the Hedgehog. "I'm just out for a little stroll."

"A stroll!" jeered the Rabbit. "I should think you could put your legs to better use than that!"

This remark wounded the Hedgehog beyond words, for he was very sensitive about his legs, which were short and somewhat crooked. So now he bristled up and cried in fury, "Oh, yes? You must think that your legs are better than mine!"

"That's exactly what I think," replied the Rabbit calmly.

"Yes, that's what you think," cried the Hedgehog, "but I'll wager that if we ran a race, I'd win it."

"That's a joke!" cried the Rabbit. "You with your stumpy little legs! However, if you are so bent on making a fool of yourself, I'll take you on. What shall be the prize for the winner?"

"A golden coin and a bottle of brandy," said the Hedgehog.

"Agreed!" cried the Rabbit. "Get in line and let's start."

"Oh, no hurry about it," said the Hedgehog, carelessly. "I haven't even had breakfast yet. You get the prizes; I'll be right back here on the same spot in half an hour."

With that they parted, for the Rabbit was satisfied with this plan.

On the way home, the Hedgehog was busy with his thoughts. That Rabbit will depend upon his long, fleet legs, he thought. My legs are—well, they're neither long nor fleet, but I'll beat him to it all the same. He may be a grand gentleman, yes—but he's an old muddle-noodle; and as for me, I'm not as stupid as I may look.

Upon reaching home, the Hedgehog said to his wife, "Come, hurry and get yourself ready. I need you out in the field."

"What's going on, then?" asked his wife.

"Oh, nothing much. I told the Rabbit I would run a race with him, and I'd like to have you around while it's going on."

"My heavens, man!" cried his wife. "Are you out of your head? How could you ever hope to win a race against a rabbit?"

"No words, wife!" cried the Hedgehog sternly. "That's my business. Don't poke your nose into men's affairs. March along now! Are you ready?"

What could the wife do? She had to obey whether she wanted to or not, and as they waddled along side by side, the Hedgehog said to her, "Now listen well to what I'm telling you. In this big field is where we'll run our race, the Rabbit and I. See these long deep furrows?"

"Yes," said his wife, "but——"

"Silence!" cried her husband, and then continued: "The Rabbit of course will run in one furrow and I in the next, and we'll start over there at the upper end of the field. Now, all you have to do is to sit at the lower end of my furrow. Understand? Don't move from that place; just sit there quietly, and when you hear the Rabbit coming along, just pop up your head and say, 'Here I am already!' "

So that's the way it was done. The Hedgehog left his wife hiding in the lower end of his furrow, had a final meeting with the Rabbit, and—one, two, three!— off they went like a whirlwind down the field.

That is, the Rabbit did. The Hedgehog only ran a few steps, then ducked down in his furrow and crouched there, out of sight and quiet as a mouse.

The Rabbit ran for his life, his ears flapping in the wind. He thought he was doing remarkably well, but as he neared the lower end of the field someone cried, "Here I am already!"

The Rabbit couldn't believe his ears and, when he looked over into the next furrow, he could hardly believe his eyes, either. What he saw, of course, was the Hedgehog's wife but, since she looked exactly like her husband, the Rabbit couldn't tell the difference between them.

Well, it's the Hedgehog all right, he thought. Just the same, I don't like the looks of the whole thing. Then, still panting for breath, he cried, "Another race! The other way around!" and off he went, so fast that it was a wonder his ears stayed on his head.

The Hedgehog's wife didn't move; she still stayed quietly in the lower end of the furrow.

In a twinkling-and-a-half the Rabbit had returned to the upper end of the furrow, yet there sat the Hedgehog, calling, "Here I am already!"

The Rabbit, now almost out of his head with fury, cried out wildly, "Another race—the other way around again!"

"As often as you wish, for all I care," said the Hedgehog.

Back and forth went the Rabbit, forth and back, then back and forth again—but always when he reached the end of the furrow it was the same old story: there sat the Hedgehog, calling, "Yoo hoo! Here I am already."

Seventy-three times he tried, this racing Rabbit, but at the seventy-fourth try he had to give up. His legs folded up under him, his ears flopped sideways over his head, and then, with his breath coming in weary gasps, he sank down in his furrow and lay there with closed eyes.

The Hedgehog picked up the prizes and called his wife out of the furrow, saying, "The race is over and, as you see, I won it."

Then they both went home together in great delight, and, if they're not dead, for all I know they're living there still.

Yes, that is the way the story goes, my children, and it must be true—or how could it be that, ever since that time, no rabbit in the Buxtehuder Heath has dared to pass a remark about a hedgehog's legs? Yes? No? Well, what do you think about it?

JAKOB AND WILHELM GRIMM, TRANSLATED BY WANDA GÁG

THUMBELINA

HERE WAS once a woman who wanted to have a tiny little child, but she did not know where to get one. So one day she went to an old witch and said to her, "I should so much like to have a tiny little child. Can you tell me where I might get one?"

"Oh, we have one ready now!" said the witch. "Here, take this barleycorn. It's not the kind the farmer sows in his field or feeds the cocks and hens with, I can tell you. Put it in a flowerpot and then you will see what happens."

"Oh, thank you," said the woman and gave the witch twelve pennies, for that was what the barleycorn cost. Then she went home and planted it. Immediately there grew from it a large and beautiful flower which looked like a tulip, but the petals were tightly closed as if it were still only a bud.

"What a beautiful flower!" exclaimed the woman, and she kissed the red and yellow petals. As she kissed them the flower burst open. It was a real tulip, the kind we usually see, but in the middle of the blossom, on the soft velvety petals, sat a tiny girl, delicate and pretty. She was scarcely as big as a thumb, so the woman and her husband called her Thumbelina.

An elegant polished walnut shell served Thumbelina as a cradle, the blue petals of a violet were her mattress and a rose petal was her quilt. There she lay at night, but in the daytime she used to play about on the table. Here the woman had put a bowl, which was surrounded by a ring of flowers, their stems dipping into the water, where a great tulip petal floated. In this, Thumbelina sat and sailed from one side of the bowl to the other, rowing herself with two white horsehairs for oars. It was such a pretty sight! She would sing, too, with a voice more soft and sweet than had ever been heard before.

One night, when she was lying in her pretty bed, an old Toad crept in through a broken pane in the window. She was very ugly and clumsy, and she hopped onto the table where Thumbelina lay asleep under the red rose petal.

"This would make a beautiful wife for my son," said the Toad. Taking up the walnut shell with Thumbelina inside, she hopped with it through the window into the garden.

Here there flowed a great wide stream, with slippery and marshy banks, where the Toad lived with her son. Ugh, how ugly and clammy he was, just like his mother!

"Croak, croak, croak!" was all he could say when he saw the pretty little girl asleep in the walnut shell.

"Don't talk so loud, or you'll wake her," said the old Toad. "She might escape us even now. She is as light as a feather. We will put her out on a broad water-lily leaf in the stream. She is so small and light it will be just like an island for her. She can't run away from us there, while we are preparing the guest room under the marsh where she will live."

Growing in the stream were many water lilies with broad green leaves which looked as if they were floating on the water. The farthest leaf was the largest, and to this the old Toad swam with Thumbelina in her walnut shell.

The tiny Thumbelina woke up very early in the morning, and when she saw where she was she began to cry bitterly. On every side of the great green leaf was water and she could not get back to the land.

The old Toad was down under the marsh, decorating her room with rushes and yellow marigold petals to make it grand for her new daughter-in-law. After she had finished she swam out with her ugly son to the leaf where Thumbelina lay. She wanted to take the pretty cradle to the room before Thumbelina herself went there. The old Toad bowed low in the water before her, and said, "Here is my son. You shall marry him and the two of you will live in great magnificence down under the marsh."

"Croak, croak, croak!" was all the son could say. Then they took the neat little cradle and swam away with it. Thumbelina sat alone on the great green leaf and wept, for she did not want to live with the Toad or marry her ugly son.

The little fishes swimming about under the water had seen the old Toad quite plainly and heard what she said. They raised their heads to see Thumbelina and thought her so pretty they were very sorry she was going down to live with the ugly Toad. No, that must not happen, they decided. They assembled in the water around the green stalk which supported the leaf on which the tiny girl was sitting and nibbled the stem in two. Away floated the leaf down the stream, bearing Thumbelina far beyond the reach of the Toad.

On she sailed past several towns, and the birds sitting in the bushes saw her and sang, "What a pretty little girl!" The leaf floated farther and farther away. Thus Thumbelina left her native land.

A beautiful little white Butterfly fluttered above her and at last settled on the leaf. Thumbelina pleased him and she, too, was delighted. Now the Toads could not reach her, and everything was so beautiful where she was sailing. The sun shone on the water and made it sparkle like the brightest silver. She took off her sash and tied one end around the Butterfly; the other end she fastened to the leaf, so that he glided along with her faster than ever.

Soon after, a great Beetle came flying past. He caught sight of Thumbelina and in a moment had put his legs around her slender waist and had flown off with her to a tree. The green leaf floated away down the stream and the Butterfly with it, for he was fastened to the leaf and could not get loose. How terrified poor little Thumbelina was when the Beetle flew off with her to the tree! And she was especially distressed for the beautiful white Butterfly because she had tied him to the leaf. If he did not get away he might starve to death.

But the Beetle did not trouble himself about that. He sat down with her on a large green leaf, gave her honey out of the flowers to eat and told her she was very pretty, although she wasn't in the least like a beetle. Later on, all the other beetles who lived in the same tree came to pay calls. They examined Thumbelina closely, and remarked, "Why, she has only two legs! How disgusting!"

"She has no feelers!" cried another.

"How ugly she is!" said all the lady beetles—and yet Thumbelina was really very pretty.

The Beetle who had stolen her knew this very well. But when he heard all the ladies saying she was ugly, he began to think so too and decided not to keep her. She could go wherever she liked. So he flew down from the tree with her and put her on a daisy. There she sat and wept, thinking she must be very ugly, because the

Beetle would have nothing to do with her. Yet she was the most beautiful creature imaginable, so soft and delicate, like the loveliest rose petal.

The whole summer poor little Thumbelina lived alone in the great wood. She wove a bed for herself of blades of grass and hung it up under a clover leaf so she was protected from the rain. She gathered honey from the flowers for food and drank the dew on the leaves every morning. Thus the summer and autumn passed. But then came winter—the long, cold winter. All the birds who had sung so sweetly about her had flown away. The trees had shed their leaves, the flowers were dead. The great clover leaf under which she lived had curled up and nothing remained but the withered stalk. She was terribly cold, for her clothes were ragged and she herself was so small and thin. Poor little Thumbelina would surely be frozen to death very soon. It began to snow, and every snowflake that fell on her was like a whole shovelful, for she was only an inch high. She wrapped herself up in a dead leaf, but since it was torn in the middle, it gave her no warmth. She was trembling with cold.

Now, just outside the wood where she was living lay a great grainfield. The grain had been harvested a long time before. Only dry, bare stubble was left standing in the frozen ground. This made a forest for her to wander about in. All at once she came across the door of a Field Mouse, who had a little hole under a knoll. There the Mouse lived warm and snug, with a storeroom full of grain, a splendid kitchen and dining room. Poor little Thumbelina went up to the door and begged for a little piece of barley, for she had not had anything to eat for two days.

"Poor little creature!" said the Field Mouse, for she was a kindhearted old thing. "Come into my warm room and have some dinner with me." Because Thumbelina pleased her, she said, "As far as I am concerned you may spend the winter with me. You must keep my room clean and tidy and tell me stories, for I like them very much." And Thumbelina did all that the kind Field Mouse asked and did it remarkably well, too.

"I am expecting a visitor tonight," said the Field Mouse. "My neighbor comes to call on me once a week. He is in better circumstances than I am, has great big rooms and wears a fine black velvet coat. If you could only marry him, you would be well provided for, though he is blind. You must tell him all the prettiest stories you know."

But Thumbelina did not trouble her head about him, for he was only a mole. He came and paid them a visit in his black velvet coat.

"He is so rich and accomplished," the Field Mouse told her. "His house is twenty times larger than mine. He possesses great knowledge, but he cannot bear the sun and the beautiful flowers and speaks slightingly of them, for he has never seen them."

Thumbelina had to sing to him, so she sang "Lady-bird, ladybird, fly away home!" and other songs so prettily that the Mole fell in love with her. He did not say anything. He was a very cautious man. A short time before, he had dug a long passage through the ground from his own house to that of his neighbor. He gave the Field Mouse and Thumbelina permission to walk in this as often as they liked, but he begged them not to be afraid of the dead Bird that lay in the passage. It was a real bird with beak and feathers and must have died a long time ago. It now lay buried just where the Mole had made his tunnel.

One day the Mole led Thumbelina and the Field Mouse into the tunnel. He took a piece of tinder wood in his mouth, for that glows in the dark, and went ahead of them, lighting their way through the long dark passage. When they came to the place where the dead Bird lay, the Mole put his broad nose against the ceiling and pushed a hole through so the daylight could shine down. In the middle of the path lay a dead Swallow, his pretty wings pressed close to his sides, his claws and head drawn under his feathers; the poor Bird had evidently died of cold.

Thumbelina was very sorry, for she was fond of all little birds. They had sung and twittered so beautifully to her all through the summer. But the Mole kicked the Bird with his bandy legs and said, "Now he can't sing anymore! It must be miserable to be a little bird! I'm thankful that none of my children are. Birds always starve in winter."

"Yes, you speak like a sensible man," said the Field Mouse. "What has a bird, in spite of all his singing, in the wintertime? He can only starve and freeze, and that must be very unpleasant for him, I must say!"

Thumbelina did not say anything. When the other two had passed on, she bent down to the Bird, brushed aside the feathers from his head and kissed his closed eyes gently. "Perhaps he sang to me in the summer," she said. "How much pleasure he did give me, dear little Bird!"

The Mole closed up the hole which let in the light and then escorted the ladies home. But Thumbelina could not sleep that night. She got out of bed and wove a big blanket of straw and carried it off and spread it over the dead Bird. She piled upon it thistledown as soft as cotton wool, which she had found in the Field Mouse's room, so that the poor little thing should lie warmly buried.

"Farewell, pretty little Bird!" she said. "Farewell, and thank you for your beautiful songs in the summer, when the trees were green and the sun shone down warmly on us!" Then she laid her head against the Bird's heart. But the Bird was not dead. He had been frozen, but now that she had warmed him, he was coming to life again.

In autumn the swallows fly away to foreign lands.

But there are some who are late in starting and then they get so cold that they drop down as if dead, and the snow comes and covers them over.

Thumbelina trembled, she was so frightened. The Bird was very large to her, for she was only an inch high. But she took courage, piled up the down more closely around the poor Swallow, fetched her own little quilt and laid it over his head.

Next night she crept out again to him. There he was, alive but very weak. He could only open his eyes for a moment and look at Thumbelina, who was standing in front of him with a piece of tinder wood in her hand, for she had no other lantern.

"Thank you, pretty little child!" said the Swallow to her. "I am so beautifully warm! Soon I shall regain my strength and I shall be able to fly out once more into the warm sunshine."

"Oh," she said, "it is very cold outside. It is snowing and freezing! Stay in your warm bed. I will take care of you!"

Then she brought him water in a petal, which he drank. He told her how he had torn one of his wings on a bramble so he could not keep up with the other swallows, who had flown far away to warmer lands. At last he had dropped down exhausted, and then he could remember no more. The whole winter he remained down there, and Thumbelina looked after him and nursed him tenderly. She told neither the Mole nor the Field Mouse anything of this, for they could not bear the poor Swallow.

When the spring came, and the sun warmed the earth again, the Swallow said farewell to Thumbelina, who opened for him the hole in the roof the Mole had made. The sun shone brightly down upon her, and the Swallow asked her if she would go with him. She could sit upon his back. Thumbelina wanted very much to fly far away into the greenwood, but she knew that the old Field Mouse would be sad if she ran away. "No, I mustn't come!" she said.

"Farewell, dear good little girl!" said the Swallow, and flew off into the sunshine. Thumbelina gazed after him with tears in her eyes, for she was very fond of the Swallow.

"Tweet, tweet!" sang the Bird, and flew into the greenwood. Thumbelina was very unhappy. She was not allowed to go out into the warm sunshine. The grain which had been sowed in the field over the Field Mouse's home grew up high into the air and made a thick forest for the poor little girl, who was only an inch high.

"Soon you are to be a bride, Thumbelina," said the Field Mouse one day, "for our neighbor has said he wishes to marry you. What a piece of fortune for a poor child like you! Now you must set to work on your trousseau, for nothing must be lacking if you are to become the wife of our neighbor, the Mole!"

Thumbelina had to sew all day long, and every evening the Mole visited her and told her that when the summer was over the sun would not shine so hot. Now it was burning the earth as hard as a stone. Yes, when the summer had passed, they would have the wedding.

But she was not at all pleased about it, for she did not like the stupid Mole. Every morning when the sun was rising, and every evening when it was setting, she would steal out of the house door, and when the breeze parted the stalks of grain so that she could see the clear sky through them, she thought how bright and beautiful it must be outside and longed to see her dear Swallow again. But he never came. No doubt he had flown far away into the great greenwood.

By the autumn Thumbelina had finished her whole trousseau.

"In four weeks you will be married," said the Field Mouse, but Thumbelina wept and declared she would not marry the ugly old Mole.

"Don't be obstinate, or I shall bite you with my sharp white teeth! You are getting a fine husband. The King himself does not possess such a velvet coat. His storeroom and cellar are full, and you should be thankful for that."

The wedding day arrived. The Mole had come to fetch Thumbelina to live with him deep down under the ground, never to come out into the warm sun again, for that was what he didn't like. The poor little girl was very sad, for now she must say good-bye to the beautiful sun.

"Farewell, bright sun!" she cried, stretching out her arms toward it and taking another step outside the house. Now the grain had been harvested and only the stubble was left standing. "Farewell, farewell!" she said, and put her arms around a little red flower that grew there. "Give my love to the dear Swallow when you see him!"

"Tweet, tweet!" sounded in her ear all at once. She looked up. There was the Swallow flying past! He was delighted when he saw Thumbelina. She told him how unwilling she was to marry the ugly Mole, because then she would have to live underground where the sun never shone, and while she said this she could not help bursting into tears.

"The cold winter is coming now," said the Swallow. "I must fly away to warmer lands. Will you come with me? You can sit on my back, and we will fly far away from the ugly Mole and his dark house, over the mountains to the warm countries. There the sun shines more brightly than here. There it is always summer and beautiful flowers always bloom. Do come with me, dear little Thumbelina, who saved my life when I lay frozen in the dark tunnel!"

"Yes, I will go with you," said Thumbelina, and climbed on the Swallow's back, with her feet on one of his outstretched wings. Up into the air he flew, over

THE WORLD'S BEST FAIRY TALES

woods and seas, over the great mountains always covered with snow. When she felt cold she crept under his warm feathers, only keeping her little head out to admire all the beautiful things in the world beneath. At last they came to warm lands. There the sun was brighter, the sky seemed twice as high, and in the hedges hung the finest green and purple grapes. In the orchards grew oranges and lemons. The air was scented with myrtle and mint and on the roads were pretty little children running about and playing with great gorgeous butterflies. But the Swallow flew on farther, and the country became more and more beautiful. Under the most splendid green trees beside a blue lake stood a glittering white marble castle. Vines trailed from the high pillars and at the top there were many swallows' nests. In one of these lived the Swallow who was carrying Thumbelina.

"Here is my house!" said he. "But it won't do for you to live with me. I am not tidy enough to please you. Find a home for yourself in one of the pretty flowers that grow down there. Now I will set you down and you can do whatever you like."

"That will be lovely!" said she, clapping her hands.

There lay a great white marble column which had fallen to the ground and broken into three pieces, but between these grew the most beautiful white flowers. The Swallow flew down with Thumbelina and set her upon one of the broad leaves. There, to her astonish-

ment, she found a tiny little man sitting in the middle of the flower, as white and transparent as if he were made of glass. He had the prettiest golden crown on his head and the most beautiful wings on his shoulders. He himself was no bigger than Thumbelina. He was the spirit of the flower. In each blossom there lived a tiny man or woman. But this one was King of them all.

"How handsome he is!" whispered Thumbelina to the Swallow.

The little King was very much frightened by the Swallow, for in comparison with one as tiny as himself the Bird seemed a giant. But when he saw Thumbelina, he was delighted, for she was the loveliest girl that he had ever seen. He took his golden crown off his head and put it on hers, asking her her name and if she would be his wife, and then she would be Queen of all the flowers. Yes, he was a different kind of husband from the son of the Toad and the Mole with the black velvet coat. So she said "Yes" to the King. And out of each flower came a lady or a gentleman, so tiny and pretty that it was a pleasure to see them. Everyone brought Thumbelina a present, but the best of all was a pair of lovely wings which they fastened to her back, and now she too could fly from flower to flower. They wished her joy, and the Swallow sat above in his nest and sang the wedding march as well as he could. But he was sad, as he was very fond of Thumbelina and did not want to be separated from her.

"You shall not be called Thumbelina!" said the spirit of the flower. "That is an ugly name, and you are much too pretty. We will call you May Blossom."

"Farewell, farewell!" said the little Swallow with a heavy heart, and he flew away to farther lands, far, far away, to the country of Denmark. There he had a little nest above the window of a man who tells such nice fairy stories. "Tweet, tweet!" he sang to the man. And that is the way we learned the whole story.

HANS CHRISTIAN ANDERSEN, ANDREW LANG COLLECTION

THE SORCERER'S APPRENTICE

A MAN FOUND himself in need of a helper for his workshop, and one day as he was walking along on the outskirts of a little hamlet he met a boy who was carrying a bundle slung over his shoulder.

Stopping him, the man said, "Good morning, my lad. I am looking for an apprentice for my shop. Have you a master?"

"No," said the boy, "I have just this morning said

good-bye to my mother and am now off to find myself a trade."

"Good," said the man. "You look as though you might be just the lad I need. But wait, do you know anything about reading and writing?"

"Oh, yes!" said the boy.

"Too bad!" said the man. "You won't do after all. I have no use for an apprentice who is able to read and write."

"Pardon me?" said the boy. "If it was reading and writing you were talking about, I misunderstood you. I thought you asked if I knew anything about eating and fighting—those two things I am able to do well, but as to reading and writing, those are things I know nothing about."

"Well!" cried the man. "Then you are just the fellow I want. Come with me to my workshop, and I will show you what to do."

The boy, however, had had his wits about him. He could read and write well enough and had only pretended to be a fool. Wondering why a man should prefer to have an unschooled helper, he thought to himself, I smell a rat. There is something strange about all of this business, and I had better keep my eyes and ears open.

While he was pondering over this, his new master was leading him into the heart of a deep forest. Here in a small clearing stood a house, and as soon as they entered it the boy could see that this was no ordinary workshop.

At one end of a big room was a huge hearth with a copper caldron hanging in it; at the other end was a small alcove lined with many big books, and from the ceiling there hung a huge, many-toothed fish. A mortar and pestle stood on the floor; bottles and sieves, measuring scales and oddly shaped glassware were strewn about on the table.

Well! It did not take the clever young apprentice very long to realize that he was working for a magician or sorcerer of some kind and so, although he pretended to be quite stupid, he kept his eyes and ears open and tried to learn all he could.

"Sorcery—that is a trade I would dearly love to master!" said the boy to himself. "A mouthful of good chants and charms would never come amiss to a poor fellow like me, and with them I might even be able to do some good in the world."

There were many things the boy had to do. Sometimes he was ordered to stir the evil-smelling broths which bubbled in the big copper caldron; at other times he had to grind up herbs and berries—and many things too gruesome to mention—in the big mortar and pestle. It was also his task to sweep up the workshop, to keep the fire burning on the big hearth and to gather the strange materials needed by the man for the broths and brews he was always mixing.

This went on day after day, week after week and month after month, until the boy was almost beside himself with curiosity. He was most curious about the thick heavy books in the alcove. How often he had wondered about them and how many times had he been tempted to take a peep between their covers! But, remembering that he was not supposed to know how to read or write, he had been wise enough never to show the least interest in them. At last there came a day when he made up his mind to see what was in them, no matter what the risk.

I'll try it before another day dawns, he thought.

That night he waited until the sorcerer was sound asleep and snoring loudly in his bedchamber. Then, creeping out of his straw couch, the boy took a light into the corner of the alcove and began paging through one of the heavy volumes. What was written in them has never been told, but they were conjuring books, each and every one of them; and from that time on, the boy read them silently, secretly, for an hour or two, night after night. In this way he learned many magic tricks: chants and charms and countercharms; recipes for philters and potions, for broths and brews and witches' stews; signs mystic and cabalistic; and other helpful spells of many kinds.

The boy memorized all these tricks of the magician carefully, and it was not long before he sometimes was able to figure out what kind of charms his master was working, what brand of potion he was mixing, what sort of stews he was brewing.

And what kind of charms and potions and stews were they? Alas, they were all wicked ones! Now the boy knew that he was not working for an ordinary magician, but for a cruel, dangerous sorcerer. And because of this, the boy made a plan, a bold one.

He went on with his nightly studies until his head was swarming with magic recipes and incantations. He even had time to work at them during the day, for the sorcerer sometimes left the shop for hours—working harm and havoc on mortals, no doubt. At such times the boy would try out a few bits of his newly learned wisdom. He began with simple things, such as changing the cat into a bee and back to the cat again, making a viper out of the poker, an imp out of the broom and so on. Sometimes he was successful, but often he was not; so the boy said to himself, "The time is not yet ripe."

Not long after, the sorcerer again went forth on one of his mysterious trips. The boy hurried through his work and had just settled down with a large conjuring book on his knees, when the master returned unexpectedly. The boy, thinking fast, pointed smilingly at a few of the pictures, after which he quietly closed the book and went on with his work as though nothing were amiss.

But the sorcerer was not deceived. If the wretch

can read, he thought, he may learn how to outwit me. And I can't send him off with a beating and a "Bad speed to you," either. Doubtless he knows too much already and will reveal all my fine mean tricks, and then I can't have any more sport working mischief on man and beast.

He acted quickly. With one leap he rushed at the boy, who in turn made a spring for the door.

"Stop!" cried the sorcerer. "You shall not escape from me!"

He was about to grab the boy by the collar when the quick-witted lad mumbled a powerful incantation by which he changed himself into a bird, and—wootsch!—he had flown into the woods.

The sorcerer, not to be outdone, shouted a charm, thus changing himself into a larger bird, and—whoosh!—he was after the little one.

With another incantation the boy changed himself into a fish, and—whish!—he was swimming across a big pond.

But the master was equal to this, for with a few words he made himself into a fish too, a big one, and swam after the little one.

At this the boy changed himself into a still bigger fish, but the magician, by a master stroke, turned himself into a tiny kernel of grain and rolled into a small crack in a stone where the fish couldn't touch him.

Quickly the boy changed himself into a rooster, and

See page 202

205

—peck! peck! peck!—with his sharp beak he snapped at the kernel of grain and ate it up.

That was the end of the wicked sorcerer, and the boy became the owner of the magic workshop. And wasn't it fine that all the powers and ingredients which had been used for evil by the sorcerer were now in the hands of a boy who would use them only for the good of man and beast?

JAKOB AND WILHELM GRIMM, TRANSLATED BY WANDA GÁG

RED RIDING HOOD

ONCE UPON a time there was a sweet little maiden who was loved by all who knew her, but she was especially dear to her grandmother, who did everything she could for the child. Once she gave her a little red velvet cloak. It was so becoming and the little girl liked it so much that she would never wear anything else, and so she got the name of Red Riding Hood.

One day her mother said to her, "Come here, Red Riding Hood! Take this cake and bottle of wine to

Grandmother. She is weak and ill, and they will do her good. Go quickly, before it gets hot. Don't loiter by the way, nor run, or you will fall and break the bottle, and then there will be no wine for Grandmother. And when you get to her house, don't forget to say 'Good morning' prettily to Grandmother, without staring about you."

"I will do just as you tell me," Red Riding Hood promised her mother.

Her grandmother lived far into the wood, a good half-hour from the village. When she got to the wood, Red Riding Hood met a Wolf, but she did not know what a wicked animal he was, so she was not a bit afraid of him.

"Good morning, Red Riding Hood," he said.

"Good morning, Wolf," she answered.

"Whither away so early, Red Riding Hood?"

"To Grandmother's."

"What have you in your basket?"

"Cake and wine. We baked yesterday, so I'm taking a cake to Grandmother. She needs something to make her well."

"Where does she live, Red Riding Hood?"

"A good quarter of an hour farther into the wood. Her house stands under three big oak trees, near a hedge of nut trees which you must know," said Red Riding Hood.

The Wolf thought: This tender little creature will

be a plump morsel! She will be much nicer to eat than the old woman. I must be very cunning and snap them both up.

He walked along with Red Riding Hood for a while, then he said, "Look at the pretty flowers, Red Riding Hood. Why don't you look about you? I don't believe you even hear the birds sing. You are as solemn as if you were going to school, and everything else is so gay out here in the wood."

Red Riding Hood raised her eyes, and when she saw the sunlight dancing through the trees, and all the bright flowers, she thought: I'm sure Grandmother would be pleased if I took her a bunch of fresh flowers. It is still quite early. I shall have plenty of time to pick them.

So she left the path and wandered off among the trees to pick flowers. Each time she picked one, she always saw another even prettier one farther on. So she went deeper and deeper into the forest.

In the meantime the Wolf went straight off to the grandmother's cottage and knocked at the door.

"Who is there?"

"Red Riding Hood, bringing you a cake and some wine. Open the door!"

"Lift the latch," called out the old woman. "I am too weak to get up."

The Wolf lifted the latch and the door sprang open. He went straight in and up to the bed without saying a word, and ate up the poor old woman. Then he put on her nightdress and cap, got into bed and drew the curtains.

Red Riding Hood picked flowers till she could carry no more, and then she remembered that she had promised not to loiter on the way to her grandmother's. She was astonished when she got to the house to find the door open, and when she entered the room everything seemed so strange. She felt quite frightened but she did not know why.

"Good morning, Grandmother," she cried. But she received no answer.

Then she went up to the bed and drew the curtain back. There lay her grandmother, but she had drawn her cap down over her face and she looked very odd.

"Oh, Grandmother, what big ears you have," she said.

"The better to hear you with, my dear."

"Grandmother, what big eyes you have."

"The better to see you with, my dear."

"What big hands you have, Grandmother."

"The better to catch hold of you with, my dear."

"But, Grandmother, what big teeth you have."

"The better to eat you with, my dear."

Hardly had the Wolf said this when he made a spring out of bed and swallowed up poor little Red Riding Hood. When the Wolf was quite full, he went back to bed, and soon he was snoring loudly.

A huntsman went past the house and thought: How loudly the old lady is snoring! I must see if there is anything the matter with her. He went into the house and up to the bed, where he found the Wolf fast asleep. "So—do I find you here, you old sinner?" he said. "Long enough have I looked for you!"

He had just raised his gun to shoot, when it occurred to him that perhaps the Wolf had eaten up the old lady and that she might still be saved. So he took a knife and began cutting open the sleeping Wolf. At the first cut he saw a little red cloak, and after a few more slashes, the little girl jumped out and cried, "Oh, how frightened I was! It was so dark inside the Wolf!" Next the old grandmother came out, alive but hardly able to breathe.

Red Riding Hood brought some big stones with which they filled the Wolf. He woke up and tried to dash away, but the stones dragged him back and he fell down dead.

They were all happy now. The huntsman skinned the Wolf and took its fur home. The grandmother ate the cake and drank the wine which Red Riding Hood had brought, and she soon felt quite strong.

And Red Riding Hood said to herself, "I will never again wander off into the forest as long as I live, when my mother forbids it."

JAKOB AND WILHELM GRIMM, COLLECTION OF
MRS. E. V. LUCAS, LUCY CRANE AND MARIAN EDWARDES

THE LITTLE MERMAID

FAR OUT AT sea, the water
is as blue as the bluest cornflower and as clear as the
clearest crystal, but it is very deep—deeper than any
anchor cable can fathom. Many church steeples would
have to be piled one on top of the other to reach from
the very bottom to the surface of the water. And down
in the depths live the sea folk.

Now, don't imagine for a moment that there is nothing but bare white sand on the bed of the ocean—no,
the most fantastic trees and flowers grow there, and
all kinds of fishes, big and small, flit in and out among
the branches, just as birds do in the air up here. At
the very lowest depth stands the palace of the Sea
King; the walls are made of coral and the high, pointed
windows of the clearest amber, but the roof is made
of mussel shells which open and close with the gentle
motion of the water. It is a wonderful sight, for every
mussel shell contains gleaming pearls—any single
one of which would be a perfect ornament for a
queen's crown.

The Sea King had been a widower for many years,

but his old mother kept house for him. She was very intelligent, although proud of her noble birth, and that is why she went about with twelve oysters on her tail, while the other highborn ladies were allowed just six. Apart from this, she deserved a great deal of praise because she was so fond of her grandchildren, the Princesses. They were six beautiful little girls, but the youngest was the prettiest of them all: her skin was as clear and delicate as a rose petal, her eyes were as blue as the deepest sea, but, like the other mermaids, she had no feet, only a fish's tail.

All day long they used to play down in the palace, in the great galleries where living flowers grew out of the walls. When the tall amber windows were opened, fishes swam in just as swallows fly into our rooms when we open the windows, but the fishes swam right up to the little Princesses, ate from their hands and allowed themselves to be patted.

Outside the palace there was a large garden with trees of fiery red and deep blue, their fruits glimmering like gold, and flowers like a blazing fire, ceaselessly moving their stems and leaves. The ground itself was of the finest sand, but blue as a sulfur flame. Down there a strange blue mist enveloped everything; you would have thought you were standing high in the air, with only the sky above and beneath you, and not down in the depths of the ocean. When the surface was dead calm you could just faintly perceive the sun, looking like a crimson flower from which streamed a flood of light.

Each of the small Princesses had her own little plot in the garden where she could dig and plant as she liked. One of them gave her flower bed the shape of a whale, another thought it nicer to have hers formed like a mermaid, but the youngest made hers as round as the sun and used only flowers as red as the sun itself. She was a strange child, quiet and pensive, and, while the other sisters decorated their gardens with all kinds of extraordinary things that they had taken from sunken ships, she would have nothing in hers but a beautiful statue and her red flowers. It was the statue of a handsome boy, in the purest white marble, that had sunk to the bottom of the sea after a shipwreck. Next to the statue she planted a rose-red weeping willow which grew splendidly and shaded the statue with its delicate branches.

Nothing gave the youngest Princess greater pleasure than to hear about the world of human beings up above. She made her grandmother tell all she knew about ships and towns, people and animals; but what fascinated her beyond words was that the flowers on earth were scented, while those at the bottom of the sea were not, that the woods were green and that the fishes one saw among the branches could sing so loudly and sweetly that it was a delight to hear them. Grandmother called the little birds of the air fishes, because otherwise the mermaids would not have understood her, for they had never seen a bird.

"As soon as you are fifteen," said their grandmother, "you will all be allowed to rise up above the water and sit on the rocks in the moonlight to watch the big ships sail by."

The following year the eldest sister was to have her fifteenth birthday, but as there was one year between each of them, the youngest still had five whole years to wait before her turn came to see what things are like on the earth. And the very one who had the longest time to wait was the most curious of them all. Many a night she stood by the open window and looked up through the dark blue sea where the fishes were lashing the water with fins and tails. She could just perceive the moon and the stars, though their light was very faint, but through the water they looked much bigger than they do to us; and if something like a black cloud passed under them, she knew that it was either a whale swimming above her or a ship with many people on board. They probably never dreamed that a lovely little mermaid was standing below, raising her white hands toward the keel of their ship.

The eldest Princess had now reached her fifteenth birthday, and was allowed to rise above the surface.

When she came back, she had hundreds of things to tell the others. But the most wonderful of all, she said, was to lie in the moonlight on a sandbank in the calm sea, gazing at the huge town close to the shore, where the lights twinkled like hundreds of stars; to listen to the music and the church bells, and to the noise and stir of carriages and people. But just because she could not get there, that was the very thing the mermaid longed to do most of all.

Oh, how eagerly the youngest sister listened; and whenever after this she stood at the open window in the evening looking up through the deep blue sea, she thought of the great town with its noise and bustle, and seemed to hear the sound of the church bells coming right down to her.

The following year, the second sister was allowed to rise up through the waves. She reached the surface just at sunset, and that sight was the most magnificent she had ever seen. The heavens looked like liquid gold, she told them, and the clouds, well, she never tired of describing their beauty—all rosy-red and violet as they sailed over her. Faster than the clouds, like a long white veil flung out toward the sky, a flock of wild swans flew away over the water beyond which the sun was setting. She swam toward the sun, but it sank, and the rosy tint faded away from sea and cloud.

The year after that, the third sister went up; she was the most daring of them, so she swam up a broad river which flowed into the ocean. She saw beautiful green hills and vineyards; palaces and farms were faintly visible among splendid forests. In a tiny cove she found a crowd of little human children, splashing about quite naked; she wanted to play with them, but she gave them a fright, and they ran away. Then came a little black animal—it was a dog, but she had never seen one before. It barked at her so furiously that she was frightened and took refuge in the open sea, but she could never forget the beautiful woods, the green hills and the lovely children who could swim in the water although they had no fishes' tails.

The fourth sister was not so daring: she remained far out in the stormy ocean and told her sisters that staying there was the best part of her adventures. You could see for miles and miles around, and the sky above was like a great glass dome. She had seen ships, but only far, far away; they looked like sea gulls. The amusing dolphins had turned somersaults, and the gigantic whales had spouted water through their nostrils, giving the effect of hundreds of fountains playing.

Now it was the turn of the fifth sister. Her birthday happened to be in the winter, so she saw things which none of the others had seen when they first went up to the surface. The sea was quite green, and large icebergs were floating about; they looked like pearls, she said. They appeared in the most wonderful shapes and sparkled like diamonds. She sat down on one of the largest, and every ship gave it a wide berth when the sailors saw her sitting there with her long hair floating in the wind. Late in the evening, the sky became overcast, thunder crashed and lightning stabbed the sky, while the black waves lifted the huge icebergs high up on their crests. Sails were furled on all the ships, the sailors stood in fear and trembling, but she sat quietly on her floating iceberg, watching the blue lightning flash in zigzags down into the shining sea.

The first time the sisters rose above the water, they were all delighted with the new and beautiful things they had seen, but as they were now grown up and were allowed to go up to the surface whenever they liked, they lost interest in it. They longed for their home, and after a month had gone by, each said that no place was more delightful than the bottom of the sea—besides, one felt so comfortably at home there.

Many an evening the five sisters would appear on the surface arm in arm. They had beautiful voices, more beautiful than those of any human beings, and when storms threatened to wreck the ships, the mermaids would swim in front of them. They sang their most seductive songs of the wonders in the depths of the sea and tried to persuade the people not to be afraid of coming down to them. But the seafarers could not understand them; they thought it was the storm they heard. Nor did they ever see the promised splendors, for when the ships sank, they drowned, and never reached the palace of the Sea King alive.

At night, when the sisters rose up through the water, the youngest remained behind quite alone, gazing after them. She would have wept, but a mermaid has no tears, and so she suffers all the more.

"Oh, if I were only fifteen!" she said. "I know I shall love that Upper World!"

At last she, too, reached the age of fifteen.

"Well, now we are getting you off our hands," said her grandmother, the old Dowager Queen. "Come here, let me dress you up like your sisters!" And she put a wreath of white lilies on her head, but each petal was formed of half a pearl; then the old Queen made eight large oysters fasten themselves to the Princess' tail to show her high rank.

"Oh, how it hurts!" said the little mermaid.

"Well, one must suffer to be beautiful," declared her grandmother.

The youngest mermaid would gladly have shaken off all this finery and laid aside the heavy wreath. The red flowers in her garden suited her much better, but she did not dare to change. "Good-bye, good-bye," she said and she rose up through the waters.

The sun had just set when her head appeared above the surface, but the clouds were still tinted with rose and gold, and in the pink-flushed sky the evening star twinkled bright and clear. The air was mild and fresh and the sea dead calm. She saw a big three-masted ship with only a single sail set, for not a breath of wind stirred, and sailors were sitting on the rigging.

She heard music and singing on board the ship,

and as the darkness was gathering, hundreds of colored lanterns were lighted; they looked like the flags of every nation waving in the air. The little mermaid swam right up to the porthole of the cabin, and every time the swell lifted her, she could see crowds of people in evening dress, but the handsomest of them all was a young Prince with great coal-black eyes. He could hardly have been more than sixteen years old; it was his birthday, and that was the reason for the party. The sailors danced on deck, and when the Prince appeared among them, hundreds of rockets shot up into the air, turning night to day and frightening the little mermaid so much that she had to dive under the water; but she soon ventured to put her head up again, and it looked as if all the stars were falling down to her from the sky. Never had she seen such a display. It was so light on board ship that one could see every rope, to say nothing of the people. Oh, how handsome the young Prince was, laughing and smiling while the music rang out in the beauty of the night.

It got quite late, but the little mermaid could not turn her eyes away from the ship and the beautiful Prince. The colored lanterns were put out, no more rockets shot up through the air, no more guns were fired, but deep down in the sea there was a dull humming and rumbling. The water was lifting her up and down so that she could look into the cabin, but the ship started to move, sail after sail opened to the wind, the waves grew mightier, great clouds gathered, and lightning flashed along the horizon. Oh, there was terrible weather ahead, so the sailors furled the sails. The great ship plowed on, pitching and tossing in the angry sea; waves, like enormous black mountains, were threatening to crash down upon the mast, but the ship disappeared like a swan in the trough of the waves and was lifted again the next moment to the top of their towering crests. The ship creaked and groaned, the thick planks cracked under the blows of the waves, the mast broke in two like a reed, and the ship rolled over so far to one side that water rushed into the hold.

Then the little mermaid saw that the people were in peril, while she herself had to beware of the beams and pieces of wreckage which were floating about in the sea. At one moment it was pitch-dark and she could see nothing at all; then there came a flash of lightning which lit up everything on board. She looked particularly for the young Prince, and when the ship split apart, she saw him sink into the sea. Her first impulse was one of joy because he was coming down to her, but then she remembered that human beings could not live under the water and that he could not come alive down to her father's palace. No, die he must not! So she swam in among the drifting beams and planks, quite forgetting that they might crush her. She dived deep into the sea, rose high up again among the waves and at last reached the young Prince, who could hardly keep on swimming in the stormy ocean. His arms and legs were beginning to fail him, his beautiful eyes were closing, he would have died had not the mermaid been there. She held his head above the water and let the waves carry her with him wherever they pleased.

At dawn the storm was over; not a trace of the ship was to be seen. The sun rose red and shining out of the water and seemed to bring life and color back into the Prince's cheeks, but his eyes remained closed. The mermaid kissed his high, noble brow and stroked back his wet hair. She thought he looked like the marble statue down in her little garden; she kissed him again and wished from the bottom of her heart that he might live.

In front of her she saw land, with snow-capped mountains in the distance. Near the shoreline were glorious green forests, and close by was a church or a convent—she could not be certain just what it was. Lemon and orange trees grew in the garden, and outside the gate were tall palm trees. There the sea had formed a cove where the fine white sand had been washed up. She swam toward it with the handsome Prince, and laid him on the sand with his head turned to the warm rays of the sun.

Then the bells rang out from the white building, and a group of young girls came through the garden. The little mermaid swam farther out and hid behind some large rocks, covering her hair and her breast with sea foam so that no one could catch sight of her face, and then kept watch to see who would come to the rescue of the poor shipwrecked Prince.

It was not long before one of the young girls arrived. For a moment, she seemed quite frightened, but she ran for help, and the mermaid saw the Prince come to and smile at those who stood around him. But he did not smile at her far out in the sea, for he did not know that she had saved him. She felt very sad, and when he was carried into the great building, she dived sorrowfully down into the depths of the water and returned to her father's palace. There her sisters asked what she had seen on her first visit to the surface, but she would tell them nothing.

Many an evening and many a morning she rose up to the place where she had left the Prince. She saw how the fruit in the garden ripened and was gathered, how the snow melted on the distant mountains, but she never saw the Prince, so she would return home sadder than before. Her only consolation was to sit in her little garden and throw her arms around the beautiful marble statue which was so like him. She neglected her flowers, and they grew into a wilderness all over the paths and wove their long stems and leaves in and out of the branches of the trees until the whole place was shrouded in darkness.

When she could endure it no longer, she confided in one of her sisters. At once the others knew about it, but nobody else—except for a few more mermaids who told just their most intimate friends. One of them knew who the Prince was; she too had seen the party held in his honor and heard where his kingdom lay.

"Come, little sister," said the other Princesses, and with their arms about each other's shoulders, they rose in a long line up through the water opposite the place where they knew the Prince's palace stood.

It was built of a kind of pale yellow stone, with a great flight of marble steps leading down to the sea. Splendid gilded cupolas were seen above the roof, and in between the pillars surrounding the whole building stood marble statues which looked as if they were alive. Through the clear glass windows one looked into magnificent halls where costly silk curtains and tapestries were hung and where all the walls were covered with large paintings. In the middle of the biggest hall a great fountain was playing, its jets soaring high up toward the glass dome through which the sun shone down upon the water and upon the beautiful plants growing in the great basin.

Now she knew where he lived, and many an evening and many a night she haunted the palace. She swam much closer to land than any of her sisters had dared to do, and she even went up the narrow creek running under the splendid balcony which cast its long shadow upon the water. Here she would sit and gaze at the young Prince, who thought he was quite alone in the bright moonlight.

Often in the evening she saw him sailing to the sound of music in a splendid new ship with waving flags. She peeped through the reeds, and if the wind caught her long silver-white veil, those who saw it thought it was a swan spreading its wings.

Many a night she heard the fishermen praising the young Prince and she rejoiced that she had saved his life. She thought how closely his head had rested on her bosom and how lovingly she had kissed him, though he knew nothing about it and could not even dream of her.

She became more and more fond of human beings, and more and more did she long to be among them. Their world seemed much larger than her own: they were able to fly over the sea in ships and climb the lofty mountains; the lands they possessed stretched farther than her eyes could reach. There was so much she wanted to know, but her sisters could not answer all her questions, so she asked her old grandmother who knew so well that Upper World, as she rightly called the countries above the sea.

"If human beings aren't drowned," asked the little mermaid, "can they live forever? Don't they die as we do down here in the depths of the sea?"

"Yes," answered the old lady, "they must die too, and their lifetime is even shorter than ours. We can live to be three hundred years old, but when we cease to exist, we turn to foam on the water, and so we don't even have a grave down here among our dear ones. We have no immortal soul, we never have another life; we are like the green reed—once it is cut, it never grows again. Human beings, on the contrary, have a soul which lives forever, which lives after the body has turned to dust. It rises up through the limpid air, up to the shining stars! Just as we rise out of the water and see the countries of the earth, so do they rise up to unknown beautiful regions which we shall never be able to see."

"Why were we not granted an immortal soul?" asked the little mermaid in a melancholy voice. "I know that I would gladly give the three hundred years I have to live if I could be a human being for only one single day, and then have some part in that heavenly world!"

"You must not brood over that," said her grandmother. "We have a much happier life than the people up there."

"So I am fated to die and float like foam upon the sea? Can I do nothing to win an immortal soul?"

"No," answered the old lady, "that could only happen if a human being held you so dear that you were more to him than father and mother. If he loved you with all his heart and soul and if his right hand were joined to yours by a monk, with the promise to be faithful to you here and in all eternity, then his soul would pass into your body and you would have a share in the happiness of mankind. He would give you a soul and yet retain his own. But that can never happen. The very thing that is considered beautiful here in the sea —your fish's tail—is considered ugly on the earth. People have very poor judgment indeed; they have two clumsy supports which they call 'legs,' and think them beautiful.''

Then the little mermaid sighed, and looked sadly at her fish's tail.

"Come, let us be happy!" said her grandmother. "Let us leap and jump about during the three hundred years we have to live; that seems a fair enough amount of time. After that we can rest the more merrily. Tonight we are giving a court ball."

Truly it was a magnificent affair such as one never sees on earth. The walls and ceiling of the great ballroom were made of thick, transparent glass. In rows on each side stood several hundred gigantic shells, rose-red and grass-green; a blue fire was burning in each— they lit up the entire room and, shining through the walls, lit up the sea as well. Innumerable fishes, great and small, could be seen swimming near the glass walls; some had scales gleaming scarlet, while others shone just like silver and gold. Down through the middle of the hall there flowed a broad stream on which the mermen and mermaids danced to their own beautiful singing. No voices such as theirs are ever heard among people of the earth. The little mermaid sang more beautifully than anyone else. Everyone applauded her, and for a moment her heart was filled with joy, for she knew she had the loveliest voice of all, on the earth or in the sea. But she could not forget the handsome Prince nor her sorrow at not having an immortal soul. So she stole out of her father's palace and, while everything within was joy and gaiety, sat sadly outside in her little garden.

Suddenly she heard bugles sounding down through the water and she thought: He is sailing up there, he whom I love more than my father or grandmother, he to whom my thoughts are clinging and in whose hand I would gladly place the happiness of my life. I will risk everything in my world to win him and an immortal soul. While my sisters are dancing in my father's palace, I shall go to see the old Sea Witch. She has always terrified me, but perhaps now she can advise and help me.

So she left her garden and set out toward the roaring whirlpools, for beyond them lived the witch. The little mermaid had never been that way before. No flowers grew there. Only the bare, gray sandy bottom stretched as far as the whirlpools which swirled around like roaring mill wheels, sweeping everything within reach down into the fathomless sea. She had to pass right through those crushing, whirling waters to enter the territory of the Sea Witch; then for a long way the only road went over a hot, bubbling morass—her peat bog, as the witch called it. Behind it lay her house, in the midst of a strange-looking forest. All the trees and bushes were polyps—half animal and half plant. They looked like hundred-headed snakes growing out of the ground. The branches were long slimy arms with slithery wormlike fingers, moving joint by joint from the root up to the very tip. They twined around anything they could reach, never loosening their grip. Terror-stricken, the little mermaid stopped on the edge of this forest. Her heart beat faster with fear and she almost turned back, but then she thought of the Prince and of the human soul, and her courage returned. She bound her long flowing hair tightly around her head so that the polyps might not seize her by it, she folded her arms closely across her breast and darted off as a fish darts through the water, in among the hideous polyps which stretched out their supple arms and fingers to catch her. She saw how each of them clung tightly to something it had caught.

People who had perished at sea and sunk deep down to the bottom were visible as white human bones among the arms of the polyps. The polyps also clutched ships' rudders, sea chests and skeletons of land animals, and, most horrible of all, she even saw a little mermaid whom they had caught and strangled.

She came next to a great slimy clearing in the forest, where big fat water snakes writhed and rolled, showing their ugly yellowish-white bellies. In the center of

the clearing was a house built of the bones of shipwrecked men; there sat the Sea Witch, letting a toad
feed out of her mouth exactly as we let a canary eat
sugar. She called the hideous, fat water snakes her little
chickens and let them creep and crawl over her great
spongy bosom.

"I know what you want," said the Sea Witch. "It is
very foolish of you, for it will bring trouble upon you,
my pretty one, but all the same you shall have your
way. You want to get rid of your fish's tail and to have
two bits of stumps to walk with instead, like the people of the earth, so that the young Prince will fall in
love with you and you will win both him and an immortal soul."

Here the witch let out a laugh so loud and so ghastly
that the toad and the snakes she had been fondling
tumbled down to the ground, where they lay wallow-
ing about.

"You have just come in time," said the witch. "Had
you waited until sunrise tomorrow, I could not have
helped you for a whole year. I am going to brew a potion for you. Before the sun rises, you must swim to
land with it, sit down on the shore and drink it. Then
your tail will part in two and shrink to what the people
of the earth call 'pretty legs,' but it will hurt as if a
sharp sword were cutting through you. Everybody
who sees you will say that you are the prettiest human
being they have ever seen. You are to keep your gliding

motion, no dancer will be able to move as gracefully as you, but at every step it will feel as if you were treading on a sharp-edged knife, so sharp that your feet will seem to be bleeding."

She paused for a moment, then went on, "If you can bear all this, I shall be able to help you."

"I can," said the little mermaid in a quivering voice, and she thought of the Prince and of winning an immortal soul.

"But remember," said the witch, "once you have taken human shape, you can never become a mermaid again. You can never return to your father's palace, and if you do not win the love of the Prince, so that for your sake he forgets father and mother and clings to you with heart and soul and lets the monk join your hands, making you man and wife, then you will not win an immortal soul. On the very morning after he has married someone else, your heart will break and you will become foam on the sea."

"I am willing," said the little mermaid, who was as pale as death.

"But you will also have to pay me," said the witch, "and it is not a trifle that I require. You have the most beautiful voice of anyone down here in the depths of the sea. You think that you will be able to charm the Prince with it, but you must give that voice to me. I want the best thing you possess in exchange for my precious potion. I must drop some of my own blood into it so that the draught may be as sharp as a two-edged sword."

"But if you take my voice," said the little mermaid, "what shall I have left?"

"Your beautiful form," said the witch, "your gliding motion and your eloquent eyes—they will be enough for you to beguile any human heart.

"Well," she went on after a moment, "have you lost your courage? Put out your little tongue, and I will cut it out and take it as my payment, and you shall have the potent draught in return."

"So be it," said the little mermaid, and the witch put her caldron on the fire to brew the magic draught. "Cleanliness is a good thing," she said, and she scoured out the caldron with the snakes that she had tied up into a knot. Then she made a cut in her finger and let her black blood drip into the caldron. The witch kept on throwing in different ingredients, and when the mixture finally started to bubble it sounded like a crocodile sobbing. The steam coming from the caldron shaped itself into the most terrifying and horrible forms. When at last the potion was ready, it looked as clear as the clearest water.

"There you are," said the witch, and she cut out the tongue of the little mermaid. Now she had become mute and could neither sing nor speak.

"If the polyps should clutch you when you are on your way back through my forest," said the witch, "just throw one single drop of this draught upon each of them, and their arms and fingers will scatter into a thousand pieces."

But there was no need for the little mermaid to do that—the polyps shrank back in terror when they saw the shining potion gleaming in her hand like a twinkling star; thus she passed quickly through the forest, the bog and the roaring whirlpools.

She could see her father's palace. The torches had been extinguished in the great ballroom; her family were probably all asleep, but she had not the courage to approach them now that she was mute and was leaving them forever.

It seemed as if her heart was going to break with sorrow. She stole into the garden, picked one flower from each of her sisters' flower beds, blew a thousand kisses toward her home and rose up through the deep blue sea.

It was not yet sunrise when she saw the Prince's palace and went up the stately marble steps. The moon was still shining beautifully clear. The little mermaid drank the sharp, burning draught given her by the witch, and she felt as if a two-edged sword had cut through her delicate body; she swooned with agony and lay as if she were dead.

When the sun spread its rays over the sea she awoke and felt a stinging pain, but before her stood the handsome young Prince. He fixed his coal-black eyes upon her, and under his gaze she lowered her eyes and saw that her fish's tail had gone and that she had the prettiest pair of white legs any young girl could desire; but her body was naked, so she veiled herself with her long thick hair.

The Prince asked who she was and how she had come there, and she looked up at him with her dark blue eyes, so mild and yet so full of sadness, for she could not speak. Then he took her by the hand and led her into the palace.

As the witch had foretold, she seemed at each step to be treading on sharp knives and pointed daggers, but she bore the pain gladly. Led by the Prince, she moved lightly as a bubble, and he and everyone else marveled at her graceful gliding motion.

They clad her in costly robes of silk and muslin. She was the fairest of all in the palace, but she was mute and could neither speak nor sing. Beautiful slave girls, dressed in silk and gold, came before them and sang for the Prince and his royal parents. One of them sang more delightfully than any of the others, and the Prince clapped his hands and smiled at her, which saddened the little mermaid, for she knew that she herself used to sing far more beautifully; and she thought, Oh, if he only knew that I gave away my voice forever in order to be with him!

The slave girls now danced gracefully to the accompaniment of the loveliest music imaginable, and then the little mermaid lifted her pretty white arms and, rising on the tips of her toes, flitted across the floor, dancing as no one had ever danced before. With each of her movements her beauty became more and more evident, and her eyes spoke more deeply to the heart than the song of the slave girls.

Everyone was enchanted, especially the Prince, who called her his own little foundling. And she danced again and again, though every time her foot touched the ground it seemed to her as if she were treading on sharp knives.

The Prince said that she must always remain with him, and she was allowed to sleep on a velvet cushion outside his door.

He had a page's dress made for her, so that she might accompany him on horseback. They rode through the fragrant woods, where the green boughs brushed her shoulders and the little birds sang hidden among the leaves.

She climbed the highest mountains in the kingdom with the Prince, and though her delicate feet bled so that even the others in the group with them noticed it, she only laughed and followed him until they could see the clouds moving far below them like flocks of birds on their way to distant lands.

At night, when the others were asleep in the Prince's palace, she would go out onto the broad marble steps and cool her burning feet in the cold seawater, and then she would think of her dear ones in the depths of the sea.

One night her sisters appeared arm in arm, singing mournful songs as they swam along. She beckoned to them and they recognized her and told her how much she had grieved them all. They visited the little mermaid every night after that and once, in the far, far distance, she saw her old grandmother, who had not been above the water for many years, and the Sea King with his crown upon his head. They stretched out their hands toward her, but did not venture so near the land as her sisters.

Day by day she grew dearer to the Prince. He loved her as one loves a good child, but had no thought of making her his Queen. Yet his wife she must be, or she could never win an immortal soul, but would become merely a cloud of foam on the sea the morning after he wed another.

"Am I not dearer to you than anyone else?" her eyes seemed to ask, when he took her in his arms and kissed her fair brow.

"Yes, you are the dearest of all to me," said the Prince, "for you have the kindest heart of all. You are more devoted to me than anyone else, and you look like a young girl whom I once saw, but whom I shall probably never see again. I was on board a ship which was wrecked; the waves carried me ashore near a holy temple where a group of young maidens were serving.

The youngest of them found me and saved my life. I saw her but twice. She is the only one in the world I could ever love, but you look so much like her that you almost take the place of her image in my heart. She belongs to that holy temple, and therefore destiny sent you to me. We will never part."

Alas, he does not know that I saved his life, thought the little mermaid. It was I who carried him over the water to the forest where the temple stands. I stayed hidden in the foam to see if anyone would come. I saw the pretty maiden whom he loves better than me. And she gave a deep sigh—for as a mermaid she had no tears. The maiden belongs to the holy temple, he tells me, she will never come out into the world, so they will never meet again. I am with him, I see him every day. I will cherish him, love him and give up my life to him.

But soon it was rumored that the Prince was going to marry the beautiful daughter of a neighboring King, and that was why he was fitting out such a splendid ship. They said that the Prince was paying a state visit to the country of that King, but the real reason was to see the King's daughter. He was to have a great entourage with him.

The little mermaid shook her head and laughed, for she knew the Prince's thoughts far better than anyone else.

"I must go away," he had said to her. "I must go

and see the beautiful Princess—my parents insist upon it; but they will not compel me to bring her home as my bride. I cannot love her! She is not like the beautiful maiden in the temple or as you are. If I ever had to choose a bride, I would sooner choose you, my dear mute foundling with the speaking eyes." And he kissed her red lips, played with her long hair and laid his head on her heart, so that she dreamed of human happiness and an immortal soul.

"I hope you are not afraid of the sea, my poor mute child," he said, when they stood on the splendid ship which was to carry him to the country of the neighboring King. Then he told her of storm and calm at sea, of strange fishes in the depths of the ocean and what divers had seen down there, and she smiled at his description, for she knew more than anyone else about the bottom of the sea.

In the moonlit night, when all were asleep except the helmsman at the wheel, she sat by the rail and, gazing down through the water, she fancied she could see her father's palace. On the top stood her old grandmother with a silver crown on her head, gazing at the keel of the ship through the fast-flowing current. Then her sisters came up above the water and looked at her with deep sorrow in their eyes and wrung their white hands. She beckoned to them, smiling, and tried to make them understand that she was well and happy, but when the cabin boy came toward her, her sisters dived down again, so he felt quite certain that the gleam of white he had seen was nothing but foam.

Next morning the ship sailed into the harbor of the neighboring King's magnificent city. All the church bells rang, and from the tall towers trumpets were blown, while the soldiers stood at attention with flying colors and glittering bayonets. Each day brought new festivity, balls and parties were given all the time, but the Princess had not yet arrived. People said she was being brought up in a holy temple, where she was learning every royal accomplishment. At last she appeared on the scene.

The little mermaid waited anxiously to see her beauty, and she had to admit that she had never seen a more graceful form. The Princess' skin was fine and delicate, and behind the long dark eyelashes smiled a pair of dark blue eyes, full of devotion.

"It is you! You who saved me when I lay like a corpse on the shore!" said the Prince, and he clasped his blushing bride-to-be in his arms. "Oh, I am more than happy!" he said to the little mermaid. "My dearest wish, the thing I have never dared to hope for, has been granted me. You will rejoice in my happiness, for you are more devoted to me than anyone else." Then the little mermaid kissed his hand, and already her heart seemed to be breaking. The morning after his wedding would bring death to her and change her to foam on the sea.

All the church bells rang out; heralds rode about the streets and proclaimed the betrothal. On every altar fragrant oil was burning in costly silver lamps. The priests swung their censers, and bride and bridegroom joined hands and received the bishop's blessing. The little mermaid, clad all in silk and gold, was holding the bride's train, but her ears heard nothing of the festive music, her eyes saw nothing of the holy ceremony; she thought of the last night she had to live and of all she had lost in this world.

That very evening, bride and bridegroom went on board the ship. Cannons were fired, banners fluttered in the wind, and in the middle of the ship a royal tent of gold and purple was set up, furnished with great sumptuous cushions on which the bridal couple were to sleep in the calm, cool night.

The sails swelled out in the breeze, and the ship glided smoothly and without any perceptible motion over the limpid sea.

When it grew dark, colored lanterns were lighted, and the sailors danced merry dances on the deck. The little mermaid could not help thinking of the first time she rose to the surface of the sea and saw a similar sight of splendor and joy. Light as a swallow in full flight she joined in the dance, and to the sound of cheers and shouting danced as she had never danced before. Her delicate feet seemed to be cut by sharp knives, but the anguish of her heart was so great that she did not feel the pain. She knew only that this was the last evening she was ever to see the Prince, for whom she had forsaken her people and her home, had given up her beautiful voice to the Sea Witch and had daily suffered untold agony, while he remained unaware of it all.

The gaiety and merriment lasted until long past midnight, and the little mermaid laughed and danced like the others, but with the thought of death in her heart. The Prince kissed his beautiful bride, and she played with his black hair, and arm in arm they went to rest in the splendid tent.

A hushed silence fell upon the ship; only the helmsman stood at the wheel. The little mermaid laid her white arms on the rail and gazed toward the east, waiting to see the red tinge of the dawn—the first rays of the sun, she knew, would kill her. Then she saw her sisters rising out of the sea; they were pale like herself, their long, beautiful hair no longer fluttered in the wind—it had all been cut off.

"We have given it to the witch so that she may give you help and save you from dying before dawn. She has given us a knife, look, here it is! Do you see its sharp edge? Before the sun rises you must plunge it into the Prince's heart, and when his warm blood splashes over your feet, they will grow into a fish's tail, and you will become a mermaid again; you will be able to come down to us in the water and live your three hundred years before you turn into dead salt sea foam. Make haste! Either he or you must die before the sun rises. Our old grandmother has been mourning till her white hair has fallen out as ours fell under the witch's scissors. Kill the Prince and come back! Make haste! Do you see that red streak in the sky? In a few minutes the sun will rise and you must die!" Having said this, they uttered a strange deep sigh and disappeared in the waves.

The little mermaid drew back the purple curtains of the tent and saw the beautiful bride sleeping with her head on the Prince's breast. She bent down and kissed him on his fair brow, then she looked up at the sky where the first faint flush of dawn became brighter and brighter. She looked at the sharp knife and again fixed her eyes on the Prince, who in his sleep was murmuring the name of his bride. She and only she was in his thoughts. The knife quivered in the mermaid's hand, but then—she flung it far out into the waves! They gleamed red where it fell; it seemed as if drops of blood were bubbling up through the water. Once more she looked with dimming eyes upon the Prince. Then she threw herself from the ship into the water, and felt her body dissolving into foam.

The sun rose out of the sea. Its rays fell mild and warm upon the death-cold sea foam, and the little mermaid felt not the hand of Death. She saw the bright sun, and above her floated hundreds of beautiful ethereal beings, so transparent that through them she could see the white sails of the ship and the rosy clouds of the sky; their voices were music, but so unearthly that no human ear could grasp it, just as no human eye could see their forms. Without wings they floated by their own lightness through the air. The little mermaid saw that she too had a body like theirs, and that it was gradually freeing itself more and more from the foam.

"Toward whom am I floating?" she asked, and her voice sounded like that of the other beings, so ethereal that no earthly music could possibly render it.

"To the daughters of the air," answered the others. "The mermaid has no immortal soul and can never gain one unless she wins the love of a human being. Her eternal life depends upon a power outside herself. The daughters of the air have no immortal souls either, but they can gain one by their good deeds. We fly to the hot countries where the torrid air of pestilence kills men; we bring cool breezes to them, we spread the fragrance of flowers through the air and send to them solace and healing. When we have tried for three hundred years to do all the good we can, we receive an immortal soul and share in the everlasting happiness of mankind. You, poor little mermaid, have tried with your whole heart to do the same. By your sufferings and by your courage in enduring them, you have raised yourself into the world of the spirits of the air, and now you can gain an immortal soul by good deeds accomplished in the course of three hundred years."

The little mermaid raised her translucent arms toward God's sun, and for the first time she felt tears in her eyes.

Noise and bustle had started again on the ship. She saw the Prince and his beautiful wife searching for her; then they gazed with sorrow in their hearts at the bubbling foam, as if they knew that she had thrown herself into the waves.

Invisible by now, the little mermaid kissed the bride on her forehead, smiled at the Prince and soared with the other children of the air toward the rose-colored cloud floating through space.

"In this way we shall float into the Heavenly Kingdom in three hundred years."

"We may even reach it sooner," whispered one of them. "Invisibly we float into the houses of human beings where there are children, and for every day on which we find a good child who brings joy to his parents and deserves their love, our time of probation is shortened by God. The child is unaware of it when we float through the room, and if we smile at him in our joy, one year is taken from the three hundred. But if we see a bad and naughty child, then we must weep tears of sorrow over him, and every tear adds one day to our time of probation."

HANS CHRISTIAN ANDERSEN, TRANSLATED BY PAUL LEYSSAC

FIVE WISE WORDS

ONCE THERE lived a handsome young man named Ram Singh who, though a favorite with everyone, was unhappy because he had a sharp-tongued, nagging stepmother. All day long she went on talking, until the youth was so distracted he determined to go away and seek his fortune. No sooner had he decided to leave his home than he made his plans, and the very next morning he started off with a few clothes wrapped in a bundle and a little money in his pocket.

But there was one person in the village to whom the young man wished to say good-bye, and that was a wise old guru, or teacher, who had taught him a great deal. So he turned his face first of all toward his master's hut and, before the sun was well up, was knocking at his door.

The old man received his pupil affectionately; but he was wise in reading faces, and saw at once that the youth was troubled. "My son," he said quietly, "what is the matter?"

"Nothing, father," replied the young man, "but I

have determined to go out into the world and seek my fortune."

"Be advised," said the guru, "and remain in your father's house. It is better to have half a loaf at home than to seek a whole one in distant countries."

But Ram Singh was in no mood to heed such advice, and very soon the old man ceased to press him.

"Well," said he at last, "if your mind is made up, I suppose you must have your way. But listen carefully, and remember five parting counsels which I will give you; if you keep these no evil shall befall you. First, always obey without question the orders of him whose service you enter. Second, never speak harshly or unkindly to anyone. Third, never lie. Fourth, never try to appear the equal of those above you in station. And fifth, wherever you go, if you meet those who read or teach from the holy books, stay and listen, if but for a few minutes, that you may be strengthened in the path of duty."

Then Ram Singh started out upon his journey, promising to bear in mind the old man's words.

After some days he came to a great city. He had spent all the money he had brought with him, and therefore resolved to look for work, however humble it might be. Catching sight of a prosperous-looking merchant standing in front of a grain shop, Ram Singh asked whether he could give him anything to do.

The merchant gazed at him so long the young man

began to lose heart, but at length the merchant answered him, "Yes, of course; there is a place waiting for you."

"What do you mean?" asked Ram Singh.

"Why," replied the other, "yesterday our Rajah's chief Wazir dismissed his body servant and is looking for another. Now you are just the sort of person he needs, for you are young and tall and handsome. I advise you to apply there."

Thanking the merchant for this advice, the young man set out at once for the Wazir's house. On account of his good looks and appearance, he was engaged as the great man's servant.

One day, soon after this, the Rajah started on a journey, and his chief Wazir accompanied him. With them was an army of servants and attendants, soldiers, muleteers, camel drivers, merchants with grain and stores for man and beast, singers to make entertainment along the way and musicians to accompany them, besides elephants, camels, horses, mules, ponies, donkeys, goats and carts and wagons of every kind and description. The caravan seemed more like a large town on the march than anything else.

Thus they traveled till they entered a country that was like a sea of sand, where the swirling dust floated in clouds, and men and beasts were half choked by it. Toward the close of day they came to a village. The headmen hurried out to salute the Rajah and to pay him their respects, but they soon began, with very long and serious faces, to explain that, while they and all they had were of course at the disposal of the Rajah, the coming of so large a company had put them into dreadful difficulty. They had neither a well nor a spring in their country, and so they had no water to give drink to such an army of men and beasts!

Great fear fell upon the caravan at the words of the headmen, but the Rajah merely told the Wazir that he must get water somehow, and that settled the matter as far as he was concerned. The Wazir sent off in haste for all the oldest men in the town and began to question them as to whether there were any wells in the neighborhood.

The men all looked helplessly at each other and said nothing; but at length one old graybeard replied, "Truly, Sir Wazir, there is, within a mile or two of this village, a well which some former king made hundreds of years ago. It is, they say, great and inexhaustible, covered in by heavy stonework, with a long flight of steps leading down to the water in the very bowels of the earth. But no man ever dares to go near it because it is haunted by evil spirits, and it is known that whosoever disappears down the well shall never be seen again."

The Wazir stroked his beard and considered a moment. Then he turned to Ram Singh, who stood behind his chair. "There is a proverb," said he, "that no man

can be trusted until he has been tried. Go you and get the Rajah and his people water from this well."

Then there flashed into Ram Singh's mind the first counsel of the old guru: "Always obey without question the order of him whose service you enter." So he replied at once that he was ready, and he left to prepare for his adventure. He fastened two great brass vessels to a mule, two lesser ones he bound upon his shoulders, and thus provided he set out with the old villager for his guide.

In a short time they came within sight of a spot where some big trees towered above the barren country, while in their shadow lay the dome of an ancient building. This the guide pointed out as the well, but he excused himself from going farther, saying he was an old man and tired, and it was already sunset. So Ram Singh bade him farewell and went on alone.

Arriving at the trees, Ram Singh tied up his mule, lifted the two large vessels down and, having found the opening of the well, descended a flight of steps into the darkness. The steps were broad white slabs of alabaster which gleamed in the shadows as he went lower and lower. All was very silent. Even the sound of his bare feet upon the steps seemed to wake an echo in that lonely place, and, when one of the vessels he was carrying fell, it clanged so loudly that he jumped.

Still he went on, until at last he reached a wide pool of sweet water, where he washed his jars with care, then filled them and began to remount the steps, carrying the lighter vessels. The big ones were so heavy that he could only take up one at a time.

Suddenly, something moved, and above him he saw a great giant standing on the stairway! In one hand the giant held clasped to his heart a dreadful-looking mass of bones, in the other was a lamp which cast long shadows about the walls and made him seem even more terrible than he really was.

"What think you, O mortal," said the giant, "of my fair and lovely wife?" And he held the light toward the bones in his arms and looked lovingly at them.

Now this poor giant had had a very beautiful wife whom he loved dearly; but, when she died, he refused to believe in her death and always carried her about even long after she had become nothing but bones. Ram Singh of course did not know of this, but there came to his mind the second wise saying of the guru, which forbade him to speak harshly or inconsiderately to others; so he replied, "Truly, sir, I am sure you could nowhere find such another."

"Ah, what eyes you have!" cried the delighted giant. "You at least can see! I do not know how often I have slain those who insulted her by saying she was but dried bones! You are a fine young man, and I will help you."

So saying, he laid down the bones with great tenderness and, snatching up the huge brass vessels, carried them up and put them on the mule with such ease that it was all done by the time Ram Singh had reached the open air with the smaller jars.

"Now," said the giant, "you have pleased me, and you may ask of me one favor. Whatever you wish I will do for you. Perhaps you would like me to show you where lies buried the treasure of dead kings?" he added eagerly.

But Ram Singh shook his head at the mention of buried wealth. "The favor I would ask," said he, "is that you will leave off haunting this well, so men may freely go in and out to obtain water."

Perhaps the giant expected some favor more difficult to grant, for his face brightened and he promised to depart at once. As Ram Singh went off through the gathering darkness with his precious burden of water, he beheld the giant striding away with the bones of his dead wife in his arms.

Great was the wonder and rejoicing in the camp when Ram Singh returned with the water. He said nothing about his adventure with the giant, but merely told the Rajah there was nothing to prevent the well from being used. And used it was, and nobody ever saw any more of the giant.

The Rajah was so pleased with the bearing of Ram Singh that he ordered the Wazir to give the young man to him in exchange for one of his own servants. So Ram Singh became the Rajah's attendant; and as the days went by, the Rajah became more and more delighted with the youth because, being ever mindful of the old guru's third counsel, he was always honest and spoke the truth. He grew in favor rapidly, until at last the Rajah made him his treasurer, and thus he reached a high place in the court and had wealth and power in his hands.

Unluckily, the Rajah had a brother who was a very bad man. This brother thought that if he could win the young treasurer over to his side he might by this means manage to steal, little by little, as much of the Rajah's treasure as he needed. Then, with the money, he could bribe the soldiers and some of the Rajah's counselors to dethrone and kill his brother, and he would reign himself.

He was too wary, of course, to tell Ram Singh of these wicked plans, but he began by flattering him whenever he saw him and at last he offered him his daughter in marriage. But Ram Singh remembered the fourth counsel of the old guru—never to try to appear the equal of those above him in station—therefore he respectfully declined the great honor of marrying a princess. The Prince, thwarted at the very beginning of his enterprise, was furious. He determined to bring about Ram Singh's ruin and he told the Rajah that his treasurer had spoken insulting words about his sovereign and also about the Princess.

What these words were nobody knew, and as the

story was not true, the wicked Prince did not know either. But the Rajah grew very angry and red in the face as he listened, and declared that until Ram Singh's head was cut off neither he nor the Princess nor his brother would eat or drink.

"But," the Rajah added, "I do not wish anyone to know that this was done by my desire, and anyone who mentions the subject will be severely punished." And with this the Prince was forced to be content.

Then the Rajah sent for an officer of his guard and told him to take some soldiers and ride at once to a tower outside the town. If anyone came to inquire when the building was going to be finished or asked any other questions about it, the officer must chop his head off and bring it to him. As for the body, that should be buried on the spot. The old officer thought these instructions rather odd, but it was no business of his, so he saluted and went off to do his master's bidding.

Early in the morning, the Rajah, who had not slept all night, sent for Ram Singh. He bade him go to the new hunting tower and ask the people there how it was getting on and when it was going to be finished, and then to hurry back with the answer. Away went Ram Singh upon his errand but, on the road, as he was passing a little temple on the outskirts of the city, he heard someone inside reading aloud. Remembering the guru's fifth counsel, he stepped inside and sat down to listen. He did not mean to stay long, but became so interested in the wisdom of the teacher that he sat and sat, while the sun rose higher and higher.

In the meantime, the wicked Prince, who dared not disobey the Rajah's command, was feeling very hungry, and the Princess was quietly crying in a corner, waiting for the news of Ram Singh's death so that she might eat her breakfast.

Hours passed, and stare as he might from the window, the Prince could see no messenger. At last he could not bear it any longer and, hastily disguising himself so that no one should recognize him, he jumped on a horse and galloped out to the hunting tower where the Rajah had told him the execution was to take place. But, when he arrived, there were only some men engaged in building and a number of soldiers idly watching them.

He forgot that he had disguised himself and that no one would know him and he cried out, "Now then, you men, why are you idling about here instead of finishing what you came to do? When is it to be done?"

At his words the soldiers looked at the commanding officer, who was standing a little apart from the rest. Unnoticed by the Prince, he made a slight sign, a sword flashed in the sun, and off flew a head to the ground beneath!

As part of the Prince's disguise had been a thick beard, the men did not recognize the dead man as the

Rajah's brother. They wrapped the head in a cloth and buried the body as their commander bade them. When this was ended, the officer took the cloth and rode off in the direction of the palace.

Meanwhile the Rajah came home from his council and to his great surprise found neither head nor brother awaiting him. As time passed, he became uneasy and thought he had better go and see what the matter was. So, ordering his horse, he rode off alone.

Just as the Rajah came near the temple where Ram Singh still sat, the young treasurer, hearing the sound of a horse's hooves, looked over his shoulder and saw that the rider was the Rajah himself! Feeling much ashamed for having forgotten his errand, he jumped up and hurried out to meet his master, who reined in his horse and seemed very surprised (as indeed he was) to see him. At that moment the officer arrived, carrying his parcel. He saluted the Rajah gravely and, dismounting, laid the bundle in the road and began to undo the wrappings, while the Rajah watched him with wonder and amazement.

When the last string was undone, and the head of his brother was displayed to his view, the Rajah sprang from his horse and caught the officer by the arm. As soon as he could speak he questioned the man as to what had occurred, and little by little a dark suspicion grew. Then, telling the soldier he had done well, the Rajah drew Ram Singh to one side, and in a few minutes learned from him how, in attending to the guru's counsel, he had delayed in doing his ruler's bidding.

In the end the Rajah found proof of his dead brother's treachery, and Ram Singh established his innocence and integrity. He continued to serve the Rajah for many years with unswerving fidelity, married a maiden of his own rank, with whom he lived happily, and died honored and loved by all men. Sons were born to him; and, in time, to them also he taught the five wise sayings of the old guru.

OLD PUNJÂBI TALE, ANDREW LANG COLLECTION

THE GOOSE-GIRL

ONCE UPON a time there was an old Queen who had a beautiful daughter. When she grew up she was betrothed to a Prince who lived a great way off.

Now when the time drew near for the Princess to be married and to depart into the foreign kingdom, her old mother gave her much costly baggage and many ornaments, gold and silver, trinkets and knickknacks and, in fact, everything belonging to a royal trousseau, for she loved her daughter dearly. The Queen also sent a waiting-maid, who was to ride with the Princess and hand her over to the bridegroom, and she provided each of them with a horse for the journey. Now the Princess' horse, which was called Falada, was able to speak.

When the hour for departure drew near, the old mother went to her bedroom and, taking a small knife, she cut her fingers till they bled. Then she held a white cloth under them, and, letting three drops of blood fall into it, she gave it to her daughter, saying, "Dear child, take great care of this cloth. It may be of use to you on the journey."

So they took a sad farewell of each other. The Princess put the cloth in the front of her dress, mounted her horse and set forth on the journey to her bridegroom's kingdom.

After they had ridden for about an hour the Princess became thirsty and said to her waiting-maid, "Please dismount and fetch me some water in my golden cup from yonder stream. I would like a drink."

"If you are thirsty," said the maid, "dismount yourself, and lie down by the water and drink. I do not mean to be your servant any longer."

The Princess was so thirsty that she got down and bent over the stream, for the golden goblet had not been brought to her. As she drank she murmured,

"Oh, Heaven, what am I to do?" And the three drops of blood replied:

> If your mother only knew,
> Her heart would surely break in two.

But the Princess was meek and said nothing about her maid's rude behavior and quietly mounted her horse again. They rode on their way for several miles, but the day was hot, and the sun's rays beat fiercely on them. The Princess was soon overcome by thirst again. And as they passed another brook she called out once more to her waiting-maid, "Pray get me a drink in my golden cup," for she had long ago forgotten her maid's rude words.

But the waiting-maid answered her mistress more haughtily even than before, "If you want a drink, you can dismount and get it. I do not mean to be your servant."

Then the Princess was compelled by her thirst to dismount. Bending over the flowing water, she cried, "Oh, Heaven, what am I to do?" And the three drops of blood replied:

> If your mother only knew,
> Her heart would surely break in two.

And as she drank, leaning over the water, the cloth containing the three drops of blood fell from her bosom and floated down the stream. In her anxiety the

Princess never even noticed her loss, but the waiting-maid had observed it with delight. She knew that now she could do as she wished with the bride, for in losing the drops of blood the Princess had become weak and powerless.

When the Princess wished to get on her horse again, the waiting-maid called out, "I mean to ride Falada; you must mount my beast." And to this too the Princess had to submit. Then the waiting-maid commanded her harshly to take off her royal robes and to put on her common ones, and finally she made her swear by Heaven not to say a word about the matter when they reached the palace. If she did not do so, she would be killed on the spot. And Falada observed everything and took it all to heart.

The waiting-maid now mounted Falada, and the real bride the other horse, and so they continued their journey till at length they arrived at the palace. There was great rejoicing over the arrival, and the Prince sprang forward to meet them. Thinking that the waiting-maid was his bride, he lifted her down from her horse and led her upstairs to the royal chamber.

In the meantime the real Princess was left standing below in the courtyard.

The old King, who was looking out of his window, beheld her in this plight, and it struck him how sweet and gentle, even beautiful, she looked. He went at once to the royal chamber and asked the false bride who it was she had brought with her and left standing in the courtyard below.

"Oh," replied the bride, "I brought her with me to keep me company on the journey. Give the girl something to do, that she may not be idle."

But the old King had no work for her and could not think of anything, so he said, "I have a small boy who looks after the geese. She had better help him."

The youth's name was Curdken, and the real bride was made to assist him in herding geese.

Soon after this, the false bride said to the Prince, "Dearest bridegroom, I pray you grant me a favor."

He answered, "That I will."

"Then have the horse I rode here killed, because it behaved very badly on the journey."

But the truth was she was afraid lest the horse should speak and tell how she had treated the Princess. When the news came to the ears of the real Princess she went to the slaughterer and secretly promised him a piece of gold if he would do something for her. There was in the town a large dark gate, through which she had to pass night and morning with the geese. Would he kindly hang up Falada's head there that she might see it again?

The man said he would do as the Princess desired, and the next day he chopped off the head and nailed it firmly over the gateway.

When she and Curdken drove their flock through

the gate early the next morning, she whispered as she passed under:

> Oh, Falada, 'tis you hang there,

and the head replied:

> 'Tis you; pass under, Princess fair:
> If your mother only knew,
> Her heart would surely break in two.

Then the real Princess and Curdken left the tower and drove the geese out into the country. And when they had reached the meadow where the geese fed she sat down and unloosed her hair, which was of pure gold. Curdken loved to see it glitter in the sun and wanted very much to pull out a few hairs.

Then the Princess spoke:

> Wind, wind, gently sway,
> Blow Curdken's hat away;
> Let him chase o'er field and wold
> Till my locks of ruddy gold,
> Now astray and hanging down,
> Be combed and plaited in a crown.

A gust of wind blew Curdken's hat away, and he had to chase it over hill and dale. When he returned from the pursuit she had finished combing and curling her hair, and his chance of getting a lock was gone. Curdken was very angry and would not speak to her.

They herded the geese in silence till evening and then went home.

The next morning, as they passed under the gate, driving the geese before them, the girl said:

Oh, Falada, 'tis you hang there,

and the head replied:

'Tis you; pass under, Princess fair:
If your mother only knew,
Her heart would surely break in two.

Then she went on her way till she came to the meadow, where she sat down and began to comb out her hair.

Curdken ran up to her and wanted to pull a lock from her head, but she called out hastily:

Wind, wind, gently sway,
Blow Curdken's hat away;
Let him chase o'er field and wold
Till my locks of ruddy gold,
Now astray and hanging down,
Be combed and plaited in a crown.

Then a puff of wind came and blew Curdken's hat far away and he had to run after it. When he returned she had long finished putting up her golden locks, and he could not get one; so they watched the geese till it was dark.

But that evening when they came home Curdken went to the old King and said, "I refuse to herd geese any longer with that girl."

"For what reason?" asked the King.

"Because she does nothing but annoy me all day long," replied Curdken, and he proceeded to relate her strange behavior.

"Every morning as we drive the flock through the tower gate she says to a horse's head that is nailed on the wall:

> Oh, Falada, 'tis you hang there,

and the head replies:

> 'Tis you; pass under, Princess fair:
> If your mother only knew,
> Her heart would surely break in two."

And Curdken went on to tell what happened on the meadow where the geese fed, and how he had always to chase his hat.

The old King bade him go and drive forth his flock as usual next day. And when morning came he himself took up his position behind the dark gate and heard how the goose-girl greeted Falada. Then he followed her through the field and hid himself behind a bush on the meadow.

He soon saw with his own eyes how the goose-boy and the goose-girl looked after the geese, and how after a time the maiden sat down and loosened her hair, that glittered like gold, and repeated:

> Wind, wind, gently sway,
> Blow Curdken's hat away;
> Let him chase o'er field and wold
> Till my locks of ruddy gold,
> Now astray and hanging down,
> Be combed and plaited in a crown.

Then a gust of wind came and blew Curdken's hat away so he had to fly over hill and dale after it, and the girl in the meantime quietly combed and braided her hair. All this the old King observed and returned to the palace without anyone having noticed him. In the evening, when the goose-girl came home, he called her aside and asked her why she behaved as she did.

"I may not tell you why," she replied. "How dare I confide my woes to anyone? For I swore by Heaven not to, otherwise I should have lost my life."

The old King begged her to tell him, and left her no peace, but he could get nothing out of her. At last he said, "Well, if you will not tell me, confide your trouble to the iron stove there." And he went away, leaving her alone.

Then she crept to the stove, and began to sob and to pour out her sad little heart, and said, "Here I sit, deserted by the whole world—I who am a King's daughter, and a false waiting-maid has forced me to remove my own clothes and has taken my place with my bridegroom, while I fulfill the lowly task of goose-girl.

If my mother only knew,
Her heart would surely break in two."

But the old King stood outside at the stove chimney and listened to her words. Then he entered the room again, and he ordered royal apparel to be put on her, in which she looked amazingly lovely. Next he summoned his son and revealed to him that he had a false bride who was nothing but a waiting-maid, while the real bride, in the guise of the goose-girl, was now standing at his side.

The young Prince rejoiced with all his heart when he saw her beauty and learned how good she was, and a great banquet was prepared, to which everyone was bidden. The bridegroom sat at the head of the table, the real Princess on one side of him and the waiting-maid on the other. The waiting-maid was so dazzled she did not recognize the Princess in her glittering garments. When they had eaten and were merry, the King asked the false bride to solve a problem for him.

"What," said he, "should be done to a certain person who has deceived everyone?" And he proceeded to relate the whole story, ending up with: "Now what sentence should be passed?" Then the false bride answered, "She deserves to be put naked into a barrel lined with sharp nails, which should be dragged by two white horses up and down the street till she is dead."

"You are the person," said the King, "and you have passed sentence on yourself. And even so it shall be done to you."

The young Prince was married to his real bride, and both reigned over the kingdom in peace and happiness.

JAKOB AND WILHELM GRIMM, TRANSLATED BY MAY SELLAR

BEAUTY AND THE BEAST

ONCE UPON a time, in a far-off country, there lived a merchant who was enormously rich. He had six sons and six daughters, however, who were accustomed to having everything they fancied, and he did not find he had a penny too much. But a series of misfortunes befell them. One day their house caught fire and speedily burned to the ground, with all the splendid furniture, books, pictures, gold, silver and precious goods it contained. Then the father suddenly lost every ship he had upon the sea, because of pirates, shipwreck or fire. As though that were not enough, he heard that his clerks in distant countries, whom he had trusted, had proved dishonest. And at last from great wealth he fell into the direst poverty.

All that he had left was a little house in a desolate place a long distance from the town. The daughters at first hoped their friends, who had been so numerous while they were rich, would insist that they stay in their houses, but they soon found they were left alone. These former friends even attributed the family's misfortunes to the daughters' extravagance and showed no intention of offering any help.

So nothing was left for them but to take their departure to the cottage, which stood in the midst of a dark forest. They were too poor to have any servants, and the girls had to work hard; the sons, for their part, cultivated the fields to earn their living. Roughly clothed, and living in the simplest way, the girls never ceased to yearn for the luxuries and amusements of their former life. Only the youngest daughter tried to be brave and cheerful.

She had been as sad as anyone when misfortune first overtook her father, but soon recovered her natural gaiety. She set to work to make the best of things, to amuse her father and brothers as well as she could and to persuade her sisters to join her in dancing and singing. But they would do nothing of the sort and, because she was not as gloomy as themselves, they declared their miserable life was all she was fit for. But she was really far prettier and cleverer than they were. Indeed, she was so lovely she was always called Beauty.

After two years, their father received news that one of his ships, which he had believed lost, had come safely into port with a rich cargo. All the sons and daughters at once thought that their poverty was at an end and wanted to set out directly for the town; but their father, who was more prudent, begged them to wait a little.

Only the youngest daughter had any doubt but that they would soon again be as rich as they were before. They all loaded their father with demands for jewels and dresses which it would have taken a fortune to buy; only Beauty did not ask for anything. Her father, noticing her silence, said, "And what shall I bring for you, Beauty?"

"The one thing I wish for is to see you come home safely," she answered.

But this reply annoyed her sisters, who fancied she was blaming them for having asked for such costly things. Her father, however, was pleased, and he urged her to choose something.

"Well, dear Father," she said, "as you insist upon it, I beg that you will bring me a rose. I have not seen one since we came here, and I love them so much."

The merchant set out, only to find that his former companions, believing him to be dead, had divided his cargo among themselves. After six months of trouble and expense he found himself as poor as when he started on his journey. To make matters worse, he returned during a terrible snowstorm. By the time he was within a few miles of his home he was almost exhausted with cold and fatigue. Though he knew it would take some hours to get through the forest, he resolved to go on. But night overtook him, and the deep snow and bitter frost made it impossible for his horse to carry him any farther.

The only shelter he could find was the hollow trunk of a great tree, and there he crouched all night. The howling of the wolves kept him awake, and when at last day broke, the falling snow had covered every path, and he did not know which way to turn.

At length he made out some sort of way, but it was so rough and slippery that he fell more than once. Presently it led him into an avenue of orange trees which ended in a splendid castle. It seemed to the merchant very strange that no snow had fallen in the avenue of trees, which were covered with flowers and fruit. When he reached the first courtyard he saw before him a flight of agate steps. He went up and passed through several splendidly furnished rooms.

The pleasant warmth of the air revived him, and he felt very hungry; but there seemed to be nobody in all this vast and splendid palace. Deep silence reigned everywhere, and at last, tired of roaming through empty rooms and galleries, he stopped in a room smaller than the rest, where a cheerful fire was burning and a couch was drawn up before it. Thinking this must be prepared for someone who was expected, he sat down to wait till he should come, and very soon fell into a sweet sleep.

When extreme hunger wakened him after several hours, he was still alone; but a little table, with a good dinner on it, had been drawn up close to him. He lost no time in beginning his meal, hoping he might soon thank his considerate host, whoever he might be. But no one appeared, and even after another long sleep, from which he awoke completely refreshed, there was no sign of anybody, though a fresh meal of dainty cakes and fruit was on the little table at his elbow.

Being naturally timid, he grew terrified of the silence, and he resolved to search once more through all the rooms; but it was of no use, there was no sign of life in the palace! Then he went down into the garden, and though it was winter everywhere else, here the sun shone, the birds sang, the flowers bloomed and the air was soft and sweet. The merchant, in ecstasies at all he saw and heard, said to himself, "All this must be meant for me. I will go this minute and bring my children to share all these delights."

In spite of being so cold and weary when he reached the castle, he had taken his horse to the stable and fed it. Now he thought he would saddle it for his homeward journey, and he turned down the path which led to the stable. This path had a hedge of roses on each side of it, and the merchant thought he had never seen such exquisite flowers. They reminded him of his promise to Beauty, and he stopped and had just gathered one to take to her when he was startled by a strange noise behind him. Turning around, he saw a frightful Beast.

"Who told you you might gather my roses?" cried the Beast in a terrible voice. "Was it not enough that I sheltered you in my palace and was kind to you? This is the way you show your gratitude, by stealing my flowers! But your insolence shall not go unpunished."

The merchant, terrified by these furious words, dropped the fatal rose and, throwing himself on his knees, cried, "Pardon me, noble sir. I am truly grateful for your hospitality. It was so magnificent I could not imagine you would be offended by my taking such a little thing as a rose."

But the Beast's anger was not lessened by his speech. "You are very ready with excuses and flattery," he cried. "But that will not save you from the death you deserve."

Alas, thought the merchant, if my daughter Beauty could only know to what danger her rose has brought me! And in despair he began to tell the Beast all his misfortunes and the reason for his journey, not forgetting to mention Beauty's request. "A king's ransom would hardly have procured all that my other daughters asked for," he said. "But I thought I might at least take Beauty her rose. I beg you to forgive me, for you see I meant no harm."

The Beast said, in a less furious tone, "I will forgive you on one condition—that you will give me one of your daughters."

"Ah," cried the merchant, "if I were cruel enough to buy my own life at the expense of one of my children's, what excuse could I invent to bring her here?"

"None," answered the Beast. "If she comes at all she must come willingly. On no other condition will I have her. See if any one of them is courageous enough, and loves you enough, to come and save your life. You seem to be an honest man, so I will trust you to go home. I give you a month to see if any of your daughters will come back with you and stay here, so that you may go free. If none of them is willing, you must come alone, for then you will belong to me. And do not imagine that you can hide from me, for if you fail to keep your word I will come and fetch you!" added the Beast grimly.

The merchant accepted this proposal. He promised to return at the time appointed, and then, anxious to escape from the presence of the Beast, he asked permission to set off at once. But the Beast answered that he could not go until the next day. "Then you will find a horse ready for you," he said. "Now go and eat your supper and await my orders."

The poor merchant, more dead than alive, went back to his room, where the most delicious supper was already served on the little table drawn up before a blazing fire. But he was too terrified to eat and only tasted a few of the dishes, for fear the Beast should be angry if he did not obey his orders. When he had finished, the Beast warned him to remember their agreement and to prepare his daughter for exactly what she had to expect.

"Do not get up tomorrow," he added, "until you see the sun rise and hear a golden bell ring. Then you will find your breakfast waiting for you, and the horse you are to ride will be ready in the courtyard. He will also bring you back again when you come with your daughter a month from now. Farewell. Take a rose to Beauty, and remember your promise!"

The merchant lay down until dawn. Then, after breakfast, he went to gather Beauty's flower and mounted his horse, which carried him off so swiftly that in an instant he had lost sight of the palace. He was still wrapped in gloomy thoughts when it stopped before the door of his cottage.

His sons and daughters, who had been uneasy at his long absence, rushed to meet him, eager to know the result of his journey which, seeing him mounted upon a splendid horse and wrapped in a rich mantle, they supposed to be favorable. But he hid the truth from them at first, only saying sadly to Beauty as he gave her the rose: "Here is what you asked me to bring you. Little you know what it has cost."

Presently he told them his adventures from beginning to end, and then they were all very unhappy. The girls lamented loudly over their lost hopes, and the sons declared their father should not return to the terrible castle. But he reminded them he had promised to go back. Then the girls were very angry with Beauty and said it was all her fault. If she had asked for something sensible this would never have happened.

Poor Beauty, much distressed, said to them, "I have indeed caused this misfortune, but who could have guessed that to ask for a rose would cause so much misery? But as I did the mischief it is only just that I should suffer for it. I will therefore go back with my father to keep his promise."

At first nobody would hear of it. Her father and brothers, who loved her dearly, declared nothing should make them let her go. But Beauty was firm. As the time drew near she divided her little possessions among her sisters and said good-bye to everything she loved. When the fatal day came she and her father both mounted the horse which had brought him back. It seemed to fly rather than gallop, but so smoothly that Beauty was not frightened. Indeed, she would have enjoyed the journey if she had not feared what might happen at the end of it. Her father tried to persuade her to go back home with him, but in vain.

While they were riding the night fell. Then, to their great surprise, splendid fireworks blazed out before them and all the forest was illuminated. They even felt pleasantly warm, though it had been bitterly cold before. They reached the avenue of orange trees and saw that the palace was brilliantly lighted from roof to ground, and music sounded softly from the courtyard.

"The Beast must be very hungry," said Beauty, trying to laugh, "if he makes all this rejoicing over the arrival of his prey." But, in spite of her anxiety, she admired all the wonderful things she saw.

When they had dismounted, her father led her to the little room. Here they found a crackling fire and the table spread with a delicious supper.

Beauty, who was less frightened now that she had passed through so many rooms and seen nothing of the Beast, was quite willing to begin, for her long ride had made her very hungry. But they had hardly finished their meal when the noise of the Beast's footsteps was heard approaching, and Beauty clung to her father in terror, which became all the greater when she saw how frightened he was. But when the Beast appeared, though she trembled at the sight of him, she made a great effort to hide her horror, and faced him respectfully.

This evidently pleased the Beast. After looking at her he said, in a tone that might have struck terror into the boldest heart, though he did not seem to be angry, "Good evening, old man. Good evening, Beauty."

The merchant was too terrified to reply, but Beauty answered sweetly, "Good evening, Beast."

"Have you come willingly?" asked the Beast. "Will you be content to stay here when your father has gone away?"

Beauty answered bravely that she was quite prepared to stay.

"I am pleased with you," said the Beast. "You have come of your own accord, so you may remain. As for you, old man," he added, turning to the merchant, "at sunrise tomorrow take your departure. When the bell rings, get up quickly and eat your breakfast, and you will find the same horse waiting to take you home."

Then turning to Beauty, he said, "Take your father into the next room, and help him choose gifts for your brothers and sisters. You will find two traveling trunks there; fill them as full as you can. It is only just that you should send them something very precious as a remembrance." Then he went away.

Beauty was beginning to think with great dismay of her father's departure, but they went into the next room and were greatly surprised at the riches they found. There were splendid dresses fit for a queen, and when Beauty opened the chests she was dazzled by the gorgeous jewels lying in heaps upon every shelf. After choosing a vast quantity for each of her sisters, she opened the last chest and discovered that it was full of gold.

"I think, Father," she said, "that, as the gold will be more useful to you, we had better take out the other things and fill the trunks with it."

So they did this, but the more they put in, the more room there seemed to be, and at last they put back all the jewels and dresses they had taken out, and Beauty even added as many more of the jewels as she could carry. Even then the trunks were not too full, but they were so heavy an elephant could not have carried them!

"The Beast was mocking us!" cried the merchant. "He pretended to give us all these things, knowing that I could not carry them away."

"Let us wait and see," answered Beauty. "I cannot believe he meant to deceive us. All we can do is to fasten them and have them ready."

So they did this and returned to the little room, where they found breakfast prepared. The merchant ate with a good appetite, as the Beast's generosity made him believe he might perhaps venture to come back soon and see Beauty. But she felt sure her father was leaving her forever, so she was very sad when the bell rang sharply.

They went down into the courtyard, where two horses were waiting, one loaded with the two trunks, the other for him to ride. They were pawing the ground in their impatience to start, and the merchant bade Beauty a hasty farewell. As soon as he was mounted, the horses went off at such a pace that she lost sight of him in an instant. Then Beauty began to cry and wandered sadly back to her own room.

But she soon found she was very sleepy, and as she had nothing better to do she lay down and instantly fell asleep. And then she dreamed she was walking by a brook bordered with trees, and lamenting her sad fate, when a young Prince, handsomer than anyone she had ever seen and with a voice that went straight to her heart, came and said to her, "Ah, Beauty, you are not so unfortunate as you suppose. Here you will be rewarded for all you have suffered elsewhere. Your every wish shall be gratified. Only try to learn who I am, no matter how I may be disguised, for I love you dearly, and in making me happy you will find your own happiness. Be as truehearted as you are beautiful, and we shall have nothing left to wish for."

"What can I do, Prince, to make you happy?" said Beauty.

"Only be grateful," he answered, "and do not trust too much to your eyes. Above all, do not desert me until you have saved me from my cruel misery."

As her dream continued she found herself in a room with a stately and beautiful lady, who said to her, "Dear Beauty, try not to regret all you have left behind you; you are destined for a better fate. Only do not let yourself be deceived by appearances."

Beauty found her dream so interesting that she was in no hurry to awake, but presently the clock roused her by calling her name softly twelve times. Then she rose and found her dressing table set out with everything she could possibly want, and when she was dressed, she found dinner waiting in the room next to hers. But dinner does not take very long when one is alone, and soon she sat down cozily in the corner of a sofa and began to think about the charming Prince she had seen in her dream.

"He said I could make him happy," said Beauty to herself. "It seems, then, that this horrible Beast keeps him a prisoner. How can I set him free? I wonder why they both told me not to trust to appearances? But, after all, it was only a dream, so why should I trouble myself about it? I had better find something to do to amuse myself."

So she began to explore some of the rooms in the palace. The first she entered was lined with mirrors. Beauty saw herself reflected on every side and thought she had never seen such a charming room. Then a bracelet which was hanging from a chandelier caught her eye, and on taking it down she was greatly surprised to find that it held a portrait of her unknown admirer, just as she had seen him in her dream. With great delight she slipped the bracelet on her arm and went on into a gallery of pictures, where she soon found a portrait of the same handsome Prince, as large as life, and so well painted that as she studied it he seemed to smile kindly at her.

Tearing herself away from the portrait at last, she passed into a room which contained every musical instrument under the sun, and here she amused herself for a long while in trying them. By this time it was growing dusk, and wax candles in diamond and ruby candlesticks lit themselves in every room.

Beauty found her supper served just at the time she liked to have it, but she did not see anyone or hear a sound and, though her father had warned her she would be alone, she began to find it rather dull.

Presently she heard the Beast coming and wondered tremblingly if he meant to eat her now. However, he did not seem at all ferocious, and only said gruffly: "Good evening, Beauty."

She answered cheerfully and managed to conceal her terror. The Beast asked how she had been amusing herself, and she told him all the rooms she had seen. Then he asked if she thought she could be happy in his palace; and Beauty answered that everything was so beautiful she would be very hard to please if she could not be happy. After an hour's talk Beauty began to think the Beast was not nearly so terrible as she had supposed. Then he rose to leave and said in his gruff voice: "Do you love me, Beauty? Will you marry me?"

"Oh, what shall I say?" cried Beauty, for she was afraid to make the Beast angry by refusing.

"Say yes or no without fear," he replied.

"Oh, no, Beast," said Beauty hastily.

"Since you will not, good night, Beauty," he said.

And she answered, "Good night, Beast," very glad to find her refusal had not provoked him. After he was gone she was very soon in bed and dreaming of her unknown Prince.

She thought he came and said, "Ah, Beauty! Why are you so unkind to me? I fear I am fated to be unhappy for many a long day still."

Then her dreams changed, but the charming Prince figured in them all. When morning came she decided to amuse herself in the garden. She was astonished to find that every place was familiar to her, and presently she came to the very brook and the myrtle trees where she had first met the Prince in her dream. That made her think more than ever that he must be kept a prisoner by the Beast.

When she was tired she went back to the palace and found a new room full of materials for every kind of work—ribbons to make into bows and silks to work into flowers. There was also an aviary full of rare birds, which were so tame that they flew to Beauty as soon as they saw her and perched upon her shoulders and her head.

"Pretty little creatures," she said, "how I wish your cage was nearer my room that I might often hear you sing!" So saying, she opened a door and found to her delight that it led into her own room, though she had thought it was on the other side of the palace.

There were more birds in a room farther on, parrots and cockatoos that could talk, and they greeted Beauty by name. Indeed, she found them so entertaining that she took one or two back to her room, and they talked to her while she was at supper. The Beast paid her his usual visit and put to her the same questions he had asked before, and then with a gruff good-night he took his departure, and Beauty went to bed to dream of her mysterious Prince.

The days passed swiftly in different amusements, and after a while Beauty found another strange thing which often pleased her when she was tired of being alone. There was one room which she had not noticed particularly; it was empty, except that under each of the windows stood a very comfortable chair. The first time she had looked out of a window, it seemed a black curtain prevented her from seeing anything outside. But the second time she went into the room she happened to be tired and sat down in one of the chairs. Instantly the curtain was rolled aside, and a most amusing pantomime was acted before her. There were dances and colored lights, music and pretty dresses, and it was all so gay that Beauty was in ecstasies. After that she tried the other seven windows in turn, and there was some new and surprising entertainment to be seen from each of them, so Beauty never could feel lonely anymore. Every evening after supper the Beast came to see her, and always before saying good-night he would ask her in his terrible voice: "Beauty, will you marry me?"

It occurred to Beauty, now that she understood him better, that when she said, "No, Beast," he went away quite sad. Her happy dreams of the handsome young Prince soon made her forget the poor Beast, and the only thing that disturbed her was being told to distrust appearances, to let her heart guide her and not her eyes. Think about this as she would, she could not understand.

So everything went on for a long time, until at last, happy as she was, Beauty began to yearn for the sight of her father and her brothers and sisters. One night, seeing her looking very sad, the Beast asked what was the matter. Beauty had quite ceased to be afraid of him. Now she knew he was really gentle in spite of his ferocious looks and his dreadful voice. So she answered that she wished to see her home once more. Upon hearing this the Beast seemed distressed and cried out miserably, "Ah, Beauty, have you the heart to desert an unhappy Beast like this? What more do you want to make you happy? Is it because you hate me that you want to escape?"

"No, dear Beast," answered Beauty softly, "I do not hate you, and I should be very sorry never to see you anymore, but I long to see my father again. Only let me go for two months, and I promise to come back to you and stay for the rest of my life."

The Beast, who had been sighing unhappily while she spoke, now replied, "I cannot refuse you anything you ask, even though it should cost me my life. Take the four boxes you will find in the room next to your own and fill them with everything you wish to take with you. But remember your promise and come back when the two months are over, for if you do not return in good time you will find your faithful Beast dead. You will not need any chariot to bring you back. Only say good-bye to your father and brothers and sisters the night before you come away and, when you have gone to bed, turn this ring around upon your finger and say firmly, 'I wish to go back to my palace and see my Beast again.' Good night, Beauty. Fear nothing, sleep peacefully, and before long you shall see your family once more."

As soon as Beauty was alone she hastened to fill the boxes with all the rare and precious things she saw about her, and only when she was tired of heaping things into them did they seem to be full. Then she went to bed, but could hardly sleep for joy. When at last she began to dream of her beloved Prince she was grieved to see him stretched upon a grassy bank, sad and weary, and hardly like himself.

"What is the matter?" she cried.

But he looked at her reproachfully and said, "How can you ask me, cruel one? Are you not leaving me to my death perhaps?"

"Ah, don't be sorrowful!" cried Beauty. "I am only going to assure my father that I am safe and happy. I have promised the Beast faithfully I will come back, and I know that he would die of grief if I did not keep my word!"

"What would that matter to you?" asked the Prince. "Surely you would not care?"

"Indeed I should be ungrateful if I did not care for such a kind Beast," cried Beauty indignantly. "I would die to save him from pain. I assure you it is not his fault he is so ugly."

Just then a strange sound woke her—someone was speaking not very far away. Opening her eyes she found herself in a room she had never seen before, which was certainly not as splendid as those she had seen in the Beast's palace. Where could she be? She rose and dressed hastily and then saw that the boxes she had packed the night before were all in the room. Suddenly she heard her father's voice and rushed out to greet him joyfully. Her brothers and sisters were astonished at her appearance, for they had never expected to see her again. Beauty asked her father what he thought her strange dreams meant and why the Prince in them constantly begged her not to trust to appearances. After much consideration he answered, "You tell me yourself that the Beast, frightful as he is, loves you dearly and deserves your love and gratitude for his gentleness and kindness. I think the Prince must mean you to understand that you ought to reward the Beast by doing as he wishes you to, in spite of his ugliness.''

Beauty could not help seeing that this seemed likely; still, when she thought of her dear Prince who was so handsome, she did not feel at all inclined to marry the Beast. At any rate, for two months she need not decide but could enjoy herself with her family. Though they were rich now, and lived in a town again and had plenty of acquaintances, Beauty found that nothing amused her very much. She often thought of the palace, where she was so happy, especially as at home she never once dreamed of her beloved Prince, and she felt quite sad without him.

And her sisters seemed quite used to being without her, and even found her rather in the way. So she would not have been sorry when the two months were over but for her father and brothers. She did not have the courage to say good-bye to them. Every day when she rose she meant to say it at night, and when night came she put it off again, until at last she had a dismal dream which helped her to make up her mind.

She thought she was wandering in a lonely path in the palace gardens, when she heard groans. Running quickly to see what could be the matter, she found the Beast stretched out upon his side, apparently dying. He reproached her faintly with being the cause of his distress, and at the same moment a stately lady appeared and said very gravely: "Ah, Beauty, see what happens when people do not keep their promises! If you had delayed one day more, you would have found him dead."

Beauty was so terrified by this dream that the very next evening she said good-bye to her father and her brothers and sisters, and as soon as she was in bed she turned around upon her finger the ring which the Beast had given her, and said firmly, "I wish to go back to my palace and see my Beast again."

Then she fell asleep instantly, and only woke up to hear the clock saying, "Beauty, Beauty," twelve times in its musical voice, which told her she was really in the palace once more. Everything was just as before, and her birds were very glad to see her, but Beauty thought she had never known such a long day. She was so anxious to see the Beast again that she felt as if supper-time would never come.

But when it came no Beast appeared. After listening and waiting for a long time, she ran down into the garden to search for him. Up and down the paths and avenues ran poor Beauty, calling him. No one answered, and not a trace of him could she find. At last, Beauty saw that she was standing opposite the shady path she had seen in her dream. She rushed down it and, sure enough, there was the Beast—asleep, so Beauty thought. Quite glad to have found him, she ran up and stroked his head, but to her horror he did not move or open his eyes. "Oh, he is dead, and it is all my fault!" cried Beauty, weeping bitterly.

But then, looking at him again, she fancied he still breathed. Hastily fetching some water from the nearest fountain, she sprinkled it over his face, and to her great delight he began to revive. "Oh, Beast, how you frightened me!" she cried. "I never knew how much I loved you until just now, when I feared I was too late to save your life."

"Can you really love such an ugly creature as I am?" asked the Beast faintly. "Ah, Beauty, you came only just in time. I was dying because I thought you had forgotten your promise. But go back now and rest, and I shall see you again by and by."

Beauty, who had half expected he would be angry with her, was reassured by his gentle voice and went back to the palace. And after a while the Beast came in to visit her and talked about the time she had spent with her father, asking if she had enjoyed herself and if they had all been glad to see her.

Beauty quite enjoyed telling him all that had happened to her. When at last the time came for him to leave, he asked, as he had so often asked before: "Beauty, will you marry me?"

She answered softly, "Yes, dear Beast."

As she spoke, a blaze of light sprang up before the windows of the palace; fireworks crackled and guns boomed, and across the avenue of orange trees, in letters all made of fireflies, was written: "Long live the Prince and his bride."

Turning to ask the Beast what it could all mean, Beauty found he had disappeared, and in his place stood her long-loved Prince! At the same moment the wheels of a chariot were heard upon the terrace, and two ladies entered the room. One of them, Beauty realized, was the stately lady she had seen in her dreams; the other was so queenly that Beauty hardly knew which to greet first. But the one she recognized said to her companion: "Well, my Queen, this is Beauty, who has had the courage to rescue your son from the terrible enchantment. They love each other, and only your consent to their marriage is wanting to make them perfectly happy."

"I consent with all my heart," cried the Queen. "How can I ever thank you enough, charming girl, for having restored my dear son to his natural form?" And then she tenderly embraced Beauty and the Prince, who had meanwhile been greeting the other lady, who was a fairy, and receiving her congratulations.

"Now," said the fairy to Beauty, "I suppose you would like me to send for your father and all your brothers and sisters to dance at your wedding?"

And so she did, and the marriage was celebrated the very next day with the utmost splendor, and Beauty and the Prince lived happily ever after.

MADAME DE VILLENEUVE, ANDREW LANG COLLECTION

THE TOWN MOUSE AND
THE COUNTRY MOUSE

ONCE UPON a time a Town Mouse met a Country Mouse on the outskirts of a wood. The Country Mouse was sitting under a hazel thicket plucking nuts.

"Busy harvesting, I see," said the Town Mouse. "Who would think of our meeting in this out-of-the-way part of the world?"

"Just so," said the Country Mouse.

"You are gathering nuts for your winter store?" asked the Town Mouse.

"I am obliged to do so if we intend having anything to live upon during the winter," said the Country Mouse.

"The husk is big and the nut full this year, enough to satisfy any hungry body," said the Town Mouse.

"Yes, you are right there," said the Country Mouse, and then she related how well she lived and how comfortable she was at home.

The Town Mouse maintained that she was the better off, but the Country Mouse said that nowhere could one be so well off as in the woods and hills. And as they could not agree on this point they promised to visit each other at Christmas; then they could see for themselves which was really the more comfortable.

The first visit was to be paid by the Town Mouse.

Now, although the Country Mouse had moved down from the mountains for the winter, the road to her house was long and tiring, and one had to travel up hill and down dale. The snow lay thick and deep, so the Town Mouse found it hard work to get on, and she became tired and hungry before she reached the end of her journey. How nice it will be to get some food, she thought.

The Country Mouse had scraped together the best she had. There were nut kernels, polypody and all sorts of roots and many other good things which grow in woods and fields. She kept everything in a hole far underground so the frost could not reach it, and close by was a running spring which was free of ice all winter long, so she could drink as much water as she liked. There was an abundance of all she had, and they ate well and heartily; but the Town Mouse thought it was very poor fare indeed. "One can, of course, keep body and soul together on this," said she, "but I don't think much of it. Now you must be good enough to visit me and taste what we have."

Yes, that her hostess would, and before long she set out. The Town Mouse had gathered together all the scraps from the Christmas fare which the woman of the house had dropped on the floor during the holidays —bits of cheese and butter, candle ends, cake crumbs, pastry and many other good things. In the dish under a beer tap she had drink enough; in fact, the place was full of all kinds of dainties. They ate and fared well. The Country Mouse seemed never to have enough; she had never tasted such delicacies. But then she became thirsty, for she found the food both strong and rich, and so she wanted something to drink.

"We haven't far to go for the beer we shall drink," said the Town Mouse, and jumped upon the edge of the dish and drank till she was no longer thirsty. She did not drink too much, for she knew the Christmas beer was strong. The Country Mouse, however, thought the beer a splendid drink; she had never tasted anything but water, so she took one sip after another, but as she could not stand strong drink she became dizzy before she left the dish. The drink got into her head and down into her toes, and she began running from one beer barrel to the other and dancing about on the shelves among the cups and mugs. She squeaked and squealed as if she were intoxicated.

"You must not carry on as if you had just come from the backwoods and make such a row and noise," said the Town Mouse. "The master of the house is a bailiff, and he is very strict indeed."

The Country Mouse said she didn't care either for

See page 298

bailiffs or beggars. But the Cat sat at the top of the cellar steps, lying in wait, and heard all the chatter and noise. When the woman of the house went down to draw some beer and lifted the trapdoor, the Cat slipped by into the cellar and struck its claws into the Country Mouse. Then there was quite another sort of dance.

The Town Mouse slid back into her hole and sat in safety looking on, while the Country Mouse suddenly became sober when she felt the Cat's claws in her back.

"Oh, my dearest bailiff, be merciful and spare my life and I will tell you a fairy tale," she said.

"Well, go on," said the Cat.

"Once upon a time there were two little mice," said the Country Mouse, squeaking slowly and pitifully, for she wanted to make the story last as long as she possibly could.

"Then they were not lonely," said the Cat dryly and curtly.

"And they had a steak they were going to fry."

"Then they could not starve," said the Cat.

"And they put it out on the roof to cool," said the Country Mouse.

"Then they did not burn themselves," said the Cat.

"But there came a fox and a crow and they ate it all up," said the Country Mouse.

"Then I'll eat you," said the Cat. But just at that moment the woman shut the trapdoor with a slam, which so startled the Cat that she let go her hold of the

Mouse. One bound, and the Country Mouse found herself in the hole with the Town Mouse.

From there a passage led out into the snow, and you may be sure the Country Mouse did not wait long before she set out homeward.

"And this is what you call living at ease and being well off," she said to the Town Mouse. "Heaven preserve me from having such a fine place and such a master! Why, I only just got away with my life!"

OLD SCANDINAVIAN TALE, COLLECTION OF
KATE DOUGLAS WIGGIN AND NORA ARCHIBALD SMITH

SNOW WHITE AND THE
SEVEN DWARFS

ONCE UPON a time in the middle of winter, when the snowflakes were falling like feathers on the earth, a Queen sat at a window framed in black ebony and sewed. And as she sewed and gazed out on the white landscape, she pricked her finger with the needle, and three drops of blood fell on the snow outside.

Because the red showed up so well against the white, the Queen said to herself, "Oh, what would I not give to have a child as white as snow, as red as blood and as black as ebony!"

And her wish was granted, for not long afterward a little daughter was born to her, with a skin as white as snow, lips and cheeks as red as blood and hair as black as ebony. They called her Snow White, and not long after her birth the Queen died.

After a year, the King married again. His new wife was a beautiful woman, but so proud and overbearing that she could not stand any rival to her beauty.

The new Queen possessed a magic mirror, and when she stood before it, gazing at her own reflection, she asked:

> Mirror, mirror, on the wall,
> Who is fairest of us all?

and it always replied:

> Thou, Queen, art the fairest of all.

Then she was quite happy, for she knew the mirror always spoke the truth.

But Snow White was growing prettier and prettier every day, and when she was seven years old she was as beautiful as she could be, and fairer than even the Queen herself. One day when the Queen asked her mirror the usual question, it replied:

Thou art fair, my Queen, 'tis true.
But Snow White is fairer far than you.

Then the Queen flew into the most awful passion and turned every shade of green in her jealousy. From this hour she hated poor Snow White, and every day her envy, hatred and malice grew, for envy and jealousy are like evil weeds which spring up and choke the heart.

At last she could endure Snow White's presence no longer and, calling a huntsman to her, she said, "Take the child out into the wood and never let me see her face again. You must kill her and bring me back her lungs and heart, so that I may know for certain she is dead."

The huntsman did as he was told and led Snow White out into the wood, but as he was in the act of drawing out his knife to slay her, she said, "Oh, dear huntsman, spare my life. I promise you that I will disappear into the forest and never return home again."

Because she was so young and pretty the huntsman had pity on her and said, "Well, run along, poor child." For he thought the wild beasts would soon find her and eat her up.

And his heart felt lighter because he hadn't had to do the deed himself. As he turned away, a young boar came running past, so he shot it and brought its lungs and heart home to the Queen as a proof that Snow

White was really dead. And the wicked woman had them stewed in salt, and ate them, thinking she had made an end of Snow White forever.

Now when the poor child found herself alone in the big wood the very trees seemed to take strange shapes, and she felt so frightened she didn't know what to do. Over the sharp stones and through the bramble bushes she stumbled, and the wild beasts ran past her, but they did her no harm. She ran as far as her legs would carry her, and as evening drew in she saw a little house and stepped inside to rest.

Everything was very small in the house, but very clean and neat. In the middle of the room there stood a little table, covered with a white tablecloth and seven little plates and forks and spoons and knives and tumblers. Side by side against the wall there were seven little beds, covered with immaculate white counterpanes.

Snow White felt so hungry and so thirsty she ate a bit of bread and a morsel of porridge from each plate and drank a drop of wine out of each tumbler. Then, feeling tired and sleepy, she lay down on one of the beds, but it wasn't comfortable. Then she tried all the others in turn, but one was too long, another too short, and it was only when she tried the seventh that she found one to suit her exactly. So she lay down upon it, said her prayers like a good child and soon fell fast asleep.

When it was quite dark the masters of the little house returned. They were seven dwarfs who worked in the mines, deep down in the heart of the mountain. They lighted their seven little candles, and as soon as their eyes were accustomed to the glare they saw that someone had been in the room, for all was not in the same order as they had left it.

The first said, "Who has been sitting on my chair?"

The second said, "Who has been eating my loaf?"

The third said, "Who has been tasting my porridge?"

The fourth said, "Who has been eating out of my plate?"

The fifth said, "Who has been using my fork?"

The sixth said, "Who has been cutting with my knife?"

The seventh said, "Who has been drinking out of my tumbler?"

Then the first dwarf looked around and saw a hollow in his bed, and he asked, "Who has been lying on my bed?" The others came running around, and cried when they saw their beds, "Somebody has lain on ours, too."

But when the seventh came to his bed, he started back in amazement, for there he beheld Snow White fast asleep. Then he called the others, who turned their little candles full on the bed, and when they saw Snow White lying there they nearly fell down with surprise.

"Goodness gracious," they cried, "what a beautiful child she is!"

They were so enchanted by her beauty that they did not wake her but let her sleep on in the little bed. The seventh dwarf slept with his companions one hour in each bed, and in this way he managed to pass the night.

In the morning Snow White awoke, and when she saw the seven little dwarfs she felt frightened. But they were so friendly, and asked her what her name was in such a kind way, that she replied, "I am Snow White."

"Why did you come to our house?" continued the seven dwarfs.

Then she told them how her stepmother had wished her put to death, and how the Queen's huntsman had spared her life, and how she had run all day till she had come to their little house. The dwarfs, when they had heard her sad story, asked her, "Will you stay and keep house for us, cook, make the beds, do the washing, sew and knit? If you keep everything neat and clean, you shall want for nothing."

"Yes," answered Snow White, "I will gladly do all you ask."

And so she lived happily with them. Every morning the dwarfs went into the mountain to dig for gold, and in the evening when they returned home, Snow White always had their supper ready for them. But during the day she was left quite alone, so the

good dwarfs warned her, saying, "Beware of your stepmother. She will soon find out you are here, and whatever you do don't let anyone into the house."

Now the Queen never dreamed but that she was once more the most beautiful woman in the world; so, stepping before her mirror one day, she said:

> Mirror, mirror, on the wall,
> Who is fairest of us all?

and the mirror replied:

> You are fair, my Queen, 'tis true,
> But Snow White is fairer far than you.
> Snow White, who dwells with the seven little men,
> Is as fair as you and as fair again.

When the Queen heard these words she was nearly struck dumb with horror, for the mirror always spoke the truth. She knew now that the huntsman must have deceived her and that Snow White was still alive. She pondered day and night how she might destroy her, for her jealous heart left her no rest. At last she hit upon a plan. She stained her face and dressed herself up as an old peddler woman, so that she was quite unrecognizable. In this guise she went over the seven hills till she came to the house of the seven dwarfs. There she knocked at the door, calling out at the same time: "Fine wares to sell, fine wares to sell!"

Snow White peeped out of the window and spoke

to her, "Good day, kind lady, what have you to sell?"

"Good wares, fine wares," she answered, "laces of every shade and description." And she held one up that was made of some gaily colored silk.

"Surely I can let the honest woman in," said Snow White, and she unbarred the door and bought the pretty lace.

"Good gracious, child," said the old woman, "what a figure you have! Come! I'll lace you up properly for once."

Snow White, suspecting no evil, stood before her and let her lace up her bodice; but the old woman laced her so quickly and so tightly that it took Snow White's breath away, and she fell down as though she were dead.

"Now you are no longer the fairest," said the wicked old woman, and then she hastened away.

In the evening the seven dwarfs came home, and what a fright they had when they saw their dear Snow White lying on the floor, as still and motionless as a dead person. They lifted her up tenderly, and when they saw how tightly laced she was they cut the lacing, and she began to breathe a little and gradually came back to life. When the dwarfs heard what had happened, they said, "Depend upon it, the old peddler woman was none other than the Queen. In the future you must be sure to let no one inside if we are not at home."

As soon as the wicked old Queen reached home she went straight to her mirror and said:

Mirror, mirror, on the wall,
Who is fairest of us all?

and the mirror answered as before:

You are fair, my Queen, 'tis true,
But Snow White is fairer far than you.
Snow White, who dwells with the seven little men,
Is as fair as you, and as fair again.

When she heard this, the Queen became as pale as death, because she knew at once that Snow White must still be alive. "This time," she said to herself, "I will think of something that will make an end of her once and for all."

And by the witchcraft which she understood so well she made a poisonous comb. Then she dressed herself up in the form of another old woman. So she went over the seven hills till she reached the house of the seven dwarfs, and knocking at the door she called out, "Fine wares for sale."

Snow White looked out of the window and said, "You must go away, for I may not let anyone in."

"But surely you are not forbidden to look out?" asked the old woman and she held up the poisonous comb for her to see.

It pleased the girl so much that she opened the

door. When they had settled their bargain, the old woman said, "Come, I'll comb your hair properly."

Poor Snow White suspected no evil, but hardly had the comb touched her hair than the poison worked, and she fell down unconscious.

"Now, my fine lady, you're really done for this time," said the wicked woman and she made her way home as fast as she could.

Fortunately it was near evening and the seven dwarfs came home. When they saw Snow White lying there as if dead on the ground, they at once suspected that the wicked Queen had been at work again. So they searched till they found the poisonous comb, and the moment they pulled it out of her hair Snow White came to herself again and told them what had happened. So once more they warned her to open the door to no one.

As soon as the Queen was home she went straight to her mirror, and asked:

> Mirror, mirror, on the wall,
> Who is fairest of us all?

and it replied as before:

> You are fair, my Queen, 'tis true,
> But Snow White is fairer far than you.
> Snow White, who dwells with the seven little men,
> Is as fair as you and as fair again.

When she heard these words she literally shook with rage.

"Snow White shall die!" she cried. "Yes, though it cost me my own life."

Then she went to a secret chamber, which no one knew of but herself, and there she made a poisonous apple. Outwardly it looked beautiful, half white and half red—anyone who saw it would long to eat it. When the apple was finished, she stained her face and dressed herself up as a peasant and went over the seven hills to the house of the seven dwarfs. She knocked at the door, but Snow White put her head out of the window and called, "I may not let anyone in. The seven dwarfs have forbidden me to do so."

"Are you afraid of being poisoned?" asked the old woman. "See, I will cut this apple in half. I'll eat the white cheek and you can eat the red."

The apple was so cunningly made that only the red cheek was poisonous. Snow White longed to eat the tempting fruit, and when she saw that the peasant woman was eating it herself, she couldn't resist the temptation any longer and, stretching out her hand, she took the poisonous half. But hardly had the first bite passed her lips than she fell down dead on the ground. Then the eyes of the cruel Queen sparkled and, laughing aloud, she cried, "As white as snow, as red as blood and as black as ebony, this time the dwarfs won't be able to bring you back to life."

When she reached home she asked the mirror:

> Mirror, mirror, on the wall,
> Who is fairest of us all?

and this time it replied:

> Thou, Queen, art the fairest one of all.

Then her jealous heart was at rest—at least, as much at rest as a jealous heart can ever be.

When the little dwarfs came home in the evening they found Snow White lying on the ground, and she neither breathed nor stirred. They lifted her up and looked everywhere to see if they could find anything poisonous about. They unlaced her bodice, combed her hair, washed her with water and wine, but it was in vain: the child was dead and remained dead. Then they placed her on a bier, and the seven dwarfs sat around it, weeping and sobbing for three whole days. At last they made up their minds to bury her, but she looked as blooming as a living being, and her cheeks were still such a lovely color that they said, "We cannot hide her away in the dark ground."

So they had a coffin made of transparent glass, and they laid her in it and wrote on the lid in golden letters that she was a royal princess. Then they put the coffin on the top of the mountain, and one of the dwarfs always remained beside it and kept watch over it. And the very birds of the air came and bewailed Snow

White's death, first an owl, and then a raven, and then a little dove.

Snow White lay a long time in the coffin, and she always looked the same, just as if she were fast asleep, remaining as white as snow, as red as blood and her hair as black as ebony.

Now it happened one day that a Prince came to the wood and passed by the dwarfs' house. He saw the coffin on the hill with the beautiful Snow White inside, and when he had read the golden letters that were written there, he said to the dwarf, "Give me the coffin. You shall have whatever you ask."

But the dwarf said, "No, we wouldn't part with it for all the gold in the world."

"Well, then," he replied, "give it to me only because I cannot live without Snow White. I will cherish and love her as my dearest possession."

He spoke so sadly that the good dwarfs had pity on him and gave him the coffin, and the Prince made his servants bear it away on their shoulders. As they were going down the hill they stumbled over a bush and jolted the coffin so violently that the poisonous bit of apple fell out of Snow White's mouth. She opened her eyes, lifted up the lid of the coffin and sat up alive and well.

"Oh, dear me, where am I?" she cried.

The Prince answered joyfully, "You are with me." He told her what had happened, adding, "Snow

White, I love you better than anyone in the whole wide world. Will you come with me to my father's palace and be my wife?"

Snow White consented and went with him, and the marriage was celebrated with great pomp and splendor.

Now Snow White's wicked stepmother was one of the guests invited to the wedding feast. When she had dressed herself very splendidly for the occasion, she went to the mirror, and said:

> Mirror, mirror, on the wall,
> Who is fairest of us all?

and the mirror answered:

> You are fair, my Queen, 'tis true,
> But the Prince's bride is fairer far than you.

When the wicked woman heard these words she was beside herself with rage and mortification. At first she didn't want to go to the wedding, but at the same time she felt she would never be happy till she had seen the young Queen.

As she entered, Snow White recognized her and nearly fainted with fear. But red-hot iron shoes had been prepared especially for the wicked old Queen, and she was made to get into them and dance till she fell down dead.

JAKOB AND WILHELM GRIMM, TRANSLATED BY MAY SELLAR

THE TINDERBOX

A SOLDIER CAME marching along the highroad—Left, right! Left, right! He had his knapsack on his back and a sword by his side, for he had been to the wars and was now returning home. An old witch met him on the road. She was very ugly to look at, for her underlip hung down close to her chest.

"Good evening, soldier!" she said. "What a fine sword and knapsack you are wearing! You are quite a soldier! You ought to have as much money as you are able to carry!"

"Thank you, old witch," said the soldier.

"Do you see that great tree?" said the witch, pointing to a tree beside them. "It is hollow within. You must climb up to the top, and then you will see a hole through which you can let yourself down into the tree. I will tie a rope around your waist so I can pull you up again when you call."

"What shall I do down there?" asked the soldier.

"Get money!" answered the witch. "Listen! When you reach the bottom of the tree you will find yourself

in a large hall. It is light, for there are more than three hundred lamps burning there. Then you will see three doors, which you can open—the keys are in the locks. If you go into the first room, you will see a great chest in the middle of the floor with a dog sitting upon it; he has eyes as large as saucers, but you needn't trouble about him. I will give you my blue-checked apron, which you must spread out on the floor. Then go back quickly and pick up the dog and set him upon it. Open the chest and take as much money as you like. It is all copper there. If you would rather have silver, you must go into the next room, where there is a dog with eyes as large as mill wheels. But don't take any notice of him. Just set him upon my apron and help yourself to the money. If you prefer gold, you can get that too, as much as you can carry, if you go into the third room. But the dog that guards the chest there has eyes as large as the Round Tower at Copenhagen! He is a savage dog, I can tell you. But you needn't be afraid of him, either. Put him on my apron and he won't touch you. Then you can take as much gold out of the chest as you like!"

"Come, this is not bad!" said the soldier. "But what am I to give you, old witch, for surely you are not doing this for nothing?"

"Yes, I am!" replied the witch. "For me you shall bring nothing but an old tinderbox which my grandmother forgot last time she was down there."

"Well then, tie the rope around my waist right now!" said the soldier.

"Here it is," said the witch, "and here is my blue-checked apron."

Then the soldier climbed up the tree, let himself down through the hole and found himself standing, as the witch had said, in the large hall where more than three hundred lamps were burning.

Well, he opened the first door. There sat the dog glaring at him with eyes as big as saucers. "You are a fine fellow!" said the soldier and, putting him on the witch's apron, took as much copper as his pockets could hold.

Then he shut the chest, put the dog on it again and went into the second room. Sure enough, there sat the dog with eyes as large as mill wheels. "You had better not look at me so hard!" said the soldier. "Your eyes will pop out of their sockets!"

He set the dog on the apron. When he saw all the silver in the chest, he threw away the copper he had taken and filled his pockets and knapsack with nothing but silver.

Then he went into the third room. Horrors! The dog had two eyes as large as the Round Tower at Copenhagen, spinning around in his head like wheels.

"Good evening!" said the soldier and saluted, for he had never seen a dog like this before. But when he had examined him more closely, he thought: Now then,

I've had enough of this, and put him down on the floor on the apron and opened the chest. What a heap of gold there was! With that he could buy up the whole town and all the sugar pigs, all the tin soldiers, whips and rocking horses in the entire world. So he threw away the silver with which he had filled his pockets and knapsack, and filled them with gold instead—yes, his pockets, his knapsack, cap and boots even, so that he could hardly walk. Now he was rich indeed. He put the dog back on the chest, shut the door and called through the tree, "Pull me up again, old witch!"

"Have you the tinderbox also?" asked the witch.

"Botheration!" said the soldier. "I had clean forgotten it!" And he went back and fetched it.

The witch pulled him up, and there he stood again on the highroad, with pockets, knapsack, cap and boots filled with gold. "What do you want to do with the tinderbox?" asked the soldier.

"That doesn't matter to you," replied the witch. "You have your money. Give me my tinderbox."

"We'll see!" said the soldier. "Tell me at once what you want to do with it, or I will cut off your head!"

"No!" screamed the witch.

The soldier immediately cut off her head. That was the end of her! But he tied up his gold in her apron, slung the bundle over his shoulder, put the tinderbox in his pocket and set out toward the town.

It was a splendid town! He went straight to the

finest inn and ordered the best room and his favorite
dinner, for he had so much money he really was rich.

It certainly occurred to the servant who had to clean
his boots that they were astonishingly old for such a
rich man. But that was because he had not yet bought
new ones. The next day he appeared in a respectable
pair and fine clothes. Instead of a soldier he had become a noble lord, and people told him about the
grand doings of the town and about the King and what
a beautiful princess his daughter was.

"How can one see her?" asked the soldier.

"She is never to be seen at all!" they told him. "She
lives in a great copper castle, surrounded by many
walls and towers! No one except the King and Queen
may go in or out, for it is prophesied that she will
marry a common soldier, and the King is not happy
with the idea."

I should very much like to see her, thought the
soldier; but he could not get permission.

Now he lived most gaily, went to the theater, drove
in the King's garden and gave the poor a great deal of
money, which was quite nice of him. He remembered
so well how hard it is not to have a penny in the world.
Being so rich, he wore fine clothes and made many
friends, who said that he was an excellent man, a
real nobleman. The soldier liked that. But as he was
always spending money and never made any more, at
last the day came when he had nothing left but two

shillings, and he had to leave the beautiful rooms in which he had been living and move into a little attic under the roof, clean his own boots and mend them with a darning needle. None of his friends came to visit him there, for there were too many stairs to climb.

It was a dark evening and he could not even buy a light. But all at once it came to him that there was a little end of tinder in the tinderbox which he had taken from the hollow tree. He found the box with the tinder in it; but just as he struck a spark out of the tinderbox, the door burst open, and the dog he had seen down in the tree—with eyes as large as saucers—stood before him and said, "What does my lord command?"

"Do you mean what you say?" exclaimed the soldier. "This is a pretty fine tinderbox, if I can get whatever I want. Get me money!" he cried to the dog, and presto! he was off and back, holding a great purse of money in his mouth.

Now the soldier knew what a precious tinderbox he had. If he rubbed once, the dog that sat on the chest of copper appeared. If he rubbed twice, there came the dog that watched over the silver chest. If he rubbed three times, the one that guarded the gold appeared. So the soldier moved back to his beautiful rooms and appeared again in splendid clothes. All his friends immediately came to see him and paid him great court.

One night he thought: It is very strange that no person can see the Princess. They say she is very pretty, but what's the use of that if she has to sit forever in the great copper castle with all the towers? I must manage to see her somehow. Where is my tinderbox? He struck a spark, and presto! there appeared the dog with eyes as large as saucers.

"It is the middle of the night, I know," said the soldier, "but I should very much like to see the Princess for a moment."

The dog was already outside the door, and before the soldier could look around, in he came with the Princess. She was lying asleep on the dog's back, and was so beautiful that anyone could see she was a real princess. The soldier could not refrain from kissing her—he was such a true soldier. Then the dog ran back with the Princess. When it was morning, and the King and Queen were drinking tea, the Princess said she had had such a very strange dream about a dog and a soldier. She had ridden on the dog's back, and the soldier had kissed her.

"That is certainly a fine story," said the Queen. But the next night one of the ladies-in-waiting was sent to watch at the Princess' bed, to see if it was only a dream or if it had actually happened.

The soldier had an overpowering longing to see the Princess again, so the dog went to the castle in the middle of the night, picked her up and ran back as fast as he could. But the lady-in-waiting followed them. When she saw them disappear into a large house, she made a great cross on the door with a piece of chalk. Then she went home to bed, and the dog went back also with the Princess. But when he saw that a cross had been made on the door where the soldier lived, he took a piece of chalk and cleverly made crosses on all the doors in the town, so that the lady-in-waiting would not find the right house.

Early next morning, the King, Queen, ladies-in-waiting and officers came to see where the Princess had been. "There it is!" said the King, when he saw the first door with a cross on it.

"No, there it is, my dear!" said the Queen, when she saw a door with a cross.

"But here is one, and there is another!" they exclaimed, for wherever they looked there were crosses on the doors. Then they realized that the sign would not help them in their search.

But the Queen was a very clever woman who could do a great deal more than just drive about in a coach. She took her large golden scissors, cut up a piece of silk and made a pretty little bag of it. This she filled with the finest buckwheat grains and tied it around the Princess' neck. When this was done she cut a little hole in the bag so the grains would trickle along the road wherever the Princess went.

That night, the dog came again, took the Princess on his back and ran with her to the soldier, who had fallen so much in love with her that he would have given anything to be a prince so that he might have her for his wife.

The dog did not notice that the grains left a trail right from the castle to the soldier's window, where he ran up the wall with the Princess.

Next morning the King and the Queen saw plainly where their daughter had been and they arrested the soldier and put him into prison.

There he sat. Oh, how dark and dull it was there! And, besides, they had told him, "Tomorrow you are to be hanged." Hearing that did not exactly cheer him, and he had left his tinderbox at the inn.

Next morning he could see, through the iron grating in front of his little window, the people hurrying out of the town to see him hanged. He heard the drums and saw the soldiers marching. All the people were running to and fro. Just below his window there appeared a shoemaker's apprentice, wearing a leather apron and shoes. He was skipping along so merrily that one of his shoes flew off and fell against the wall just at the place where the soldier was peeping through the iron grating.

"Oh, shoemaker's boy, you needn't be in such a hurry!" said the soldier to him. "There's nothing going on till I arrive. If you will run back to the house where I lived, and fetch me my tinderbox, I will give you four shillings. But you must run like the wind."

The shoemaker's boy was very eager to earn four shillings, so he ran and brought the tinderbox to the soldier quickly.

Outside the town a great scaffold had been erected, and all around it were standing soldiers and hundreds of thousands of people. The King and Queen were sitting on a magnificent throne opposite the judges and the whole council.

When the soldier was standing on the top of the ladder and they wanted to put the rope around his neck, he said that one innocent request was always granted to a poor criminal before he died. He would so much like to smoke a small pipe of tobacco. It would be his last pipe in this world.

The King could not refuse him this, and so he took out his tinderbox and rubbed it once, twice and three times. And lo and behold! There stood the three dogs —the first with eyes as large as saucers, the second with eyes as large as mill wheels and the third with eyes as large as the Round Tower at Copenhagen.

"Save me! Don't let them hang me!" cried the soldier. Thereupon the dogs fell upon the judges and the entire council, seized some by the legs, others by their noses, and threw them high into the air.

"I won't stand this!" said the King. But the largest dog seized him, too, and the Queen as well, and threw them up in the air after the others. This frightened the soldiers, and the people cried, "Good soldier, you shall be our King, and marry the beautiful Princess!"

Then they put the soldier into the King's coach, and the three dogs danced in front, crying "Hurrah!" And boys whistled and soldiers presented arms.

The Princess came out of the copper castle and became Queen and that pleased her very much. The wedding festivities lasted for eight days, and the dogs sat at the table and made eyes at everyone.

HANS CHRISTIAN ANDERSEN, ANDREW LANG COLLECTION

LITTLE FIR TREE

THERE WAS once a pretty little fir tree in a forest. It grew in an excellent spot, for it could get sun and plenty of air, and all around it grew many tall companions, pines as well as firs. The little fir tree's greatest desire was to grow up. It did not care about the warm sun and the fresh air or notice the peasant children who ran about chattering when they came out to gather wild strawberries and raspberries. Often they could fill a whole basketful and would string them up on a straw. Sometimes they would sit down by the little fir tree and exclaim, "What a sweet little one this is!" The tree did not like that at all.

By the next year it had grown a whole ring wider and the year after that another ring more, for you can always tell a fir tree's age from its rings.

"Oh, if I were only as tall as the others," sighed the little fir tree, "then I could stretch my branches far and wide and look out upon the great world! The birds would build their nests in my branches, and when the wind blew I would bow politely just like the others!"

The fir tree took no pleasure in the sunshine nor in the birds nor in the rosy clouds that sailed over it at dawn and at sunset. Then the winter came and the ground was covered with sparkling white snow. Sometimes a hare would come and leap right over the little fir tree. This annoyed it very much. But when two more winters had passed, the fir tree was so tall that the hare had to run around it. "Ah, to grow and grow, and become big and old! That is the only pleasure in life," thought the tree.

In the autumn, woodcutters used to come and chop down some of the tallest trees. This happened every year, and the young fir tree would shiver as the magnificent trees fell crashing to the ground, their branches hewn off and the great trunks left bare, so that they were almost unrecognizable. Then they were loaded onto wagons and dragged out of the forest by horses.

"Where are they going? What will happen to them?" thought the fir tree.

In the spring, when the swallows and storks came, the fir tree asked them, "Do you know where they were taken? Have you met them?"

The swallows knew nothing about them, but a stork nodded his head thoughtfully, saying, "I think I know. I saw many new ships with splendid masts as I flew from Egypt. I imagine those must be the trees you mean! They had the scent of fir about them. Ah, they were grand, grand!"

"Oh, if I were only big enough to sail over the sea too! What sort of thing is the sea? What does it look like?" asked the fir tree.

"It would take much too long to tell you all that," said the stork, and off he went.

"Rejoice in your youth," said the sunbeams, "rejoice in the sweet growing time, in the young life within you." And the wind kissed it and the dew wept tears over it, but the fir tree did not understand.

Toward Christmastime, quite a few of the little trees were cut down, some not as big as the young fir tree or just the same age, and now it had no peace or rest for longing to be away. These young trees, which were chosen for their beauty, did not have their branches chopped off. They were stacked onto carts and dragged out of the forest by horses.

"Where are those going?" asked the fir tree. "They

are no bigger than I, and one was even much smaller! Why do they keep their branches? Where are they being taken?"

"We know! We know!" twittered the sparrows. "Down there in the city we have peeked in at windows, we know where they go! They are set up in the greatest splendor and magnificence you can imagine! We have looked in windows and seen them planted in the middle of a warm room and adorned with the most beautiful things—golden apples, sweets, toys and hundreds of candles."

"And then?" asked the fir tree, trembling in every limb with eagerness. "What happens then?"

"Oh, we haven't seen anything more than that. But that was simply wonderful!"

"Am I, too, destined for the same brilliant future?" wondered the fir tree excitedly. "That is even better than sailing over the sea! I am sick with longing. If it were only Christmas! I am as tall and grown up now as the ones that were taken away last year. If I were only in that warm room with all that splendor and magnificence! Oh! I am pining away! I really don't know what's the matter with me!"

"Rejoice in us," said the air and sunshine, "rejoice in your fresh youth out here in the open!"

But the fir tree took no notice, and just grew and grew. There it stood fresh and green in winter and in summer, and those who saw it said, "What a beautiful tree!" And the following Christmas it was the first to be cut down. The axe went deep into the core and the tree fell to the ground with a sigh. It felt bruised and faint. It could not think of happiness, it was sad at leaving its home, the place where it had grown up. It knew, too, that it would never again see its dear companions or the shrubs and flowers, perhaps not even the birds. Altogether the parting was not pleasant.

When the tree came to, it found itself packed in a yard with other trees, and a man was saying, "This one is perfect. This is the one we will take."

Then came two footmen in livery who carried the fir tree into a beautiful big room. There were pictures hanging upon the walls, and near the Dutch stove stood great Chinese vases with lions on their lids; there were armchairs, silk-covered sofas, large tables laden with picture books and toys worth lots and lots of money—at least so the children said. The fir tree was placed in a great tub filled with sand, but no one could see that it was a tub, for it was covered with greenery and stood on a gaily colored carpet.

How the tree trembled! What was coming now? Young ladies and men servants began to decorate it. On its branches they hung little baskets cut out of bright paper, each full of sugarplums. Gilded apples and nuts hung down as if they grew there, and over a hundred red, blue and white candles were fastened among the branches. Dolls as lifelike as human beings

—the fir tree had never seen any before—were suspended among the branches, and at the top was fixed a gold tinsel star. It was gorgeous, quite gorgeous! "Tonight," they all said, "tonight it will be lighted!"

"Ah," thought the tree, "if only it were evening! If only the candles were already lit! What will happen then? I wonder whether the trees will come from the forest to see me, or if the sparrows will peek in at the windows? Am I to stand here decked out thus through winter and summer?"

It was not a bad guess, but the fir tree had real barkache from sheer longing, and barkache in trees is just as bad as headache in human beings.

At last the candles were lighted. What glittering splendor! The tree quivered so much in all its branches that one of the candles singed a twig. "Take care!" cried one of the young ladies, and they extinguished that candle.

Now the tree did not even dare to quiver. It was really terrible! It was so afraid of losing any of its ornaments and it was quite bewildered by the radiance.

Then the folding doors were opened, and a crowd of children rushed in, so excitedly it seemed as if they would overturn the whole tree, while the older people followed more calmly. The children stood perfectly still, but only for a moment, and then they started to shout with excitement and dance around the tree, and snatch off one present after another.

"What are they doing?" thought the tree. "What is going to happen?" The candles burned low on the branches, and were put out one by one, and then the children were given permission to plunder the tree. They rushed at it so that all its branches creaked. If it had not been fastened to the ceiling by the gold star, it would have toppled over.

The children danced around with all their splendid toys, and no one looked at the tree except the old nurse, who came and poked among the branches just to see if by chance a fig or an apple had been forgotten.

"A story! A story!" cried the children, and dragged a stout little man to the tree. He sat down beneath it, saying, "Here we are in the greenwood, and the tree will be delighted to listen! But I am only going to tell one story. Shall it be Chicken Little or Humpty Dumpty, who fell downstairs and yet won great honors and married a princess?"

"Chicken Little!" cried some. "Humpty Dumpty!" cried others. There was absolute bedlam! Only the fir tree kept silent, and thought, "Am I not to be in it? Am I to have nothing to do with it?"

But it had already been in it and played out its part. And the man told them about Humpty Dumpty, who fell downstairs and married a princess. The children clapped their hands and cried, "Another, another!" They wanted the story of Chicken Little too, but they had to be satisfied with Humpty Dumpty. The fir tree stood quite astonished and thoughtful. The birds in the forest had never related anything like that. "Humpty Dumpty fell downstairs and yet married a princess! Yes, that is the way of the world!" thought the tree, and was sure it must be true, because such a nice man had told the story. "Well, who knows? Perhaps I shall fall downstairs and marry a princess." And it rejoiced, thinking that next day it would be decked out again with candles and toys, tinsel and fruit. "Tomorrow I shall quiver again with excitement. I shall enjoy all my splendor. Tomorrow I shall hear Humpty Dumpty again, and perhaps Chicken Little, too." And the tree stood silent and thoughtful through the night.

Next morning the servants came in. "Now the decorating will begin again," thought the tree. But they dragged it out of the room and up the stairs to the attic. There they put it in a dark corner where no ray of light could penetrate. "What does this mean?" said the tree. "What am I to do here? What am I to hear?" And it leaned against the wall and thought and thought. There was time enough for that, for days and nights went by, and no one came up. At last when someone did come, it was only to put some big boxes into the corner. Now the tree was so hidden it seemed as if it had been completely forgotten.

"It is winter outdoors now," thought the fir tree. "The ground is hard and covered with snow. They cannot plant me at this time, and that is why I am staying here under cover till the spring. How thoughtful they are! Only I wish it were not so terribly dark and lonely here; not even a little hare! It was so nice out in the forest when the snow lay on the ground and the hare raced past me; yes, even when he leaped over me, but I didn't like it then. The loneliness up here is more than I can stand."

"Squeak, squeak!" said a little mouse, scampering out, followed by a second. They sniffed at the fir tree and then crept between its boughs. "It's frightfully cold," said the little mice. "How nice it is to be here! Don't you think so too, you old fir tree?"

"I'm not at all old," said the tree. "There are many much older than I am."

"Where do you come from?" asked the mice, "and what do you know?" They were extremely inquisitive. "Do tell us about the most beautiful place in the world. Is that where you come from? Have you been in the storeroom, where cheeses lie on the shelves and hams hang from the ceiling, where one dances on tallow candles and where one goes in thin and comes out fat?"

"I know nothing about that," said the tree. "But I know the forest, where the sun shines and the birds sing." And then it told them about its young days, and the little mice had never heard anything like that before. "Oh," they said, "how much you have seen! How happy you must have been!"

"I?" said the fir tree and then thought it over.

"Yes, on the whole those were very happy times." But it went on to tell them about Christmas Eve, when it had been adorned with sweets and candles.

"Oh," said the little mice, "how lucky you have been, you old fir tree!"

"I'm not at all old," said the tree. "I just came out of the forest this winter. I am just a little backward, perhaps, in my growth."

"How beautifully you tell stories!" said the little mice. And the next evening they came with four others, who wanted to hear the tree's story, and it told still more, for it remembered everything so clearly and said, "Those were happy times! But they may come again. Humpty Dumpty fell downstairs, and yet he married a princess. Perhaps I shall also marry a princess!" And then it thought of a pretty little birch tree that grew out in the forest and it seemed to the fir tree that it was a real princess, and a very beautiful one, too.

"Who is Humpty Dumpty?" asked the little mice.

And then the tree told the whole story. It could remember every single word, and the little mice were ready to leap to the topmost branch out of sheer joy! The next night many more mice came, and on Sunday even two rats appeared; but they did not care about the story, and that troubled the little mice, for now they thought less of it too.

"Is that the only story you know?" asked the rats.

"The only one," answered the tree. "I heard that on

my happiest evening, but I did not realize then how happy I was."

"That's a very dull story. Don't you know one about bacon or tallow candles? A storeroom story?"

"No," said the tree.

"Then we are much obliged to you," said the rats, and they went back to their friends.

At last the little mice went also, and the tree said, sighing, "Really it was very pleasant when the lively little mice sat around and listened while I told them stories. But now that's over too. Perhaps I should think of the time when I shall be taken out of here."

But when would that happen? Well, it happened one morning when the servants came to tidy up the attic. The boxes were set aside. The tree was brought out and thrown rather roughly on the floor. Then a servant dragged it off downstairs, where there was daylight once more.

"Now life begins again!" exclaimed the tree. It felt the fresh air, the first sunbeams, and there it was out in the yard! Everything happened so quickly that the tree forgot to think of itself, there was so much to see all around. The yard opened on a garden full of flow- ers; the roses were so fragrant and pretty, hanging over a little trellis, the lime trees were in blossom, and the swallows flew about, saying, "Quirre-virre-vit, my love has come home." But it was not the fir tree they meant.

"Now I am really going to live," said the tree

joyfully, stretching out its branches wide. Alas! they were dry, withered and yellow, and it was lying in a corner among weeds and nettles. The golden star was still fastened to its top, and it glittered in the bright sunlight. Some of the merry children who had danced so gaily around the tree at Christmas were playing in the yard. One of the little ones ran up and tore off the gold star. "Look what was left on the ugly old fir tree!" he cried, and stamped on the branches so that they crackled under his feet.

And the tree looked at all the splendor and beauty of the flowers in the garden, and then looked at itself, and wished that it had been left lying in the dark corner of the attic. It thought of its fresh green youth in the woods, of the merry Christmas Eve and of the little mice who had listened so happily to the story of Humpty Dumpty. "Too late! Too late!" thought the discarded tree. "If only I had enjoyed them while I could. Now all is over and gone."

And a servant came and cut the tree into small pieces; there was quite a stack of them. A huge fire blazed up, and the logs flickered brightly under a great copper vat. The tree sighed deeply, and each sigh was like a pistol shot. The children who were playing there ran up and sat in front of the fire, gazing at it and crying, "Piff! Puff! Bang!" But for each crack, which was really a sigh, the tree was thinking of a summer's day in the forest, or of a star-filled winter's night there;

it thought of Christmas Eve and of Humpty Dumpty, which was the only story it had heard, or could tell, and then the tree became a heap of ashes.

The children played on in the garden, and the youngest had on his breast the golden star which the tree had worn on the happiest evening of its life. Now that was past—and the tree had passed away—and the story too, ended and done with.

And that's the way with all stories!

HANS CHRISTIAN ANDERSEN, ANDREW LANG COLLECTION

THE BRONZE RING

ONCE UPON a time in a certain country there lived a King whose palace was surrounded by a spacious garden. And though the gardeners were many and the soil was good, this garden yielded neither flowers nor fruits, not even grass nor shady trees.

The King was in despair about it when a wise old man said to him: "Your gardeners do not understand their business. But what can you expect of men whose fathers were cobblers and carpenters? How could they have learned to garden?"

"You are quite right," cried the King.

"Therefore," continued the old man, "send for a gardener whose father and grandfather have been gardeners before him. Soon your garden will be full of green grass and gay flowers, and you will enjoy its delicious fruit."

So the King sent messengers to every town, village and hamlet in his dominions to look for a gardener whose forefathers had been gardeners also. And, after forty days, one was found.

"Come with us and be gardener to the King," the messengers said to him.

"How can I go to the King," asked the gardener, "a poor wretch like me?"

"That is of no consequence," they answered. "Here are new clothes for you and your family."

"But I owe money to several people."

"We will pay your debts," they said.

So he allowed himself to be persuaded and he went away with the messengers, taking his wife and his son with him. The King, delighted to have found a real gardener, entrusted him with the care of his grounds. The man found no difficulty in making the royal garden produce flowers and fruit, and at the end of a year the park was a mass of glowing colors. In gratitude, the King showered gifts upon his new servant.

The gardener's son was a very handsome young man with most agreeable manners. Every day, he carried the best fruit from the garden to the King and all the loveliest flowers to his daughter. Now this Princess, who was wonderfully pretty, was just sixteen years old, and the King was beginning to think it was time she should be married.

"My dear child," said he, "you are of an age to take a husband, therefore I am thinking of marrying you to the son of my prime minister."

"Father," replied the Princess, "I will never marry the son of the minister."

"Why not?" asked the King.

"Because I love the gardener's son," answered the Princess.

On hearing this the King was at first very angry, and then he wept and sighed and declared that a gardener's son was not worthy of his daughter. But the young Princess was not to be persuaded to change her mind. So the King consulted his ministers.

"This is what you must do," they said. "To get rid of the gardener you must send both suitors to a far distant country. The one who returns first shall marry your daughter."

The King followed this advice. The minister's son was presented with a splendid horse and a purse full of gold pieces, while the gardener's son had only an old lame horse and a purse full of copper money, and everyone thought he would never come back from his hopeless journey.

The day before they started, the Princess met the gardener's son and said to him, "Be brave, and remember always that I love you. Take this purse full of jewels and make the best use you can of them for love of me. Then come home again quickly and ask my father for my hand."

The two suitors left the town together, but the minister's son went off at a gallop on his good horse and very soon was lost to sight behind the distant hills. He traveled on for some days and presently reached a fountain beside which an old woman all in rags sat upon a stone.

"Good day to you, young traveler," said she.

But the minister's son made no reply.

"Have pity upon me, traveler," she said again. "I am dying of hunger, as you see. Three days have I been here, and no one has given me anything."

"Let me alone, old witch," cried the young man, "I can do nothing for you." And so saying he went on his way.

That same evening, the gardener's son rode up to the fountain upon his lame gray horse.

"Good day to you, young traveler," said the beggar woman.

"Good day, good woman," answered he.

"Young traveler, have pity upon me."

"Take my purse, good woman," said he, "and if you wish, ride behind me on my horse, for your legs cannot be very strong."

The old woman did not wait to be asked twice but mounted behind him, and in this style they reached the chief city of a powerful kingdom.

The minister's son was lodged in a grand inn, but the gardener's son and the old woman dismounted at the inn for beggars.

The next day, the gardener's son heard a great noise in the street, and the King's heralds passed, blowing all kinds of instruments and crying: "The King, our master, is old and infirm. He will give a great reward to whosoever will cure him and give him back the strength of his youth."

Then the old beggar woman said to her benefactor, "This is what you must do to obtain the reward which the King promises. Go out of the town by the south gate and there you will find three little dogs of different colors. The first will be white, the second, black, the third, red. You must kill them, burn them separately and gather up the ashes.

"Put the ashes of each dog into a bag of its own color, then go before the door of the palace and cry out, 'A celebrated physician has come from Janina in Albania! He alone can cure the King and give him back the strength of his youth.' The King's physicians will say, 'This is an impostor and not a learned man,' and they will make all sorts of difficulties. But you will overcome them at last and will present yourself before the King.

"You must then demand as much wood as three mules can carry and a great caldron and shut yourself up in a room with the King. When the caldron boils, throw him into it and leave him there until his flesh is completely separated from his bones. Then arrange the bones in their proper places and throw over them the ashes out of the three bags. The King will come back to life and will be just as he was when he was twenty years old.

"For your reward, demand the bronze ring which has the power to grant everything you desire. Go, my son, and do not forget any of my instructions."

The young man followed the old woman's directions. On going out of the town, he found the white, red and black dogs, just as she had said, and he killed and burned them, gathering the ashes into three bags —white, red and black. Then he ran to the palace and cried: "A celebrated physician has just come from Janina in Albania! He alone can cure the King and give him back the strength of his youth."

The physicians at first laughed at the unknown wayfarer, but the King ordered that the stranger be admitted. The gardener's son asked the servants to bring a great caldron and three loads of wood, and very soon the King was boiling away.

Toward midday, the youth arranged the bones in their places and had hardly scattered the dogs' ashes over them before the old King revived and found himself once more young and hearty.

"How can I reward you, young man?" he cried. "Will you take half my treasures?"

"No," said the gardener's son.

"My daughter's hand?"

"No."

"Take half my kingdom!"

"No. Give me only the bronze ring which can instantly grant me anything I wish for."

"Alas!" said the King, "I set great store by that marvelous ring. Nevertheless, you shall have it." And he gave it to him.

The gardener's son went back to say good-bye to the old beggar woman. Then he said, "Bronze ring, obey thy master. Prepare a splendid ship for my journey. Let the hull be of fine gold, the masts of silver and the sails of brocade. Let the crew consist of twelve young men of noble appearance, dressed like kings. St. Nicholas will be at the helm. As for the cargo, let it be diamonds, rubies, emeralds and garnets."

And immediately such a ship appeared upon the sea. Stepping on board, he set forth on his journey. Presently he arrived at a great town and established himself in a splendid palace. After several days, he met his rival, the minister's son, who had spent all his money

and was reduced to being a carrier of dust and rubbish. The gardener's son said to him: "Tell me, what is your name, what is your family and from what country do you come?"

"I am the son of the prime minister of a great nation, and yet you see to what a degrading occupation I am reduced."

"Listen to me. Though I don't know anything more than that about you, I am willing to help you. I will give you a ship to take you back to your own country, but only upon one condition," said the son of the gardener.

"Whatever it may be, I accept it willingly."

"Follow me to my palace."

The minister's son followed the rich stranger, whom he had not recognized. When they reached the palace, the gardener's son made a sign to his slaves, who completely undressed the newcomer.

"Make this ring red hot," commanded the master, "and mark the man with it upon his back."

The slaves obeyed him.

"Now, young man," said the rich stranger, "I am going to give you a vessel which will take you back to your own country." And, going out, he took the bronze ring and said: "Bronze ring, obey thy master. Prepare for me a ship of which the half-rotten timbers shall be painted black. Let the sails be rags and the sailors infirm and sickly. One shall have lost a leg, another an arm, and most of them shall be covered with scars. Go, and let my orders be executed."

The minister's son embarked in this old vessel and, thanks to favorable winds, at length reached his own country. In spite of the pitiable condition in which he returned he was received joyfully.

"I am the first to come back," said he to the King. "Now fulfill your promise and give me the Princess in marriage."

So they began to prepare the wedding festivities. And the poor Princess was sorrowful and angry enough about it.

The next morning, at daybreak, a wonderful ship with every sail set came to anchor before the town. The King happened that moment to be at the palace window.

"What strange ship is this," he cried, "that has a golden hull, silver masts and silken sails, and who are the young men like princes who man it? Do I not see St. Nicholas at the helm? Go at once and invite the captain of the ship to come to the palace." Very soon, in came an enchantingly handsome young man, dressed with rich silk ornamented with pearls and diamonds.

"Young man," said the King, "you are welcome, whoever you may be. Do me the favor to be my guest as long as you remain in my capital."

"Many thanks, sire," replied the captain. "I accept your offer."

"My daughter is about to be married," said the King. "Will you give her away?"

"I shall be charmed, sire."

Soon after, in came the Princess and her betrothed.

"Why, how is this?" cried the young captain. "Would you marry this charming Princess to such a man?"

"But he is my prime minister's son!"

"What does that matter? I cannot give your daughter away. The man she is betrothed to is one of my servants."

"Your servant?"

"Certainly! I met him in a distant town working as a dustman and rubbish collector. I had pity on him and engaged him as one of my servants."

"It is impossible!" cried the King.

"Do you wish me to prove what I say? This young man returned in a vessel which I fitted out for him, an unseaworthy ship with a black battered hull. The sailors were infirm and crippled."

"It is quite true," said the King.

"It is false!" cried the minister's son. "I do not know this man."

"Sire," said the young captain, "order him to be stripped and see if the mark of my ring is not branded upon his back."

The minister's son, to save himself from such an indignity, admitted the story was true.

"And now, sire," said the young captain, "guess who I am."

"I recognize you," said the Princess. "You are the gardener's son whom I have always loved, and it is you I wish to marry."

"Young man, you shall be my son-in-law and no one else," cried the King. "The marriage festivities are already begun."

And that very day the gardener's son married the beautiful Princess.

Several months passed. The young couple were as happy as the day was long, and the King was more and more pleased with himself for having acquired such a son-in-law.

But, presently, the gardener's son found it necessary to take a long voyage on his golden ship, and, after embracing his wife tenderly, he embarked.

Now in the outskirts of the capital there lived a wicked man who had spent his entire life in studying the black arts—alchemy, astrology, enchantment and magic. This magician found out one day that the gardener's son had succeeded in marrying the young Princess only through the help of the genies who obeyed the bronze ring.

"I will have that ring," said he to himself. So he went down to the seashore and caught some little red fishes that were wonderfully pretty. Then he went back and, passing before the Princess' window, he began to cry out: "Who wants some pretty little red fishes?"

The Princess heard him and sent out one of her slaves, who said to the old man, "What will you take for your fishes?"

"A bronze ring."

"A bronze ring, old simpleton! And where shall I find one?"

"Under the cushion in the Princess' room."

The slave went back to her mistress. "The old madman will take neither gold nor silver," said she.

"What does he want, then?"

"A bronze ring that is hidden under a cushion in your room."

"Then find the bronze ring and give it to him," said the Princess.

The slave found the bronze ring which the Princess' husband had accidentally left behind. She carried it to the magician, who made off with it at once.

Hardly had he reached his own house when, taking the ring, he said, "Bronze ring, obey thy master. I desire that the golden ship shall turn to black wood and the crew to hideous old men. St. Nicholas shall leave the helm, and the only cargo that it shall carry will be black cats."

And the genies of the bronze ring obeyed him.

Finding himself upon the sea in this miserable condition, the young captain understood someone must have stolen the bronze ring and he lamented his misfortune loudly. But that did him no good. "Alas," he said to himself, "whoever has taken my ring has probably taken my dear wife also. What good will it do to go back to my own country?"

And he sailed about from island to island and from shore to shore. Soon his poverty was so great that he and his crew and the poor black cats had nothing to eat but herbs and roots. After wandering about a long time, they reached an island inhabited by mice. There were mice everywhere—nothing but mice. The black cats, not having been fed for several days, were fearfully hungry and made terrible havoc among the little creatures.

Then the Queen of the Mice held a council. "These cats will certainly eat every one of us," she said, "if the captain of the ship does not shut the ferocious animals up. Let us send the bravest among us to him to ask him this."

Several mice offered themselves for this mission and set out to find the young captain.

"Captain," said they, "go away quickly from our island with your black cats or we shall perish, every mouse of us."

"Willingly," replied the young captain, "upon one condition. Bring me back the bronze ring which some clever magician has stolen from me."

The mice withdrew in great dismay.

"What is to be done?" said the Queen. "How can we find this bronze ring?"

She held a new council, calling in mice from every quarter of the globe, but nobody knew where the bronze ring was.

Suddenly three mice arrived from a far distant country. One was blind; the second, lame; and the third had had her ears cropped.

"Ho, ho, ho!" said the newcomers. "We come from a far distant country."

"Do you know where the bronze ring is which the genies obey?"

"Ho, ho, ho! We know. A wicked man has it. He keeps it in his pocket by day and in his mouth by night."

"Go and take it from him, and bring it back to us as soon as possible," the Queen of the Mice instructed them.

So the three mice made themselves a boat and set sail for the magician's country. When they reached the capital, they landed and ran to the palace, leaving only the blind mouse on the shore to take care of the boat. Then they waited till it was night. The man lay down in bed and put the bronze ring into his mouth, and very soon he was asleep.

"Now, what shall we do?" said the two little mice to each other.

The mouse with the cropped ears found a lamp full

of oil and a bottle full of pepper; so she dipped her tail first in the oil and then in the pepper and held it to the man's nose.

"Achoo! Achoo!" sneezed the man. He did not awaken, but the shock made the bronze ring jump out of his mouth. Quick as a wink, the lame mouse snatched up the precious talisman and carried it off to the boat.

Imagine the despair of the magician when he awoke and the bronze ring was nowhere to be found! But by that time the three mice had set sail with their prize. A favoring breeze was carrying them toward the island where the Queen of the Mice was awaiting them. Naturally they began to talk about their daring rescue of the bronze ring.

"Which of us deserves the most credit?" each cried, all at once.

"I do," said the blind mouse. "Without my watchfulness, our boat certainly would have drifted away to the open sea."

"No, indeed," cried the mouse with the cropped ears, "the credit is mine. Did I not cause the ring to jump out of the magician's mouth?"

"No, it is mine," cried the lame mouse, "for I ran off with the ring."

And from high words they soon came to blows and, alas, while the quarrel was raging, the bronze ring fell into the sea.

"How are we to face our Queen," said the three mice, "when by our folly we have lost the talisman and condemned our people to death by the cats? We cannot go back to our country; let us land on this desert island and there end our miserable lives."

No sooner said than done: the boat reached the island, and the mice landed.

As the blind mouse wandered sadly along the shore, she found a dead fish and was eating it when she felt something very hard. At her cries the other two mice ran up.

"It is the bronze ring! It is the talisman!" they cried joyfully, and, getting into their boat again, they soon reached the mouse island and returned the ring to the captain.

"Bronze ring," commanded the young man, "obey thy master once again. Let my ship appear as it was before."

Immediately the genies of the ring set to work, and the old black vessel became once more the wonderful golden ship with sails of brocade. The sailors, young and handsome again, swiftly ran to the silver masts and the silken ropes, and very soon they set sail for the capital.

Ah! How merrily the sailors sang as they flew over the glassy sea! At last the port was reached.

The captain landed and ran to the palace, where he found the magician asleep. The Princess clasped her husband in a long embrace. The magician tried to escape, but he was seized and bound with the strongest of cords.

The next day the magician was tied to the tail of a mule loaded with nuts and broken into as many pieces as there were nuts upon the mule's back.

HENRI CARNOY, ANDREW LANG COLLECTION

THREE BILLY GOATS GRUFF

ONCE UPON a time there were three Billy Goats and their name was Gruff.

They were going up the mountain to get fat. On their way up, they had to cross a bridge, and under this bridge there lived a Troll, with eyes as big as saucers and a nose as long as a broomstick.

The Billy Goats did not know that the Troll lived there.

First of all came Little Billy Goat Gruff. He went trip-trap, trip-trap, trip-trap over the bridge.

The Troll poked up his head and said, "Who goes trip-trap, trip-trap, trip-trap over my bridge?"

The Little Billy Goat said, "It is I, Little Billy Goat Gruff, and I'm going up the mountain to get fat."

"Oh, no, you're not," said the Troll, "because I'm going to eat you."

"Oh," said Little Billy Goat Gruff, "you wouldn't eat me, would you?—I am so small. Just wait for my brother, Second Billy Goat Gruff, and you eat him. He is much larger than I."

"Very well then," said the Troll, "be off with you." And trip-trap, trip-trap, trip-trap went Little Billy Goat Gruff.

Presently along came Second Billy Goat Gruff, and he went TRIP-TRAP! TRIP-TRAP! TRIP-TRAP! over the bridge.

The Troll poked up his head and said, "Who goes TRIP-TRAP! TRIP-TRAP! TRIP-TRAP! over my bridge?"

The Second Billy Goat Gruff tried to make his voice sound very weak, and he said, "It is I, Second Billy Goat Gruff, and I'm going up the mountain to get fat."

"Oh, no, you're not," said the Troll, "because I'm going to eat you." Then the Second Billy Goat said, "Oh, you wouldn't eat me, would you?—I am so small. You wait for my brother, Great Billy Goat Gruff, and you eat him. He is much larger than I."

"Very well then," said the Troll, "be off with you." And TRIP-TRAP! TRIP-TRAP! TRIP-TRAP! went Second Billy Goat Gruff.

Last of all came Great Billy Goat Gruff. Oh, he was

a great, large fellow. His great shaggy fur hung down to his feet, he had two large horns coming out of his forehead. When he walked, the bridge shook. He went TRIP-TROP! TRIP-TROP! TRIP-TROP! "Oh!" went the bridge—he was so heavy.

The Troll poked up his head and said, "Who goes TRIP-TROP! TRIP-TROP! TRIP-TROP! over my bridge?"

The Great Billy Goat stood there and said, "It is I, Great Billy Goat Gruff, and I'm going up the mountain to get fat."

"Oh, no, you're not," said the Troll, "because I am going to eat you."

"Come along, then," said Great Billy Goat Gruff, and up came the Troll. The Great Billy Goat caught him with his two horns and tossed him way up into the sky.

That was the end of the Troll; and TRIP-TROP! TRIP-TROP! TRIP-TROP! away went Great Billy Goat Gruff over the bridge.

By this time the three Billy Goats are so fat that they couldn't come back across the bridge even if they wanted to. So—

Snip, snap, snout
My tale is out.

PETER C. ASBJÖRNSEN AND JÖRGEN E. MOE,
RETOLD BY VERONICA S. HUTCHINSON

THE BOY WHO KEPT A SECRET

ONCE UPON a time there lived a poor widow who had one son. At first sight you would not have thought that he was different from a thousand other little boys. Then you noticed that by his side hung a scabbard, and as the boy grew bigger the scabbard was growing bigger, too. The sword which belonged in the scabbard was found sticking out of the ground in the garden, and every day the boy pulled it up to see if it would go into the scabbard. But though the scabbard was plainly becoming longer, it would be some time before the two fitted together.

However, there came a day finally when the sword slipped into the scabbard quite easily. The child was so delighted he could hardly believe his eyes, but, pleased though he was, he determined not to tell anyone about it, particularly not his mother, who never could keep anything from her neighbors.

Still, in spite of his resolutions, he could not hide altogether that something had happened. When he went in to breakfast later his mother asked him what was the matter. "Oh, Mother, I had such a nice dream

See page 362

last night," he said, "but I can't tell it to anybody."

"You can tell it to me," she answered.

"No, Mother, I can't tell it to anybody," returned the boy, "till it comes true."

"I want to know what it was, and know it I will," she cried. "I will beat you till you tell me."

But it was no use; neither words nor blows would get the secret out of the boy. When she stopped beating him, the child ran into the garden and knelt weeping beside his sword. It was working around and around all by itself, and anyone except the boy trying to catch hold of it would have been badly cut. But the moment he stretched out his hand it stopped turning and slid quietly into the scabbard.

For a long time the child sat sobbing, and the noise was heard by the King as he was driving by. "Go and see who is crying so," he said to one of his servants.

The servant returned saying, "Your Majesty, a young boy is sobbing because his mother has beaten him."

"Bring him to me at once," commanded the monarch, "and tell him that it is the King who sends for him. Tell him the King has never cried in all his life and cannot bear anyone else to do so." On receiving this message, the boy dried his tears and went with the servant to the royal carriage.

"Will you be my son?" asked the King.

"Yes, if my mother will let me," answered the boy. And the King sent his servant for the mother and told her that if she gave her boy to him, he would live in the palace and marry the King's prettiest daughter as soon as he was a man.

The widow's anger now turned to joy, and she kissed the King's hand. "I hope you will be more obedient to His Majesty than you were to me," she said, and the boy shrank from her half-frightened. But when she had gone back to her cottage, he asked the King if he might fetch something that he had left in the garden. Given the permission, he pulled up his sword, which he slid into the scabbard. Then he climbed into the coach and was driven away.

After they had gone some distance the King said, "Why were you crying so bitterly in the garden when we came along?"

"Because my mother had been beating me," replied the boy.

"And why did she do that?" asked the King.

"Because I would not tell her my dream."

"And why wouldn't you tell it to her?"

"Because I will never tell it to anyone till it comes true," answered the boy.

"And won't you tell it to me either?" asked the King in surprise.

"No, not even to you, Your Majesty."

"Oh, I am sure you will when we get home," said the King, smiling, and he talked to him about other things till they came to the palace.

"I have brought you such a nice present," he said to his daughters. And as the boy was very charming, they were delighted to see him and gave him all their best toys.

"You must not spoil him," observed the King one day, when he had been watching the children playing together. "He has a secret which he won't tell to anyone."

"He will tell me," answered the eldest Princess. But the boy only shook his head.

"He will tell me," said the second girl.

"Not I," replied the boy.

"He will tell me," cried the youngest, who was the prettiest, too.

"I will tell nobody till it comes true," said the boy, as he had said before, "and I will beat anybody who asks me."

The King was very sorry when he heard this. He loved the boy dearly, but he thought it would never do to keep anyone near him who would not do as he was bidden. So he commanded his servants to take him away and not let him enter the palace until he had come to his right senses.

The sword clanked loudly as the boy was led off, but the child said nothing, though he was very unhappy at being treated so when he had done nothing wrong. However, the servants were very kind to him, and their children brought him fruit and all sorts of nice things. Soon he grew cheerful again and lived among them for many years till he reached his seventeenth birthday.

Meanwhile, the two eldest Princesses had become women and had married powerful kings who ruled over great countries across the sea. The youngest one was also old enough to be married, but she was very particular and turned up her nose at every young prince who sought her hand.

One day she was sitting in the palace, feeling rather bored and lonely, and suddenly she began to wonder what the servants were doing and whether it was not more amusing down in their quarters. The King was at his council and the Queen was ill in bed, so there was no one to stop the Princess, and she hastily ran across the gardens to the houses where the servants lived. Outside one of them she noticed a youth who was handsomer than any prince she had ever seen, and in a moment she knew him to be the little boy she had once played with.

"Tell me your secret and I will marry you," she said to him, but the boy only gave her the beating he had promised her long ago, when she asked him the same question.

The girl was very angry, besides being hurt, and ran home to complain to her father.

"If he had a thousand lives, I would take them all," swore the King.

That very day a gallows was built outside the town. The people crowded around to see the execution of the young man who had dared to beat the King's daughter.

The prisoner, his hands tied behind his back, was brought to the scene by the hangman. His sentence was being read by the judge, amid deathly silence, when the sword clanked against his side.

Suddenly a great noise was heard and a golden coach with a white flag waving from the window rumbled over the stones. It stopped underneath the gallows, and from it stepped the King of the Magyars, the ruler of Hungary. He begged that the life of the boy might be spared.

"Sir, he has beaten my daughter, who merely asked him to tell her his secret. I cannot pardon that," answered the Princess' father.

"Give him to me. I'm sure he will tell me the secret. If not, I have a daughter who is like the Morning Star, and he is sure to tell it to her."

The sword clanked again, and the King said angrily, "Well, if you want him so much you can have him; only never let me see his face again." And he made a sign to the hangman.

The cords were removed from the young man's wrists, and he took his seat in the golden coach beside the King of the Magyars. Then the coachman whipped up his horses, and they set out for Buda.

The King talked very pleasantly for a few miles, and when he thought that his new companion was quite at ease with him, he asked him what was the secret which had brought him into such trouble. "That I cannot tell you," answered the youth, "until the day it comes true."

"You will tell my daughter, I am sure," said the King, smiling.

"I will tell nobody," replied the youth, and as he spoke the sword clanked loudly.

The King said not another word, but he was confident that his daughter's beauty would get the secret from him.

The journey to Buda was long, and it was several days before they arrived there. The beautiful Princess happened to be picking roses in the garden when her father's coach drove up.

"Oh, what a handsome youth! Have you brought him from Fairyland?" she cried, when they all stood upon the marble steps in front of the castle.

"I have brought him from the gallows," answered the King, rather vexed at his daughter's words, as never before had she consented to give attention to any man.

"I don't care where you brought him from," said the spoiled girl. "I shall marry him and nobody else, and we will live together till we die."

"You may tell another tale," replied the King,

"when you ask him his secret. After all, he is no better than a servant."

"That is nothing to me," said the Princess, "for I love him. He will tell his secret to me and will always have a place in my heart."

But the King shook his head and gave orders that the lad was to be lodged in the summer house.

One day, about a week later, the Princess put on her finest dress and went to pay him a visit. She looked so beautiful that, at the sight of her, the book he held dropped from his hand, and he stood up speechless with wonder.

"Tell me," she said, coaxingly, "what is this wonderful secret? Just whisper it in my ear, and I will give you a kiss."

"My angel," he answered, "be wise and ask no questions, if you wish to get safely back to your father's palace. I have kept my secret all these years and do not mean to give it up now."

However, the girl would not listen and went on pressing him, till at last he slapped her face so hard that her nose bled. She shrieked with pain and rage, and ran screaming back to the palace where her father was waiting to hear if she had succeeded.

"I will starve him to death, the son of a dragon," cried he, when he saw her streaming with blood. Then he ordered all the masons and bricklayers in the town to come before him.

"Build me a tower as fast as you can," he said, "and see that there is room inside for a stool and a small table and for nothing else."

The men set to work and in two hours the tower was built. Then they started for the palace to inform the King that his orders had been followed. On the way, they met the Princess, who began to talk to one of the masons. When the rest were out of hearing she asked if he could manage to make a hole in the tower which nobody could see, large enough for a bottle of wine and food to pass through.

"To be sure I can," said the mason, turning back, and in a few minutes the hole was bored.

At sunset a large crowd assembled to watch the youth being led to the tower and, after his misdeeds had been proclaimed, he was solemnly walled up. But every morning the Princess passed food to him through the hole. Every third day the King sent his secretary to climb up the tower on a ladder and look down through a little window to see if the boy was dead, but the secretary always came back with the report that he was fat and rosy.

"There is some magic about this," said the King.

This state of affairs lasted a long time, till one day a messenger arrived from the Sultan of Turkey bearing a letter for the King, and also three canes. "My master bids me say," said the messenger, bowing low, "that if you cannot tell him which of these three canes grows nearest the root, which in the middle and which at the top, he will declare war against you."

The King was very much frightened when he heard this, and, though he took the canes and examined them closely, he could see no difference between one or the other. He looked so sad that his daughter noticed it and inquired the reason.

"Alas, my daughter," he answered, "how can I help being sad? The Sultan has sent me three canes and says that if I cannot tell him which of them grows near the root, which in the middle and which at the top, he will make war upon me. And you know that his army is far greater than mine."

"Oh, do not despair, my father," said she. "We shall be sure to find out the answer," and she quickly ran away to the tower and told the young man what had occurred.

"Go to bed as usual," he replied, "and, when you wake, tell your father you have dreamed that the canes must be placed in warm water. After a little while, one of them will sink to the bottom; that is the one which grows nearest the root. The one which neither sinks nor comes to the surface is the cane that is cut from the middle; and the one that floats is cut from the top."

The next morning the Princess told her father of her dream, and on her advice he cut tiny notches in each of the canes when he took them out of the water, so he might make no mistake when he handed them back to the messenger.

The Sultan, who could not imagine how the King had found out the answer to the puzzle, did not declare war against Buda.

The following year, the Sultan again wanted to pick a quarrel with the King of the Magyars, so he sent another messenger, this one bearing a letter and three foals. The letter required the King to say which of the animals was born in the morning, which at noon and which in the evening. If an answer was not ready in three days, war would be declared at once.

The King's heart sank when he read the letter. He could not expect his daughter to be lucky enough to dream rightly a second time. To add to his troubles, a plague which was raging through the country had killed off many of his soldiers and his army was even weaker than before. At this thought his face became so gloomy that his daughter noticed it and inquired what was the matter.

"I have had another letter from the Sultan," replied the King, "and he says that if I cannot tell him which of three foals he has sent was born in the morning, which at noon and which in the evening, he will declare war at once."

"Oh, don't be downcast," she said, "something is sure to happen." And she ran down to the tower to consult the youth.

"Go home, idol of my heart, and when night comes, pretend to scream out in your sleep, so your father hears you. Then tell him that you dreamed he was just being carried off by the Turks—because he could not answer the question about the foals—when the lad whom he had walled in the tower ran up and told them which had been born in the morning, which at noon and which in the evening."

So the Princess did exactly as the youth had bidden her. No sooner had she spoken than the King ordered the tower to be pulled down and the prisoner brought before him.

"I did not think that you could have lived so long without food," said he, "and as you have had plenty of time to repent your wicked conduct, I will grant you pardon, on condition that you help me solve a terrible problem. Read this letter from the Sultan; you will see that if I fail to answer his question about the foals, a dreadful war will be the result."

The youth took the letter and read it through. "Yes, I can help you," he replied. "But first you must bring me three troughs, all exactly alike. Into one you must put oats, into another, wheat, and into the third, barley. The foal which eats the oats is the one which was foaled in the morning; the foal which eats the wheat is the one which was foaled at noon; and the foal which eats the barley is the one which was foaled at night."

The King followed the youth's directions and, marking the foals, sent them back to Turkey, and there was no war that year. Now the Sultan became very angry that both of his plots to get possession of Hungary had been such total failures, so he sent for his aunt, who was a witch, to consult her about what he should do next.

"It is not the King who has answered your questions," observed the aunt, when he had told his story. "He is far too stupid ever to have done that! The person who has solved the puzzle is the son of a poor woman. If he lives, he will become King of Hungary. Therefore, if you want the crown yourself, you must get him here and kill him."

After this conversation, another letter was written to the King of Hungary, saying that if the youth in the palace was not sent to Turkey within three days, a large army would cross the border. The King's heart was sorrowful as he read, because he was grateful to the lad for what he had done to help him. The boy only laughed, bade the King fear nothing and to search the town instantly for two youths who looked exactly alike. Then he would paint himself a mask that would make him a replica of them. And the sword at his side clanked loudly.

After a long search, twin brothers were found, so identical that even their own mother could not tell the difference between them. The youth painted a mask

that was a precise copy of their faces and, after he had
put it on, no one would have known one boy from the
other two.

They set out for the Sultan's palace, and as soon
as they reached it, they were taken straight into his
presence. He made a sign for them to come near;
they all bowed low in greeting. He asked them about
their journey; they answered his questions all together,
and in the same words. If one sat down to supper,
the others sat down at the same instant. When one got
up, the others got up too, as if there had been one
body instead of three. The Sultan could not detect
any difference between them and told his aunt that
he could not be so cruel as to kill the three of them.

"Well, you will see a difference tomorrow," replied
the witch, "for one will have a cut on his sleeve. That
is the youth you must kill." And one hour before midnight, when witches are invisible, she glided into the
room where the three lads were sleeping in the same
bed. She took out a pair of scissors and cut a small
piece out of the boy's coat sleeve and then crept silently from the room. But in the morning the youth
saw the slit and marked the sleeves of his two companions in the same way, and all three went down to
breakfast with the Sultan.

The old witch was standing in the window and pretended not to see them, but witches have eyes in the
backs of their heads, and she knew at once that not one

sleeve but three were cut, and they were alike as before. After breakfast, the Sultan, who was getting tired of the whole affair and wanted to be alone to invent some other plan, told them they might return home. So, bowing together, they went.

The Princess welcomed the boy back joyfully, but the poor youth was not allowed to rest long in peace, for one day another letter arrived from the Sultan, saying that he had discovered that the young man was a very dangerous person—and he must be sent to Turkey at once. The girl burst into tears when the boy told her what was in the letter which her father had bade her carry to him.

"Do not weep, love of my heart," said the boy, "all will be well. I will start at sunrise tomorrow."

So next morning at sunrise, the youth set forth; and in a few days he reached the Sultan's palace. The old witch was waiting for him at the gate and whispered as he passed, "This is the last time you will ever enter it." But the sword clanked, and the lad did not even look at her.

As he crossed the threshold, fifteen armed Turks barred his way, with the Sultan in the lead. Instantly, the sword darted forth and cut off the heads of everyone but the Sultan and then went quietly back into its scabbard. The witch, who was looking on, saw that as long as the youth had possession of the sword her schemes would be in vain. She tried to steal the sword that night, but it jumped out of its scabbard and sliced off her nose, which was made of iron. And in the morning, when the Sultan brought a great army to capture the lad and take away his sword, they were all cut to pieces, while the boy remained without a scratch.

Meanwhile the Princess was in despair because the days slipped by and the young man did not return. She never rested until her father let her lead some troops against the Sultan. Dressed in uniform, she rode proudly before them, but they had just left the town when they met the lad and his sword.

When he told them what he had done, they shouted for joy and carried him back in triumph to the palace. There the King declared that the youth had shown himself worthy to become his son-in-law, and that he should marry the Princess and succeed to the throne at once, because he himself was getting old and the cares of government were becoming too much for him. But the young man said he must first go and see his mother, and the King sent him in state, with a troop of soldiers as his bodyguard.

The old woman was quite frightened at the array which drew up before her little house. She was still more surprised when a handsome young man, whom she did not know, dismounted and kissed her hand, saying: "Now, dear Mother, you shall hear my secret at last! I dreamed that I should become King of Hungary, and my dream has come true. When I was a child and you begged me to tell you, I had to keep silence or the Magyar King would have killed me. And if you had not beaten me, nothing would have happened that has happened, and I should not now be King of Hungary." FROM FOLK TALES OF THE MAGYARS, ANDREW LANG COLLECTION

THE MAGIC KETTLE

RIGHT IN the middle of Japan, high in the mountains, an old man lived in his little house. He was very proud of his home and never tired of admiring the whiteness of his straw mats and the pretty papered walls, which in warm weather slid back to allow the fragrance of the trees and flowers to come in.

One day he was standing looking at the mountain opposite his home, when he heard a rumbling noise in the room behind him. He turned around and in the corner he beheld a rusty old iron kettle, which could not have seen the light of day for many years. How the kettle got there the old man did not know, but he took it up and looked it over carefully, and when he found that it was quite whole he cleaned off the dust and took it into his kitchen. "That was a piece of luck," he said, smiling to himself. "A good kettle costs money, and it is always well to have a second one at hand in case of need. My kettle is nearly worn out now, and the water is already beginning to leak through its bottom."

Then he took the old kettle off the fire, filled the new one with water and put it in its place.

No sooner was the water in the kettle getting warm than a strange thing happened, and the man, who was standing nearby, thought he must be dreaming. First the handle of the kettle gradually changed its shape and became a head, and the spout grew into a tail, while out of the body sprang four paws, and in a few minutes the man found himself watching—not a kettle, but a living creature which the people of Japan called a *tanuki*.

It jumped off the fire and bounded about the room like a kitten, running up the walls and over the ceiling, till the old man was in an agony lest his pretty room be spoiled. He cried to a neighbor for help, and between them they managed to catch the *tanuki* and shut it up safely in a wooden chest.

Then, quite exhausted, they sat down and consulted together about what they should do with this troublesome beast. At length they decided to sell it and asked a child who was passing by to send them a certain tradesman called Jimmu.

When Jimmu arrived, the old man told him that he had something which he wished to get rid of, and he lifted the lid of the wooden chest where he had shut up the *tanuki*. But, to his surprise, no *tanuki* was there, nothing but the kettle he had found in the corner. It was certainly very odd, but the man remembered what had taken place on the fire and did not want to keep the kettle in his house anymore, so, after a little bargaining about the price, Jimmu went away carrying the kettle with him.

Now Jimmu had not gone very far before he felt that the kettle was getting heavier and heavier. By the time he reached home he was so tired that he was thankful to put it down in the corner of his room and then forgot all about it.

In the middle of the night, however, he was awakened by a loud noise in the corner where the kettle stood and raised himself up in bed to see what it was. But nothing was there except the kettle, which seemed quiet enough. He thought he must have been dreaming and fell asleep again, only to be roused a second time by the same disturbance. He jumped up and went to the corner and, by the light of the lamp that he always kept burning, he saw that the kettle had become the *tanuki*, which was running around after its tail. After it grew weary of that, the *tanuki* turned several somersaults on the balcony from pure gladness of heart.

The tradesman was much troubled as to what to do with the creature, and it was almost morning before he managed to get any sleep. But when he opened his eyes, there was no *tanuki*, only the old kettle he had left in the corner the night before.

As soon as he had tidied his house, Jimmu set off to tell his story to a friend next door. The man listened quietly and did not appear so surprised as Jimmu expected, for he recollected having heard, in his youth, something about a wonder-working kettle.

"Go and travel with it; display it," said he, "and you will become a rich man. But be careful first to ask the *tanuki*'s permission. It would be wise also to perform some magic ceremonies to prevent it from running away at the sight of people."

Jimmu thanked his friend for his counsel, which he followed exactly. The *tanuki*'s consent was obtained, a booth was built and a notice was hung up outside inviting the people to come and witness the most wonderful transformation that ever was seen.

They came in crowds, and the kettle was passed from hand to hand. They were allowed to examine it all over and even to look inside. Then Jimmu took it back and, setting it on the platform, commanded it to become a *tanuki*. In an instant the handle began to change into a head and the spout into a tail, while the four paws appeared at the sides.

"Dance," said Jimmu, and the *tanuki* did its steps, moving first on one side and then on the other, till the people could not stand still any longer and began to dance too. Gracefully the *tanuki* led a fan dance and glided without a pause into a shadow dance and an umbrella dance, and it seemed as if it might go on dancing forever. And very likely it would have, if Jimmu had not declared that the *tanuki* had danced enough and the booth must now be closed.

Day after day the booth was so full it was hardly possible to enter it, and what the neighbor foretold came to pass and Jimmu was a rich man. Yet he did not feel happy. He was an honest man and thought that he owed some of his wealth to the man from whom he had bought the kettle.

One morning, he put a hundred gold pieces into the kettle and, hanging it on his arm, he returned to the old man who had sold it to him. "I have no right to keep it any longer," he added when he had told his story, "so I have brought it back to you, and inside you will find a hundred gold pieces I have put there as the price of its hire."

The man thanked Jimmu, saying that few people would have been as honest. And the kettle brought them both luck; everything went well with them till they died, which they did when they were very, very old and respected by everyone.

FROM JAPANESE TALES, ANDREW LANG COLLECTION

See page 378

381

ACKNOWLEDGMENTS Collected and edited by Andrew Lang: THE PIED PIPER OF HAMELIN, THE GOLDEN GOOSE, JACK AND THE BEANSTALK, SIX SILLIES, SNOW WHITE AND THE SEVEN DWARFS, from *Red Fairy Book*, © 1948; SNOW WHITE AND ROSE RED, CINDERELLA, WHY THE SEA IS SALT, THE GOOSE-GIRL, BEAUTY AND THE BEAST, THE BRONZE RING, from *Blue Fairy Book*, © 1948; THE NIGHTINGALE, THUMBELINA, THE TINDERBOX, from *Yellow Fairy Book*, © 1948; ALI BABA AND THE FORTY THIEVES, from *Arabian Nights*, © 1898, 1946; the aforementioned books are copyrighted and published by David McKay Company, Inc. FIVE WISE WORDS, from *Olive Fairy Book*, first published by David McKay Company, Inc., in 1950. All the aforementioned books are published in Great Britain by Longmans, Green & Co. Ltd. THE SNOW QUEEN, LITTLE FIR TREE, from *Pink Fairy Book*, © 1897 and published by Longmans, Green & Co. Ltd. TWO FROGS, from *Violet Fairy Book*; THE BOY WHO KEPT A SECRET, THE MAGIC KETTLE, from *Crimson Fairy Book*; both first published by Longmans, Green & Co. Ltd. in 1951.

THE FROG PRINCE, from *Tales From Grimm*, © 1936, Wanda Gág; THE HEDGE-HOG AND THE RABBIT, THE SORCERER'S APPRENTICE, from *More Tales From Grimm*, © 1947, Estate of Wanda Gág, both translated by Wanda Gág, published by Coward-McCann, Inc. and Faber & Faber Ltd. IT'S PERFECTLY TRUE!, THE UGLY DUCKLING, THE LITTLE MERMAID, from *It's Perfectly True and Other Stories*, by Hans Christian Andersen, translated by Paul Leyssac, © 1937, Paul Leyssac; renewed, 1965, Mary Rehan, published by Harcourt, Brace & World, Inc. TOM THUMB, from *English Fairy Tales*, by Joseph Jacobs, published by G. P. Putnam's Sons. CHICKEN LITTLE, from *For the Children's Hour*, by Carolyn S. Bailey and Clara M. Lewis, © 1906, 1926 and published by Milton Bradley Company. THE PRINCESS AND THE PEA, THE TOWN MOUSE AND THE COUNTRY MOUSE, from *Tales of Laughter*, edited by Kate Douglas Wiggin and Nora Archibald Smith, © 1908, 1926 and published by Doubleday & Company, Inc. RED RIDING HOOD, from *Grimms' Fairy Tales*, translated by Mrs. E. V. Lucas, Lucy Crane and Marian Edwardes, © 1945 and published by Grosset & Dunlap, Inc. and J. M. Dent & Sons Ltd. THREE BILLY GOATS GRUFF, from *Chimney Corner Stories*, by Veronica S. Hutchinson, © 1925 and published by G. P. Putnam's Sons.